REWIND

The Siggost Chronicles

Book 1

SYDNEY ADDAE

The Siggost Chronicles Book 1: Rewind

Sydney Addae
Copyright 2017 by Addae, Sydney
ISBN: 978-1-937334-89-5
First Edition Electronic December 2017
Published by Sydney Addae

Prologue

Aldrik Sigman walked into the boardroom. His pale gray,
austere gaze swept over Remi Karo - Project manager, and Dr.
Kenn Berkhorn - lead scientist, seated at the small conference
table located in the back of the room. Karo and Berkhorn nodded
greetings, which Sigman didn't return. He took his seat at the head
of the table. "Let's get started, I've flown halfway around the
world for this. Questions regarding this project required an
unscheduled meeting with the Head Counsel and I don't
understand why. Based on the reports I've received, MERP is on
target with a few, minor inconsequential setbacks. It's my hope,
between the three of us, we'll provide responsible answers without
crippling ourselves when I meet with them in the morning." His
gaze lit on each man for a brief second.

"Tell me of the latest test results," Sigman said. His late
father's formula, Siggost, was the cornerstone of MERP - Memory
Enhancement and Replacement Project, the brainchild of
Kirtchens Holdings, a global pharmaceutical company and the
supposedly defunct MK Ultra.

Once the public found out the government had been testing
civilians without permission all hell had broken loose in the 70's.
Very few knew MK still operated in the shadows, running tests
that included torture, drugs and exotic hypnosis experiments in an
effort to explore the mind, propaganda and other related patterns.

Sigman had negotiated the use of the drug with legal
tenacity, including a top leadership spot in the program, as well as
a hefty percentage of profits. He looked over his interests with a
keen eye and sharp tongue, prepared to trim fat or incidentals, as
he referred to them, at a moment's notice. In his eyes, no one was

irreplaceable, and he made sure everyone within his small circle understood that.

Chapter One

I looked at the address in the text message from my cousin Rashan, and then at the tall numbers, 711, attached to the two-story office building in front of me. Uncertain what she'd cooked up this time, I hesitated to go inside. Lately she'd been secretive, refusing to say more than she really needed me to meet her here and used several favors to get me this far, putting her in my debt for a change.

Behind me the drone of the city bus grabbed my attention as it turned the corner across the street. Muted sounds of chatter, honking horns, the hiss of trucks in the stop and go traffic filled the air marking the passing of time. I looked up and down the street at people moving with purpose to wherever they needed to be while I remained still, uneasy and unsure of going inside.

"Psst, hey giiirrll," a guy dressed in an oversized tee-shirt, baseball cap pulled down so I couldn't see his eyes and baggy jeans yelled walking by. He blew a kiss as if he'd just made my day.

"That's why I don't come to this part of town," I murmured, rolling my eyes and ignoring him.

The large clock across the street chimed, reminding me I needed to move it if I planned to show up as summoned and still make it home on time. I would've ignored Rashan's cryptic text, loaded with exclamation marks and the word 'FUN' in all caps if I weren't curious about this new app, *"Rewind"* she and my online clan talked about.

The idea of recreating your life all the way from birth up to the present held fascinating possibilities and most of my friends had jumped off the deep end imagining the type of world they'd live in if *they* were in charge.

My cousin had been after me for weeks to accept her friend request on the app so we could share ideas about our new lives, but the idea of sharing something that personal, an entire new world created by me, for me, I couldn't do it. Of course I'd tried to be the voice of reason, explaining the obvious. The app offered the impossible and wasted hours re-building a dream world that would never happen.

No one listened to me.

Several people I thought had great lives were more than willing to toss everything out the door and start over on their terms. I have to admit, the idea of converting the living room or basement into a mega gaming room with superior sound and state of the art graphics with the ability to step into the game, yeah, that would be epic, *if* it was possible. But it wasn't, not in my world anyway.

Rashan said several of the "Rewind" crew had gotten together and were throwing a party in this building on the second floor. She wanted the unbeliever, me, to come. Why? I didn't know and that made me uneasy.

I pulled my long hair up and secured it with the band I kept on my wrist and hefted my book bag upon my shoulder. I checked the number again and pushed the glass door. The first thing I noticed was the eerie silence. I knew Rashan, the girl was loud. If she were here, there'd be music or noise.

No one sat behind the information desk.

Granted, I was 30 minutes late, but mom worked at an office and someone always greeted people in the lobby. Rather than become the star of a horror movie, I placed my bag down on the information desk and sent Rashan a message.

"I'm here where are you?"

"Hey! Come on up! 2nd floor. FUN!!"

I cringed at the caps and exclamation marks. Rashan's definition of fun and mine had changed over the years, but she'd played video games with me before I hooked up with my clan, so I owed her. At least that's the rationale she sometimes used when I said no to things she asked me to do.

Shiny letters on the wall in the lobby spelled the name of the building which I promptly forgot. I glanced at my reflection devoid of make-up and wiped the shine from the tip of my nose. Cornflower blue eyes, spaced a good distance apart, stared back at me in an unremarkable face. Rashan said my high cheekbones and narrow nose gave me an upper crust look, whatever the hell that meant. I thought it made me look even skinnier than I already did. I patted my hair, moved a few light strands behind my ear, and turned slightly. One day I'd have more on top and on the bottom, but today I'm still slim and underdeveloped. I'd mentally listed my physical faults a thousand times and didn't want to rehash them with Rashan waiting. No doubt she'd have a lot to say about me being late already.

I glanced in both directions until I saw the arrow pointing to the elevator. When I turned the corner the scent of stale coffee and cigarettes clashed with a strong deodorizer that must have been tossed on the tiled floors straight out the bottle. My eyes watered as I rushed down the hall toward the metal doors offering escape from the burn of chemicals. Clicks from the heels of my boots on the shiny floor kept time with the fast pace of my heart. Covering my nose, I pushed the button.

"No rabbit holes, please, please," I muttered. When the door opened, I stepped inside, taking a deep breath as the door closed. A brightly colored poster advertising the play Annie lay on the floor. For several moments I stared at the red hair and freckles. Rashan loved Annie when we were younger. I'd hide in my room when she came to visit to keep from watching that damn movie again. For a brief moment I wondered how she'd respond seeing her beloved on the floor of the elevator. "Probably couldn't care less." My cousin had changed, but then so had I.

When the door opened again, sounds of laughter, loud music, and chatter filled the air as I stepped over the poster into the hall.

People, lots of people, mostly teens of all ages, races, and nationalities hung out in the halls, some smoking, others talking, a few made out in the corners.

Several jocks from my school stood in a huddle, talking and laughing. I pushed through the crowd, feeling more self-conscious than ever in my ratty jeans and dark Motown tee-shirt which showcased my A cups, to find my cousin. After a few minutes I gave up and sat on the corner of a sofa with two other girls who looked just as out of place as me.

"Hello," I said, watching them tap the keys on their phone.

"Hi, I'm Casey and this is Jen." She pointed to the other girl typing furiously on her phone. "We're thinking about moving to New York, become models and work as dancers on Broadway," the girl next to me said without looking up or slowing down with her keystrokes.

Models? Dancers on Broadway? I looked at the two girls, both much shorter than my five feet six inches and silently wished them luck with the Rewind they'd need to accomplish those dreams.

"What about you?" Casey asked. Her question sounded more of a courtesy than sincere curiosity, my family had schooled me well in telling the difference.

"I'm still thinking about it," I finally said when I realized this wasn't the best place to spout all the reasons fantasizing over recreating your life was a complete waste of time. I glanced at my watch. In three hours my afternoon duties babysitting my two younger brothers began and I needed to be home.

"Shelly, I've been looking for you," Rashan said, reaching for my hand to pull me up. She didn't acknowledge Casey or Jen, they didn't exist in Rashan's world and that had nothing to do with the new game.

"There's some people I want you to meet." She pulled me through the crowd as I murmured 'excuse me' to those we barreled into. Rashan never paused and when someone slowed her down, she'd push them aside, ignoring the remarks thrown at her back.

Talk about making an entrance.

When we finally stopped, I pulled my backpack up higher and pulled the cord tight. The two guys she'd pushed me in front of were taller than my dad's six feet, but much narrower. One wore a mustache; the other's face was baby smooth.

"This is my cousin, Shelly, or Shells –"

"No, it's Shelly." I didn't bother glaring at Rashan. She knew I hated that old nickname she gave me when we were two. Instead, I watched smooth face. His eyes were an interesting combination of brown and gray, as if Mother Nature wasn't sure which color to use.

He smiled at Rashan as she giggled and spewed facts about me no one could possibly be interested in. My face burned as she blabbed to a stranger, who looked entirely too interested in her breasts, about my gaming habit. And yeah, it was an expensive habit. I gladly sunk every spare dollar I had into it, but reaching level 98 in 30 days with my clan made it worthwhile.

"Shelly is an expert gamer, she has a team that plays tournaments and wins all the time."

I tore my gaze from the guy to look at her. She wasn't remotely interested in my gaming friends, she'd been very clear on that point, often. "What are you doing?" I asked in a low whisper.

That's when I took a good look at her from head to toe. She hated wearing her dark mahogany hair loose around her shoulders and despised lipstick. At least she had a few months ago when we hung out. Not only did dark strands rest on her shoulders and her lips sport some shade of putrid pink, she wore girly shoes and a tight dress that pushed up her breast to the point they looked as if they were on display. I always hated her boobs were so much larger than mine.

"Just telling Jake and Paul why you'd be another good candidate for the test the company's running." Rashan's cheeks reddened as I stared at her a few seconds longer.

Test? Company? Not knowing which name belonged to whom, I looked at smooth face again. "What kind of test?"

"A Rewind competition. We're looking for people with the most creative ideas for a complete restart."

My gaze flew from one face to the other looking for some sign that these two guys weren't trying to make this whole "you can do it again" thing real. A quick glance at Rashan's face worried me. She'd bought into the entire idea of second chances. "What do you get if you win the competition?" I needed to hear them say it.

"A rewind of your life. Whatever it is, we make it happen," smooth face said, his gaze serious.

"Yeah, okay. Thank you very much." I took Rashan by the arm and backed away.

She stopped me after we walked a few feet. "Wait. Stop pulling me," she snapped, and straightened her top. "What are you doing? He wasn't finished explaining."

"Dude, seriously?" I stared at her. She never bought into fairy tales, not even when we were kids. I still recalled the day she laughed at my expectations from the tooth fairy. More importantly she thought video games were fake and stupid. I couldn't believe she even listened to those guys. "You're kidding right? Tell me you don't believe that shit?" No way had my normally brash, diva-on-the-rise cousin fallen for that BS. Her side of the family was Catholic for Christ's sake.

"No." She straightened as if pulling herself together and then met my gaze. "No, I'm not kidding. I'd like the chance to do some things over; it's not a bad idea."

It's a crazy, stupid, impossible idea! Her dad and my mom were brother and sister. Uncle Franco didn't have a sense of humor at the best of times and would tear this place a part if she tried something like this. A dull pain blossomed in the pit of my belly. Knowledge, deep and ripe, blossomed that somehow I'd get dragged into it. No matter what I said, if Rashan got involved with anything odd like this competition, mom and Uncle Franco would come to me.

I stared at her clenched jaw. Although I didn't see a cup or bottle in her hand I wondered if they'd slipped something into her drink. "Shon," I used her childhood nickname, hoping we could talk on a heart to heart level. "Shon you cannot rewrite the past. It's not possible. Everybody knows that."

Her brow rose. "Everybody? Look around. What do you think all these people are doing here? Not *everybody*, Shells." She held up her hand, stopping my next comment.

Looking around at the diversity in the room, I refused to accept all these people actually believed they could change their pasts.

"This isn't the first time they've done this," she said, effectively stopping the protest on my lips.

"What? How do you know that?" I didn't believe it was possible, but curiosity knocked on my door and I opened it.

She took my hand again. "I'm not crazy or stupid, as you well know. Do me a favor, listen to..." She stood on tip-toes and looked in the direction we'd just left before returning to me. "Listen to Paul, ask any question you want, and then when you're done, we'll talk. Just...just stop thinking like mom or dad for a minute and think like those games you love to play. Think what if? Okay? Is that fair?"

No, it wasn't fair to bring my gaming habit into this conversation, but that didn't stop her from misusing it to try to make her point.

"I've got to be home for the boys," I reminded her. She knew my routine, if it hadn't been the unofficial senior skip day at school I wouldn't be here now.

"Okay, talk with Paul, and I'll drive you home. Deal?"

Chapter Two

"You did what?" Celine, my clansman, asked later that night. "I thought you didn't believe in that shit."

Considering Celine was one of two clansmen who loved fantasy, but not the kind that pretended to be real, I knew I could count on her to side with me in this debate. She and I often played as teammates, discussed movies and got along well despite the two-year age difference. Also, we emailed each other outside the game and shared several social platforms. If I were hard pressed to name a bestie, it'd be Celine.

"I don't, I'm just telling you guys what happened today." I settled my headphones into a better position and spoke into the microphone while watching the monitor. Serena, my avatar, resembled a blond Zena strapped with a whip of truth on the side of her hip and cross-blades strapped to her back. The pouch on her waist contained a Blackstone, which allowed her to mimic an enemy's weapon. *Epic.*

Online, the six of us sat in our underground lair, equipped with all types of sensors, with large pillows and a table which our avatars sat around. We'd grown into a routine where we'd come early and talk a bit before defending our turf in the outlying arena.

I glanced at my watch, mom had finally arrived to take control of the boys, which allowed me some free time before going to bed. This was the third time this week she'd been late coming home, eating into my free time and that really sucked.

When I started to complain she shushed me and said how hard her day had been as if watching my two brothers was easy. Pissed she hadn't allowed me to express my discontent, I stalked to my room, locked the door and entered my cyber world. In the clan, expectations were high but we functioned as a cyber-family with everyone pulling their weight. I could live with that.

I was unable, however, to block the sound of feet running down the hall, coupled with yelling and high-pitched laughter that accompanied high energy boys. With an aggravated sigh, I turned up the volume on my headset.

"I like the game, met a lot of cool peeps in the forums, some of the things they'd change are stupid, self-serving, but really entertaining," Pete said. He was our clan leader, living in some part of Georgia and the oldest player at 20. "It's harmless fun."

Thurgood, his avatar a cross between Hulk and Iron Man, sat across the table from mine.

"Did you miss the part about a contest where they award you with a new life?" Pia, an exchange student from the states living in Ireland, asked. "How can you give someone a new life I'd like to know?"

At 17, Pia had seen and done more things in her life than any of us. She traveled all over the world with her family, and posted photos and videos on her YouTube channels. Few people would ever suspect the petite teen chose a ferocious faery avatar who ate her enemies and spit out their bones.

"The game clearly states you rewrite your life from the beginning to the present day, which means the offer is to go forward with the consequences of the life you've written," Pete said.

"Yeah, that's kinda what Paul said, there are some rules though," I said, recalling the conversation with Paul, who turned out to be smooth face. "You can't include anything from your past or present when you rewrite your life." That part troubled me the most.

Once Paul finished explaining the rules, it took a few seconds for me to understand just how fresh a start a Rewind would be. My life wasn't great, there were things I'd change in a heartbeat, but I didn't think I could walk away from everyone I loved and knew. Who would watch the boys while mama worked? What about school? I had one more year and was on a fast track to finish early. I didn't want to do that over.

Rashan, on the other hand, didn't seem bothered in the least about leaving her parents, younger sister, or anyone else behind. She thought it'd be great to live the way she'd imagined her life to be.

Until she'd spoken those words, I'd thought her life had been pretty good. At the start of this school year Uncle Franco, I preferred to call him Uncle Frank, bought Rashan a new car. She had lots of clothes, freedom to go as she pleased, and wasn't strapped into daily babysitting detail. Why would she throw all of that away?

"That makes sense," Pete said. "The whole purpose of the game is to write the world as you see it, to place your stamp on it based on what you've learned to this point. I think it's epic. I'd be down for it."

"You applied?" Arnold, another clansman living in Portland, asked with skepticism. His centaur avatar sat next to me across from Pete. He and Pete rotated as Chief in our clan, based on who remained at the highest level, which sometimes caused tension. As a 150 level player, far above the rest of us, we needed Pete to remain undefeated. No question, the dude could game.

"Yeah, I did. My application is under review," Pete answered.

"Way to go for the team," Gimple said, his British accent strong. "If you and Shelly defect, we'll lose our top ranking." His avatar, a combination of wolf and human, stood and moved from the table.

"Whoa," I said, sitting forward and turning my avatar to face his. "Who said I was going anywhere? I haven't even downloaded the app or played the game. Get your facts straight before you go spouting wrong shit." I released a breath and stared at the screen.

Gimple Pinkerton, a punk rocker from London, and I had played around with the idea of being more than clan-mates a few months ago. Cute, quirky, with strong gaming skills, I thought we might work out, especially with an ocean of distance. But I quickly learned cyber dating had more drawbacks than dating a local. The whole thing fizzled before I realized it was over. For a while things were awkward between us, and the clan stepped in for an intervention. Short story long, Gimple and I wanted different things socially, but were one for one as gamers.

"Wasn't sure where this conversation was going," Gimple said, his version of an apology.

"Pete, are you sure you want to fool around with that?" Celine, her avatar a cyborg woman with amazing abilities, stepped away from the table. "You do know it's a gimmick, right? I downloaded the app, answered the questions, and it went to a website. I saw my name and it said my application was in review. It's a marketing strategy. Coming from a marketing student, I'd say a really good one. Lots of activity in the forum, lots of people writing what they'd change in their past."

"I hear you, Celine," Pete said. "What you're forgetting is the way the questions are worded. Nowhere on the app or game do they say *they* re-write the past. They say I can rewrite my past, that's what you see on the website. So the offer is not to rewrite my past, but to put me where I'd be if what I write had been my past, and that is something that can be done."

Pete sounded like Paul, the guy at the party earlier. "That's the offer on the table," I added, unsure how I'd feel about a new life I created. Almost 17, I had a limited view of the world and would probably turn out worse than I started. Despite my reservations, in the back of my mind I couldn't help but wonder what I'd say, how I'd recreate things but was afraid I'd make things worse.

"I wish you the best," Pia said. "Since you won't remember us, is there a way for us to track your progress?"

"They can't erase a person's memories," Arnold snapped. "They'll limit his access to computers or something, but take his memories and leave his skills? That's impossible."

Arnold's comment set off a firestorm debate. Pete and Pia criticized Arnold's attitude and small-mindedness. Celine, the voice of reason, agreed with Arnold, although she used tact while stating her reasoning.

Gimple leaned against the wall, his face turned toward my back. "Are you seriously thinking of doing this?" he asked in a private message.

"No." Hadn't he heard me before? "I'd wondered how all of that worked myself, but didn't want to ask Paul too many questions since I have no intentions of using the app." Besides, Rashan had supplied the answer on the drive home.

"Good," he said

"My cousin said within the first 30 days you have some memories but those start to fade," I said, interrupting the heated debate.

"And she knows this how?" Celine asked.

"She said she researched the offer for a while, they have proof that it works. Not that I saw it," I added quickly. "Rashan's seen people who've done it."

"If they had no memory, how did they know they were in the program?" Arnold asked.

"Exactly," Celine said. "They could point out anyone and say they were in the program, but that don't mean it's proof or true."

"Don't argue with me," I said, uncomfortable repeating my cousin's comments, chances were she made them up just for me. "If you want to play the game, play or not, don't matter to me."

"For real," Pia said. "Pete, if that's what you want, I wish you the best."

"Same here, Dude," Gimple chimed in.

"You know my thoughts on it," Celine said. "But if that's what you want, go for it."

There was a brief moment of silence. I wondered if Arnold would wish Pete well. He didn't.

"There's an uprising in the northern quadrant, Chief," Pia said, breaking the quiet.

"Ready Clansmen?" Pete asked, moving his avatar to the edge of the lair.

"Ready! Game on!" We shouted.

Chapter Three

Sociology 101 wasn't a bad online college course, especially since it took place in one of my high school class slots. The professor required assignments be turned in by 10:00 pm every Monday night, which gave me plenty of time to finish homework, look up new game sites, and send messages to my gaming buddies during that hour. I'd just finished my English assignment and started Statistics when the classroom monitor, Mrs. Greer, left her desk to walk around the room.

I logged into the class blackboard and checked to see if anyone other than me had posted comments for our homework discussion on human sexuality. Three people basically agreed with what I'd said, giving as little thought to the subject matter as I had. Or rather, no one wanted to say anything that would get them flamed. I agreed with their remarks, and added everyone should be free to be themselves no matter what and prepared to log off.

"If everyone were free to be themselves, this world would be in a sad state." Patrick M.

I blinked, shook my head and then pushed a few strands of hair behind my ear. Patrick M. broke the unspoken rule in the group, never knock other people's opinions if you didn't want to start a war. Within seconds, he received three long scathing responses. One person claimed their brother was gay. Another called Patrick a homophobe who needed to get a life, and the other person ended with "you're a sack of shit."

Patrick didn't respond, at least not then, and I exhaled. Everyone had giant-sized balls in cyber-fights, people said things online they'd never say in person. I glanced at my watch, 30 minutes before the end of class. I set my statistics notes aside and stared at the screen, sociology just became a lot more interesting.

Mrs. Greer smiled as she reached my desk. "Things okay, Shelly?" she whispered. Her gaze flitted over the monitor and then back at me.

"Yes, thanks." I dicked around with the idea of showing her the discussion, get her ideas on the subject, but in the end I didn't want to weigh in on the subject more than I already had.

She nodded and moved on. In this room, students took all kinds of online courses. Based on the heated tempers and profanity filling the discussion thread, classmates seated around me looked bored, and un-engaged. I didn't think anyone else in this room shared my class.

"Just because I believe there needs to be laws, and people need to show some restraint doesn't make me an asshole, gutless wonder, homophobe, piece of shit or anything you say, so fuck you. I can feel the way I want and say what I want, I don't give a damn what you say." Patrick M.

"Bullshit, you're in the closet and ashamed to come in the light." Sharon C.

"You're probably dressed in women's panties right now, you're such a hypocrite." Lillian K.

"Fuck you," Patrick M.

I couldn't believe how fast the discussion deteriorated. Eight students had logged on and joined the fray. No one defended Patrick's right to say what he thought. The attack became personal and had nothing to do with the assignment.

"Everyone's entitled to say what they believe and be who they are. I don't see how you can accept one without the other, that's hypocritical," I typed. My finger hovered over the send button. More people joined the kill Patrick now party.

His comebacks were reduced to "fuck you" or "kiss my ass."

Did I really want to get into this? Sure I'd made the statement he commented on, but his comments didn't bother me, or change my opinions. If he was a douche, what did I care? I didn't know him, we weren't friends or anything. I canceled my comment and sat back. Five minutes before the end of class Patrick stopped responding to the cutting, colorful remarks. Nothing had been left untouched, he'd been accused of sodomizing his brothers, banging his mother and father, hanging out in adult book store glory holes, and other nasty things.

When the professor logged on later, she'd read how sensitive people were about sexual identity, which was the topic of the discussion. I doubted Patrick M was the only person who believed there should be rules in place and if he'd stated that first, the dynamics of the thread might be a lot different.

"Why not just agree to disagree?" Reginald T.

"Agreed," I wrote immediately, glad to end on a positive note.

Three others made similar remarks.

I turned off my computer and headed for my last class, Statistics. I saw a few fellow gamers in the hall and waved.

"Are you competing in the Smite tournament here at the school?" Donna asked, her bright blue and green hair hung loosely around her shoulder.

My chest tightened for a moment, I wished I could go. "No, can't. You?" I didn't bother explaining the school gaming club I'd played with found someone else who was available to meet after school because I couldn't make any practices.

"Not sure. I'd like to go to the national conference and see the finals, though."

"Seeing that live would be epic," I said, remembering the registration website and all the events.

"I know, right." She turned the corridor with a wave as I headed toward my class.

My phone vibrated. I looked at the caller ID. My cousin Rashan. "Why aren't you in class?" I asked, bypassing any greeting.

"I'm sitting at my desk, we have a sub. Did you download it yet?"

I placed my book bag on my desk and took a seat. Mr. Nork wasn't in the room but the assignment was on the board. I turned sideways and answered. "No, I told you I wouldn't."

"Please, Shells. It's a lot of fun, I want to add you as my friend and send stuff."

Rashan and several other people played Rewind, and since the party, she'd stepped up her campaign to get me to play. I glanced at the clock, the bell would ring in another minute.

"Gotta go."

"Download the app, and don't forget you promised to meet me next Friday."

Having forgotten the commitment she'd wrangled from me in a weak moment, I groaned and thought of several life-threatening things I'd rather do than meet Rashan at some party. "Mama's been talking about me doing a few things for her that day, I'll let you know."

"No. You promised, it won't take long, hour tops. Gotta go, see you Friday."

Chapter Four

That night I lay in my room with my text book open. I'd finished my homework earlier but hadn't put anything away. My gaze landed on the colorful poster of Tom Hiddleston as Loki on the wall, my all-time favorite character, there was something about him that made my heart clench. So bad and yet... good. Seconds later, Rashan's face replaced Loki's and dredged up our conversation right after dinner. She called to make sure I hadn't reneged on going with her next Friday or said anything to my parents about what we were talking about. I reminded her of my disinterest in the game and the unlikelihood of discussing the app with anyone. As usual she ignored my sarcasm and said I was the best. Assured I hadn't given away her secret, she asked if I'd go shopping with her after school tomorrow.

"Can't I'm watching the boys."

"I thought Uncle Griff was off."

"I don't think so, mama didn't say anything." Maybe my dad was off, but I'd rather be at home with him than in the streets with Rashan. Since she'd gotten a car and developed breasts, she'd exchanged her sports shoes for dancing boots. I didn't know this new person and wasn't sure I'd like her if I did.

"Hmm, what if we go later in the day, after Aunt Linda gets home."

I didn't say anything.

"Come on, they can't keep you home watching the boys all the time, you should have some fun too."

If I was in the mood, I'd blow all kinds of holes in Rashan's assumptions. It wasn't that I didn't appreciate my cousin, we used to be really close. But she thought I wanted the same things she did and that's where we clashed.

"I'll text you," I said to end the conversation.

Someone tapped on my bedroom door.

"Yes?"

"Got a minute?" Mom asked, after opening and peeking around the door. Wisps of brown hair escaped the band she wore around her head. Large hazel eyes darted around the room before settling on me.

I put the phone down and scooted up to rest against the headboard. As a sales manager, her work schedule varied, but her days were long. We rarely talked any more, other than her giving instructions for the boys or dinner. My stepdad's schedule was worse. He worked 12-hour shifts at the plant four days a week. The days he didn't work there, he helped his brother, Uncle Joe, with construction jobs to help pay child support from his first marriage. Griffin Chesney wasn't my biological father, but he was the only father I knew. When I was younger I'd asked who and where my biological father was. Back then I wanted a daddy who looked like me, so people wouldn't stare at Griffin, who was Indian, mom and me when we were out, Mama said she didn't know where my sperm-donor was, he'd disappeared before I was born. Over the years, I'd stopped asking questions and accepted the love and acceptance from my step-father.

"Sure," I said, watching her. I wasn't a l'il kid and didn't hang on mom's every word or dream of being just like her anymore. If working hard made her happy, or met some kinda warped life- goal like reaching a high rank or something, then I'd understand the long hours and missed events. Instead, her job drained her of joy and energy, something I never wanted to happen to me.

Dressed in gray sweats and a large faded green tee-shirt that seemed too long for her short, round frame, she closed the door, but not before looking behind her into the hall.

"Everything okay?" I wondered if daddy was home, they'd been arguing lately. I hadn't heard his voice or the boys calling out to him. No matter how tired he'd be, he always spent a few minutes with the boys and then came by my room to say hi when he came home.

"Not yet, how are things at school?" She picked up the shirt I'd worn the day before and placed it in the hamper. Her gaze flicked over my paper filled desk and un-made bed. We'd had several conversations about how I'd like privacy in my room, which meant I'd keep it the way I wanted.

"Good, same as usual." She put my sneakers in the closet.

I bit back a groan. "Mom. We talked about this remember?"

She paused and stared down at me with a question in her gaze. "What?"

I stood, moved next to her, and took my jeans from her hand. "My room. I'll get to it. I plan to do laundry tomorrow." I hadn't planned it before, but a quick glance at the overflowing basket in the corner made it a true statement.

"Oh, okay." She released a breath, looked around, and sat on the lone chair at my desk.

I returned to the bed, stretched out my legs, and looked at her in expectation.

"Your grandmother, my mom, wants to come visit." She shook her head and looked at the floor for a few moments before meeting my gaze. "No, she needs to come stay here for a while. She's not..." She exhaled. "She's not doing well and her doctor doesn't think she should live alone."

Shock raced through me. Not live alone? Last time I'd seen Grandma Jan, she'd promised to make me a coconut cake after mom mentioned I was allergic to coconuts. When was that? Two, three years ago? She'd been living with Aunt Gail, mom's oldest sister in Virginia.

"What happened to Aunty?"

Mom's face twisted like something nearby smelled bad. "She moved in with her boyfriend and he won't let mama move with them. Gail says it's time for me and Franco to help out." She paused. "Guess she's got a point. Franco's not much help and

Miriam says they don't have the space, which is crazy, they've got more bedrooms than us."

I nodded.

Since mama and Rashan's mom didn't get along that well, her heated comment wasn't a surprise. Still, I wasn't sure what she expected from me or where this conversation was headed.

"Sooo, mama'll be moving in next Wednesday. Gail's bringing her on her day off. I'll try to be here that day, but things are weird at work." Her voice trailed off and she stared at a spot over my shoulder.

Silence took on substance and weighed heavy in the room, making it as gray as the outfit mama wore. I couldn't see a bright spot in this announcement, and that's what it was. Another decision that would steal my time without my input. This time I wouldn't be shushed. Who would take care of grandma? Afraid I'd be a part of the answer, I chased my thoughts in another direction.

"Which room are you putting her in?" There were no spare bedrooms. I hoped she'd get Griffin's room at the front of the house.

"The boys will share Griffin's room up front, she'll be next to you in Roger's room. I'm going to need you to help out some, especially in the mornings and after school."

I jerked back, not believing she'd want more from me. "I'm already coming straight home from school to watch Griff and Roger in the afternoon, plus my bus leaves thirty minutes before theirs, what do you expect me to do in the mornings?" I had no social life as it was and tried not to be bitter about saying no to all the things I'd like to do with the few friends I had. But this crossed the line. Arguments filled my mind and crowded my throat. I deserved some kind of life other than watching kids and old people.

Mama patted my hand and then held it. Her eyes filled.

Seeing pain etched across her face snatched the angry words from my mouth and squeezed my chest tight.

"Right now I don't have answers or know how bad mama is." She sniffed and looked away a few seconds. "All I know is I've gotta help take care of her the best I can and I'll need your help, the boys are too young to understand." She paused and pressed my hand between hers. "This is hard, to see mama like this, unable to care for herself, not being sure of where she is or what she needs... it's hard." She sniffed again and wiped the tears from her face. "This is my mama. Mine. I have to help her." Her hand squeezed mine until it hurt. "She doesn't go to a home unless there's no other choice." Her voice hardened with finality.

Seeing her like this brought tears to my eyes. No, I didn't want to take care of grandma, but I'd help. I'd do anything to see mama smile again. Seems she hadn't smiled in a long time, and if it meant I'd have less time to do other stuff... well, it wouldn't last forever.

"I know. You've got to help her." I paused and hoped I said the right thing. "It's going to be okay, Mom. Don't cry."

She leaned forward, wrapped her arms around me and held tight. Hearing her sobs, feeling her chest heave against mine knocked the wind out of me. Somehow it seemed wrong for her not to have it all together, like the sky fell when I wasn't looking and didn't know what to do.

Mama always had answers, except this time she didn't, and that scared the hell out of me.

Chapter Five

The door to my room opened and closed with a soft snap. Tense, I waited for mom to ask me to do something that would take up my day. Since grandma moved in, it seemed I never had any free time, even though mama did most of grandma's personal care. *Please, don't ask me to watch the boys or take Roger to the park.* I didn't want to see any kids today. Surprised she hadn't spoken, I peeked.

Rashan, dressed in pink sweats, sneakers, and her hair pulled up in a ponytail, stood near the door wringing her hands and staring at the wall.

"No, whatever you want the answer is no," I said without closing my eyes so she'd leave.

Rather than leave she sat on the bed, scooted up against the wall, and cleared her throat.

"Still not going anywhere," I said, although it was strange for my cousin to remain silent this long.

"Wake up, I need to talk to you." Her voiced trembled.

I rolled to the side, brushed a few strands from my face and looked at her. For a few seconds I stared at her puffy face and red eyes. "You're crying?"

"I need to talk to you," she said again.

The way her voice wavered scared me, something bad had happened. "Why're you crying? Is this a new thing to get me to go and do something with you? Because if it is…" I didn't really think that, but I wanted to cover my bases, besides I didn't know what to say or do about the tears.

She held up a hand. "No. Stop, just stop," she said in a harsh whisper. Our gazes locked for a brief second before she turned away.

Flipping onto my back, I realized my words had been insensitive, especially given her emotional state. "Sorry. What's wrong?" I softened my voice so she knew the apology was real.

When she clasped her hands and licked dry lips, my gut tightened. I knew this would be bad.

"First, promise me you won't tell anybody what I'm telling you." Determination blazed across her face and I could think of a hundred reasons not to make this promise. But she'd just remind me she'd kept quiet when she read in my journal I'd tried to find information on my biological dad. As far as I know, she never told anyone after I made her swear.

"Depends on what it is." I wanted to hedge my bets with Rashan, no telling what she'd done. There could be bodies somewhere, I could become an accessory, who knew.

Lips pressed firmly together, she shook her head. "No. You tell no one."

"What's wrong? Are you in trouble?" I brushed tangled strands from my face, surprised Rashan hadn't given me her normal, totally unsolicited, comments on how much better it would be if I took the time to care for my hair properly. Perhaps, based on the whole 'my life is over' vibe she put out, this wasn't the time.

"Promise me first, and hurry up, I'm dying here."

"Okay I promise, but only because if you could say the dying thing, I know it can't be that bad." Of course we'd disagreed before, so now wasn't much different.

"I'm pregnant," she whispered.

I swear her face went white as a sheet, as if hearing her own words freaked her out more than me hearing them, which couldn't be true. Never in a million, gazillion years did I expect to hear those words from her. In fact, I didn't hear them. Couldn't have, to be pregnant there'd need to be a guy somewhere, and Rashan didn't have a guy, right?

"What?" I inched closer. "What'd you say?" I needed her say it again to be sure.

She ran the pad of her fingers across a fingernail as tears rolled down her face. My heart lurched seeing her like this. But pregnant, that was huge. *Mega.* A former clansman had gotten pregnant and stopped gaming completely, her life changed and she didn't even have the baby.

"I went to the clinic yesterday instead of cheerleading practice. I'm pregnant."

Wait, something wasn't adding up. "You're having sex?"

"I did." Sniffing, she wiped her face. "Twice. He said it'd be better the second time." She tried to shrug as if it was no big deal, but she wasn't that good an actress, not with me. We'd gone through measles, chicken pox, and daycare together, if Rashan had sex with a guy, she thought the dude was special.

"Turned out he specialized in lying and wants nothing to do with me anymore." Her face went from pale white to red.

I tried to get a grasp on what she wasn't saying even as the idea of her repeating mama's mistakes rose like a creepy shadow in the back of my mind. "Unprotected sex?"

"Obviously," she snapped, clearly pissed at the disbelief in my voice.

"Whoa, hold up." I held up my hand and met her gaze. This was my room, she'd woke me on a Saturday morning to talk, not the other way around. "I need a moment to digest what you're saying. It's too early for you to lay this kind of thing on me and not expect questions."

"Sounded like you were judging me, I don't need that from you."

"Not judging, trying to understand how this happened. I didn't know you had a boyfriend, you never mentioned anyone." Maybe that was the real problem for me. In a twisted way I assumed she'd have told me about someone special.

She avoided my gaze and my stomach dropped to the floor. Some guy had tricked her and bailed. That had to hurt.

"Just someone I'd liked for a while, we got together and it didn't work. He's not important."

I scoffed. "Hell yes, he is. Uncle Frank's going to kick his ass. You better warn him to move the hell out of town if he don't want to get dropped kick into next week." I paused, thinking about my aunt and uncle. Mama hadn't questioned me about this, hadn't mentioned it which meant one thing. "You didn't tell the parents?".

Shiny-eyed, she turned from my gaze and cleared her throat. "Can we go to that park around the corner? Talk where no one can hear?"

Not wanting to sound insensitive, especially since she was so upset, and she had come all the way over, but damn, it was Saturday morning, no school, and I could sleep in. But she's my cousin. I rolled out of bed.

"Okay."

Griffin waved as we left the house. I eyed the small compact car she drove parked in the driveway and beat down the green monster. It'd be great to have a car my senior year and not catch the school bus. "You want to drive or walk?"

"The cool air feels good, let's walk, plus I need the extra time to think and stop crying so damn much."

I looked at her, realized she was serious, and walked alongside on the sidewalk toward the park. Nearby a lawnmower roared to life. Car doors opened and closed, typical sounds of a waking neighborhood intruded our silence.

A couple blocks later, we turned from the sidewalk and headed into the park to sit on the bench.

"What are you going to do?" I asked, not knowing how I could help her.

"That's the million dollar question. I don't know."

"Thinking of having it?"

"Don't have much choice, I can't have an abortion."

"Can't?" I loaded that one word with skepticism. Mama wasn't a practicing Catholic like Rashan's parents. We never went to Mass, and Rashan rarely missed one.

"Can't," she said with narrow-eyed emphasis.

I raised my fingers and made a sign of the cross. "Ease up, I'm on your side. So you're having a baby, are you ready for that?"

"No. I don't want a baby, I'm just 16 and have no idea what to do with a kid."

"But you're having one?" I asked to be sure we were on the same page.

She closed her eyes and I saw the conflicting emotions crossing her face. "I guess."

"Whatever you decide, I've got your back." In that moment I meant it and the limited things it entailed.

"What would you do?" she asked, watching closely.

Me? I tried to keep the distasteful surprise from my face. But I couldn't imagine having sex with a guy who'd toss me aside, let alone having a baby. Watching my brothers all the time, I knew I'd probably never have a kid. Trying not to sound completely insensitive, I tempered my answer. "I don't know. But I don't think I'd have a baby, not this young."

"Oh."

"When are you going to tell Uncle Frank?" We needed to move the conversation along. She'd came to me as a sounding board, but the real issue was her parents and how they'd deal with all of this.

She shuddered. "I'm not."

"Huh?" That made no sense. "He'll see eventually."

Rashan exhaled and stood. The expressions racing across her face concerned me, she was quiet too long, no telling what she was thinking, but I was sure I wouldn't like it.

"I've thought something was wrong for a while. When I'd asked you to go shopping with me shopping or to that party, I... I knew I might be pregnant."

My gaze narrowed. That Rewind party had been over the top.

"I've been trying to think how to handle this." She twisted her hands so hard they left painful looking marks. That couldn't be good for her or the baby.

Thinking to ease her concerns, I touched her hand to help her focus on what I thought was the main issue. "Uncle Frank might be angry, but they'll help, especially if you keep the baby."

Her brow furrowed as she looked down at me. "I never said I'd keep the baby."

I frowned. "Huh?"

"Didn't you hear me say I don't want a kid?" She looked at me as if I wasn't paying attention, but she wasn't making sense.

"Right. So what... you're going to go through the pregnancy and give her up for adoption?" I said slowly.

"That's the plan."

"Not bad. I still don't see how you plan to keep that from your parents."

She stared at the ground for a few minutes. "I signed up for the Rewind contest and was accepted." She said the words so fast it took a minute for me to process them.

"What?" I jumped up. "Have you lost... Shon, listen to me. Please, don't do that. You don't have to get involved with who knows what, we can deal with this. Uncle Frank and Aunt Miriam will help --"

She laughed.

The harsh sound bordered on the edge of hysteria and scared me. Was Rashan losing it?

"You have no idea," she hissed jumping up, sounding less like my cousin and more like one of those women on TV out to right some imagined wrong. I couldn't think of any names at the moment, but my inner me totally agreed that Rashan walking in a tight circle wasn't normal.

"What?" I asked, watching her closely. "No idea about them helping or about being pregnant?" I had no experience with either, but I wanted to be sure we were talking about the same thing.

"You think daddy walks on water, turns it into wine, and bottles it for sale."

"What?" Sure I looked up to my uncle. Before mama married my stepdad, Uncle Frank had been the only man in my life that I remembered. But to say he walked on water was a huge stretch.

Straightening, she met my gaze. "Have you ever wondered why I never call you at night or if I do, it's from the house phone and it's never a long conversation."

My brow furrowed as I thought about her question. Honestly I hadn't paid much attention to anything going on with Rashan. Had I missed something? "Not really."

"Hmmm. You ask why I don't tell my parents about my situation, and the reason you had to swear never to mention it to anyone. I'm Catholic, so are my parents. Daddy's not as bad as mama, but ever since she discovered he cheated on her, she's been crazy about me and Lucy's virginity."

My mouth dropped. I had no idea my uncle had been unfaithful, but she wasn't finished.

"So whenever I go somewhere, she makes Daddy randomly check the mileage on my car to make sure I'm not out doing something with a boy. Or when I come from a game, mama checks my clothes, even my cheerleading outfit. Yes, she sniffs them to make sure I haven't been doing things I'm not supposed too. Once, she went through my cell phone and read a text a friend sent as a joke. I spent every day for two weeks on my knees in her prayer room, well, it's really a closet she converted."

I tried to connect the dots, but couldn't. "But... they bought you the car. You go shopping and ask me to do stuff all the time."

"Usually I ask when mom's around, plus that's window dressing. Daddy has to show the world he can afford the car, but the keys and my cell phone are locked away every night. That's why I couldn't call you until this morning."

"You called me?"

"Yeah, a few times, but you didn't answer. I told mama I was coming to pick you up to go with me to the math fair at school. Trust me, one of them will check the mileage when I get home."

Realizing she was serious, I tried to imagine living that way and couldn't. "That day we went to the party?"

"Senior skip day, so I skipped too, plus I took you home. I called mama from your house remember? It gave me added time and miles."

"Now that you're not a virgin...?"

Chill bumps ran across her skin. For some reason my eyes were drawn to them and I couldn't turn away. She shuddered and wrapped her arms around her waist.

"No telling what mama would do. Either spend lots of time on my knees in her prayer closet or be sent to one of those places she suggests to the parents in her prayer group. I don't know much about it, but it's a place for girls to have their babies and put them up for adoption." She looked away, but not before I saw the sheen of tears in her eyes.

My heart wept for her.

"No way she'd let me stay at home to have the baby. Like I said, you have no idea what it's like living in that place."

Disbelief raced through my mind and settled as I dragged my gaze to her face. The lack of color made her cheekbones stand out, portraying signs of her German roots. Lips trembling, she returned my gaze with an air of defiance and possibly freedom, as if sharing the horrors of home released her in some way.

Checked her clothes? Locked away her cell phone? "So you don't think your parents will help you?" I asked to be sure I understood. Never in a million years would I have guessed

Rashan went through that type of scrutiny. *How the hell did she look happy all the time? Had I seen what she wanted me to see?* My gut clenched in shame. Instead of calling her out on her recently changed behavior, I accepted that we'd grown apart, wanted different things. I never looked beyond the smiles or snappy comebacks. Inwardly I swore I'd do better.

"Help me?" Rashan snorted and walked back to the bench. "I'd be on my knees praying all day every day until mama made arrangements for me to go away and have the baby. She's a religious nut job and daddy goes along with her to keep peace. I'm sure he's still doing somebody on the side, and the more he's gone, the more whacky she becomes."

Hearing my uncle wasn't the perfect father bothered me in ways I didn't want to examine too closely, so I distanced myself from those comments. "But you met with this guy, what? Twice? So you found time."

She sat down. "I skipped school, skipped a practice, skipped going to your house. You can always find time to do what you really want, that's what makes me so mad. They're so damn hypocritical."

Hypocritical? Reeling from her confessions, I sat next to her and tried to be of some use. Realistic decisions needed to be made. After a few moments of silence, I came up with what I thought was a summation of the discussion so far. "So basically, if you stay you'll be shipped away someplace, and you don't want to do that, right?"

Rashan released a long sigh. "I don't want *them* to make that choice for me. Life at home is restrictive enough, the thought of dealing with mama's rants and that prayer closet scares me. She gets really mad sometimes, it's like she flips into this other person. When she gets like that, we lock ourselves in our rooms until she calms down."

Images of the Aunt Miriam I knew appeared like snapshots in my mind. I'd always thought she was shy, didn't have much to say. Mama didn't care much for her, but never talked bad about the woman. Everyone knew Aunt Miriam took her faith seriously, and that she'd given up her dream of being a nun to marry Uncle Frank.

"The reason I wanted you at the party was to get information on the program so you could give me your opinion," Rashan said.

In my opinion, the app thing wasn't a better option. There were too many unknowns, plus at its heart, it was a game. Games had no place in serious situations like this. Rather than blurt it was a bunch of bullshit, I took a moment and thought my answer through. Right now Rashan wasn't thinking clearly. I wasn't sure about the things she'd said about her parents, maybe she wanted me to believe she had no other options.

"Help me understand how you can get caught up with that? How do you see it as a solution?"

Her face brightened a bit as she turned to face me. "When I sign up, I'll re-write my past. I'll still be Catholic though, just not crazy."

The determined gleam in her eyes concerned me. This was real to her.

"No prayer closets. No eavesdropping. No clothes sniffing or odometer reading. I'd rather not have the car if I have to go through that."

I agreed that type of monitoring made the gift a headache.

"My new family would accept me in my condition, help put the child up for adoption, and then I'd go on to college to be an engineer like I always planned. Crisis averted."

"How? If they put you with a new family, how's that different from what your mom would do?"

"Because I get to write the terms, not her or anyone else, that's how." She nodded as if that settled the matter.

It didn't. At least not in my mind.

"But who's going to do all of that? How can you trust that? It sounds crazy."

"I'm not crazy," Rashan snapped. Her eyes narrowed and nostrils flared.

"No you're not. But going away with a company you don't know anything about... that's crazy." I held up my hands. "You asked my opinion and I'm giving it."

"But you never downloaded the app and re-created your life for a rewind. How can you have an opinion?"

"First, you asked. Second, because what you're saying you want to do, walk into a life based on a past you created is impossible."

"No it's not. Others have done it." She crossed her arms and stared out at the road. A few kids played on the bars and ran around at the park.

I moved closer for privacy even though I didn't know what to say. She's always been stubborn. "Sounds like you've made up your mind," I said into the prolonged silence. Unable to think of anything new, anything that would make her see reason, to see that this Rewind thing was riskier than talking to her parents, I covered her hand with mine.

"Not completely. But I'll make a move in the next few days or so." Rashan faced me; her large eyes filled with tears. With trembling lips, she grabbed two of my fingers. "I'm more scared of mama than anything else. If she finds out I'm pregnant, no longer a virgin, she'll lose it. That's why I went to a clinic two counties over for the test. She can't know, not until I make a decision."

Uncertain my aunt was *that* bad kept me silent. Push came to shove, Rashan and Aunt Miriam were about the same size, and Rashan had a temper too.

"Promise me, Shells. Don't mention this to anybody. If I choose the Rewind, I don't want anybody messing it up for me. I want to make my own decision."

"But you'll just disappear? No one will know where you are?" Did she really expect me to remain quiet under those circumstances? "What if the company's a scam?"

"If it is, then nothin'll happen. I'll fill out the forms, re-create my past, and take it from there. If nothing happens, it cost me what? A few hours. But if, and I know this is a big if, there is a life available based on the way I'd like to live, I want it." Her lips pressed tight together as she stared at me.

I wanted to shake her. Why couldn't she see this whole thing was crazy? "If you disappear, your parents are going to come to me. You lied and told them we were together when we weren't, so they'd think I know where you are," I reminded her.

Rashan wrapped her arms around her waist again and rocked back and forth for a few moments.

Praying she'd at least think about what I said, I placed my arm around her shoulder. We sat quietly for a few minutes.

"If I disappear, don't tell anyone anything until you check with the company. I'll put you down as my contact, that way they'll answer your questions. I get 30 days in this new life to decide if I want to stay or go back home."

Oh God, Uncle Frank would tear this city apart in 30 days. She wasn't thinking rationally. It had to be the baby. "Can't you just call and let me know you're okay?"

"No, I can't access anything from my past. That's a big rule."

"That's a red flag right there. If you can't contact me, how will I know you're safe? Don't you see this makes no sense? It's dangerous." This seemed like a bad act in one of those daytime televisions' programs with Rashan as the lead which was wrong on so many levels.

"Tell you what, if I decide to go with Rewind, I'll text you. And if you don't hear from me that evening, contact the company the next morning." She pulled out her wallet and gave me one of two identical cards. On the back were a series of numbers and alphabets. "That's my ID number." She put the other card back in her wallet.

Did my cousin have a death wish? I thought of all the things that could go wrong. Teenagers went missing every day and this company could be part of the reason. Suddenly the idea of being sent away to have the baby seemed better, brighter and more balanced than before.

"Shon, you're pregnant. If you went somewhere to have the baby, at least I'd know you were safe. We could talk or I could visit. You'd still have family who loved and cared about you. But you don't know anything about this deal." My tone took on a pleading quality I was helpless to stop. The idea of her going off to some fly-by-night company sent chills down my back.

Tears rolled down her cheek as she looked at me. "That's the thing, Shell. I'd rather take a chance with the unknown than stay with a family who'd treat me as if I were the world's worst person for screwing up." She rubbed the water from her cheeks. "I made a mistake. I admit that. But I've heard mama say horrible things about unwed mothers, and some of the things she's made me do for missing curfew or talking on the phone too long... she'd beat me first, and then toss me out. Daddy won't stop her, at least he hasn't so far."

Beat her? Toss her out? I didn't know my aunt or uncle at all. I wanted to say it wouldn't be that bad, or assure her I'd be there to help, but in the end I couldn't honestly say either of those things.

"I'd rather take my chances with the unknown than stay with them..." Rashan murmured again.

Chapter Six

Now that Rashan's secret completely wrecked my weekend, I couldn't help but think about what she'd said about Aunt Miriam and Uncle Frank all day. Granted, things at my house were cramped, I complained about my lack of freedom and wished things were different, but I believed I could tell mama anything. Maybe not about searching for my biological father, or my true feelings about staying home all the time watching the boys and now grandma, or how I'd like to stay after school to participate in some of the clubs, but most other things. Course, if I had a boyfriend in person and not online, that might be different too, I suppose.

The rest of Saturday passed in a blur as I waited to hear from Rashan. That night, I sucked royally playing games and logged out after losing a match I'd normally win with my eyes closed. Celine called later and asked what was wrong but I couldn't share Rashan's secret no matter how much I wanted. So I blamed my miserable night on family problems. Since we'd discussed my lack of freedom and heavy responsibilities before, she bought it. I battled my conscience, should I tell mama or keep my promise to Rashan? If anything happened to my cousin and I could've prevented it, I'd never forgive myself. On the other hand, if her life was so bad she'd prefer to disappear rather than stay at home, telling mom might make things worse. Neither solution worked for Rashan and I didn't know what to do.

Sunday, the next day, mama dressed grandma to go spend the day with Uncle Frank and Aunt Miriam. I'd just finished cleaning the kitchen when I overheard mama tell daddy they'd talk, spend some time together when she came back. He kissed her and it was good seeing them together like that again.

"I'll go with you to help." I grabbed a pair of sandals and met her at the car. We placed grandma in the back seat and locked her in. Mama smiled at me, but her eyes held a question she didn't ask and I was grateful.

"Things going okay at school?" Mama asked as we drove out of the subdivision.

"Yeah, end of year finals are done. Glad this is the last week, I'm ready for summer break." I glanced behind at grandma and smiled. "How's work?" I asked not because I wanted to know, but sometimes I think she likes to share what she does with me.

"Busy." She launched into the ins and outs of managing a large marketing department for a Fortune 500 company. I'd heard various scenarios for the past three years, different names, different days. But for the most part, her work remained the same. When we pulled into Uncle Frank's driveway, Rashan's car sat in the driveway. I helped Grandma out of the back seat while mom got the bag filled with supplies.

"How long will she be here?" I asked, looking at the canvas bag mama hefted onto her shoulder.

"Just until tonight. Franco will bring her home after dinner. I needed a break." The look she shared said we all needed a break.

Pleased with mama's plan, I took Grandma's elbow, it seemed thinner than before and I wondered if she'd lost weight since moving in. Now wasn't the time to talk about it, maybe on the drive home.

Mama rang the doorbell and Uncle Frank opened it.

"Hi Franco," Mama said, looking at her brother and then back at grandma. As the youngest, grandma had spoiled him and everyone knew it.

"Hey, Sis." A few inches taller than me, he took a few steps and embraced grandma. "Mama."

Standing to the side I watched the pain slide across his square face at her lack of response. Since he'd been to our house numerous times since grandma arrived, he knew she wouldn't respond, but like the rest of us, held out hope. Instead of walking her inside, he lifted and carried her across the threshold, through the large foyer, into the living area.

I followed mama inside and closed the door behind me. In the foyer, on a small table beneath an oval mirror sat a box with a slit on top and padlock on the side. Above it a five hook key rack held two sets of keys. Rashan's was missing.

The foyer opened into a large open area twice the size of ours with light colored sofas and chairs on hardwood floors. Aunt Miriam waved at me from the kitchen, her dark brown hair pulled up in a short ponytail. Lucy, Rashan's sister, stood in the dining area near the kitchen watching Uncle Frank settle grandma in a chair. I waved Lucy over. She glanced at Aunt Miriam before moving.

"Rashan's in her room," she said before I could say hi.

"Thanks, how you been? I haven't seen you for a while." I glanced at the dark mark on her shoulder and then met her gaze when she pulled up her blouse.

"Okay, how long is she going to be here?" She pointed at Grandma, who sat staring at Uncle Frank.

"Until I take her home, I've already made that clear," Uncle Frank said, standing and looking at Lucy, who seemed to shrink behind me.

"Sorry." Lucy bolted down the hall.

"Was that necessary?" Aunt Miriam asked, coming toward them holding a glass filled with ice and a clear liquid.

He pointed at her. "Don't start. This is my mama, my house, and she's welcome here any time."

"As long as you're here to watch her, it's fine," Aunt Miriam said in an icy tone as she looked at mama. "Hi Linda, how are you?"

"Good, thanks." Mama handed Uncle Frank the bag without asking Aunt Miriam the same. "Let's go over her supplies."

"Hi Shelly, you've gotten taller. So pretty. I love your hair." Aunt Miriam touched a few strands on my head. Normally I'd smile and thank her. But now I wasn't sure how to react after seeing the bruise on Lucy's shoulder and the lock box beneath the keys.

"Thanks." I stepped aside and headed toward Rashan's room, surprised she hadn't come out front yet.

"Tell Rashan to come greet her grandmother," Aunt Miriam said.

Unable to put my finger on what bothered me about that request, I nodded. Maybe it was her mocking tone, or the look she gave Uncle Frank when she said it. But the longer I stayed in this house, the more I believed Rashan hadn't exaggerated.

Lucy and Rashan's bedroom doors were closed. I tapped on Rashan's door, twisted the knob, it was locked. "Rashan?"

"Shelly?"

I heard movement and then the door opened. "Come in, I thought you were Lucy." She locked the door after I walked in. Unlike my bedroom, Rashan kept her space neat. No clothes littered the floor, open blinds filled the room with natural light, and I'd bet her private bathroom was just as clean.

"Nice poster." I pointed to the Beyoncé photo on her wall.

"Yeah, I ordered it online. When did you get here?"

Must be nice having a home so large you don't hear doorbells or guests in the front of the house. After bringing her current, I ended with the comment from her mom.

She turned off the TV and slid her feet into a pair of slippers. "Better get this over with."

I put my hand on her arm to stop her. "I talked to Lucy a few minutes ago. She has a bruise on her shoulder."

"And her back and probably on her ass, but never anyplace that can be seen, compliments of talking back to the queen of the castle. I can't wait to get the hell out of this place." Rashan opened the door and bumped into Lucy.

"Oww," Lucy said, holding her shoulder.

"Sorry," Rashan said, softening her voice. "You need anything?"

Lucy's eyes slid to mine and then she shook her head fast. "Nah, I'm good." We headed to the living room.

Aunt Miriam's gaze lingered on Lucy before meeting Rashan's. "We have company." She waved at grandma, who sat watching mama and Uncle Frank.

Rashan kissed grandma on the cheek. "Hi Grandma, it's good to see you."

Lucy did the same but didn't say anything.

Uncle Frank patted Rashan's shoulder.

Aunt Miriam's jaw tightened until she caught me staring at her. "Can I get you something to drink?" The offer was made to the room even though she looked at me.

"No, thank you," I said. After seeing Lucy's bruises my opinion of her changed from sweet aunt to wicked witch of the west.

She nodded and returned to the kitchen.

"Lucy, bring a bottle of water from the kitchen," Uncle Frank said.

"Come on, I want to show you something." Rashan touched my arm and walked away.

Avoiding mama's gaze, I followed and wasn't surprised when we passed Rashan's room and turned the corner. She went inside a room and stopped. Inside the small area that must've been a storage closet, was an altar, candles, vases, and a large opened Bible on a pedestal. Several long bamboo canes and what looked like a leather strap lay on the carpeted altar. Speechless, my gaze roamed the area for a few moments until she pulled me back, and closed the door. In silence we returned to her bedroom, where she locked the door again.

Heart heavy, I sat next to her on the bed wanting to cry. All this time I thought Rashan lived a charmed life, the princess in the castle. I placed my hand on top of hers and squeezed. She leaned her head against my shoulder and we sat quietly lost in thought. Even after seeing the room, the bruises, I still didn't want to believe Uncle Frank allowed his kids to be treated that way.

Lucy tapped on the door. "Aunt Linda's ready to go."

We headed to the living room where mom and Uncle Frank stood talking.

"Mom, can I have my phone?" Rashan asked Aunt Miriam, surprising me.

"In a little while, after your grandmother's settled."

Mama's brow rose.

Uncle Frank's jaw tightened.

Rashan gave me an I-told-you look.

Mama looked at Lucy a few seconds and then at Uncle Frank.

I walked over to my aunt and hugged her good-bye like I always did. This time I forced myself not to cringe when she patted my back.

"Such a good girl." She placed her palms on both sides of my cheeks and stared into my eyes. "So pretty, make your parents proud."

I nodded to dislodge her hands, but she held tight for a second and then released me.

In that second I understood Rashan's fear. Something in Aunt Miriam's gaze scared me, the woman wasn't right. I could've sworn I smelled liquor on her breath.

"Shelly?" Mama called, not bothering to address her sister-in-law.

Stepping back, I tried to smile at my aunt but I don't think I was successful. Rashan walked with us to the front door. "I'll call you later," she said, and I knew Uncle Frank heard her. "Maybe we can hang out tomorrow."

Understanding the game, I nodded. "Sounds good, maybe go to the mall, there's a game I've been wanting to buy."

"Games!" Mama said, throwing her hands up. "Take some of that money and buy a dress or a pair of heels instead of sneakers."

I looked at Rashan, read her eagerness to get out of the house and nodded. "Maybe."

Chapter Seven

This morning clouds littered the sky in a haphazard fashion, granting rays of the rising sun admittance into the new day. The air smelled fresh without the fumes from transporting vehicles.

Dressed for school in jeans, a green tank top, a navy blue hoodie, and blue with green stripes knock-offs sneakers, I headed toward the bus stop without stopping in the kitchen to grab a piece of fruit. Down to the last two days of school, I was ready for summer break.

My phone beeped and I looked at the caller ID. "Lucy?" Dread rolled down my back. I'd talked to Rashan early yesterday; she hadn't made a decision on what she planned to do yet.

"Shelly?"

"Yeah."

"Have you seen Rashan?"

"Huh?" Heart slamming against my chest, I stopped in the middle of the sidewalk, turned and held the phone tight. "What do you mean?" I prayed a useless prayer that Lucy wasn't serious. Considering she'd called me three times tops in her life, I knew this was the real deal.

"She left yesterday after school. Mama thinks she went to the library a few blocks over, but she didn't come home last night. Did she call you?"

"No. I haven't talked to her. Hopefully she'll call soon." Or send a text as we planned.

Last night my clansman Pete said he'd been accepted in Rewind and explained the alpha-numeric code on the back of the card the company gave him. Turns out it was all he needed for the two days of testing. His session was scheduled for tomorrow. I didn't mention the card Rashan gave me as I wished him the best.

"Mama's mad. Daddy's not here yet. I called him so he could come home," Lucy said, drawing my attention back to the issue at hand.

"Good idea. Maybe they can find her."

"Maybe," Lucy said, sounding skeptical. "She didn't take her car or phone. They were locked away, so if she wanted to call she couldn't."

"Why didn't you tell me this before?" I snapped, knowing I might not get a text or call from my cousin.

"I didn't know until mama said she'd put Rashan's car in the garage and still had her cell phone. Daddy'll be mad about that."

He should be. I didn't want to get into their family drama, but my aunt was at the center of all of this and should be held accountable. That didn't matter right now. If I couldn't find Rashan as we agreed to make sure she was okay, I'd tell mama about the app, the pregnancy, and the office building. I'd prefer Rashan never speak to me again rather than lose her to some kind of con. The only reason I didn't wake mama now was because I wanted to try and do it Rashan's way first.

A quick glance at my watch propelled me toward the corner to catch public transportation. To make this work I needed to catch the early bus, get into the testing area to see if someone would page Rashan, make sure she was good and leave.

In and out.

If she wanted to stay, cool, that was on her. I'd head home to start summer break early and wait for the fallout. Approaching the large warehouse, I handed the security guard the card Rashan gave me. He typed in the number. Frowned and typed it again.

"Strange," he murmured as he pressed the buzzer opening the door. I pulled my purse strap up my shoulder and walked through as if I belonged, glad no one could see my hands shaking. Inside I handed the card to another woman. She typed in the number. "Do you have ID?"

"Yes." I gave her my high school ID and waited while she made a copy.

"Thank you, Shelley," she said and unlocked the door.

"What the hell was going on here?" I loved my cousin, but I wasn't sure I wanted to go inside electronic locking doors and security guarded entryways. Either go forward or turn back, what to do?

"Go through the doors, someone will answer questions inside," the woman said behind me, seeing my hesitation.

I looked over my shoulder at her and walked back. "I'm looking for Rashan Curten, have you seen her?"

"I don't know. Ask inside, they can help you," she said, pointing at the open door.

"This isn't like the Wizard of Oz is it?" I asked, smiling to cover my fear.

"No, several people can answer your questions, not just one person," she said, her dark eyes crinkled at the corners, easing my fears slightly.

As a gamer, the idea that a company had perfected a product to the point they used this type of security peaked my interest. Sure, I wanted to find Rashan because I promised, but I also wanted to see how the game worked. Curious, I followed the sounds of people talking and laughing. I turned the corner into a large room.

No more than twelve teenagers sat around on sofas and overstuffed chairs. Two left through a side door. Some were eating, others typing on keyboards, others talking and laughing in the relaxed environment. A large sign with the Rewind logo flashed on the wall reminding me all of this was for a game. A weight eased off my shoulder as I moved forward. Maybe this wasn't a complete scam, but I still didn't see how it could help Rashan.

A tall black female with a pixie haircut and large smile walked over to me. "Welcome, I'm Iris, glad you decided to join us. Would you like something to drink or eat?" She pointed to a table loaded with food and drink. My stomach growled at the sight of the tasty treats. I hadn't eaten since last night.

"Just something to drink, please. I'm looking for my cousin Rashan."

We walked toward the table, she grabbed and handed me a bottle of water. "Rashan? That name sounds familiar. I'll have to check a few things. Would you like to have a seat while I look?"

"Thanks." I finished that bottle and grabbed another. Eying the table of food, I picked up a plate and placed a few slices of bacon and a blueberry muffin on it.

Iris sat behind a desk while I ate.

"Hey, I've seen you around," a tall redheaded guy said, taking the seat next to me. "What school do you attend?"

In the middle of swallowing, I held up a finger to finish and then told him the name of my high school.

"Cool, I'm across town at Central. What's your dream?" Muddy brown colored eyes stared into mine as he sat next to me.

I coughed. "Oh, I'm not here for that, I'm looking for my cousin Rashan." I looked at Iris to make sure she wasn't looking. "Have you seen her? A little shorter than me, dark hair, cheerleader?"

"I wish, but I just got here a few seconds ago and you're the only person I've met so far." He kept staring at me.

"What?" I wiped my face with the napkin wondering why he stared.

"Nothing, just you're really pretty and the type of person I'd like to meet in my new life."

"Okaaay," I said, standing and moving to the trash bin to toss my plate, all the while, keeping him in my peripheral vision. I opened another bottle of water, looked around the room. Rashan wasn't here, I needed to leave. "I'm looking for my cousin Rashan, does anyone know her?" I said, raising my voice above the chatter.

Everyone stopped talking and looked at me.

Face warm, I cleared my throat. "She's sick and I need to help her."

No one spoke, eventually they went back to their conversations and I felt stupid.

Iris approached, her smile slipped some. "Rashan was in testing. If you'd waited a few seconds, I would've told you that."

"Sorry, can I talk to her?"

"Only if you're in testing and I don't think you'll make it." Iris turned and walked toward some of the others.

What did she mean I wouldn't make it? Make what? Testing? What kind of tests did they do? Those questions stumbled in my mind but didn't pass my lips. I stood on the side watching Iris talk to each person, coaxing a smile or burst of laughter. Was this all there was to it? I pulled out my phone and remembered Aunt Miriam had taken Rashan's phone.

By the time Iris made it back to me, I wasn't sure what to do.

"Think you're up for the challenge?"

"What challenge?" I asked.

"You have to play a game before you can go into testing. Rashan passed and was able to go further."

"When?"

"I'm not sure. But she was here, does that answer your questions?"

"She's missing. Is she still here?"

"I don't have access to anything other than the initial testing that happens here. Once you pass the initial challenge, you go into the next level. I don't know if she passed testing, quit, or went on to higher rounds," Iris said.

"How can I find out if she's still here?"

"You can ask one of the monitors in the first phase of testing, if you pass the test here." Her doubtful tone ticked me off.

"This sounds like some kind of game, with different rounds and levels. All I want to know is that she's okay and I'll leave."

Iris frowned. "Why wouldn't she be okay?"

I wasn't sure how much to say. "Just a feeling." I glanced at my watch, an hour had passed. Whatever I planned to do I needed to get with it. "Tell me about your test."

Iris' brow rose. "Go to a monitor, read the instructions and start. Take as much time as you need. Nothing starts until you pass this level."

Twenty minutes later, Iris escorted me to another room and wished me luck finding Rashan.

Chapter Eight

This room wasn't as large as the other. Funky background music piped through the speakers and the slight smell of wintergreen teased my nose. Good thing I wore sneakers otherwise I'd probably slip and fall on the shiny concrete floor. One older woman sat at a desk in the middle of the room. Looking around and seeing no one else, I headed toward her.

"Excuse me, I'm looking for my cousin, Rashan Curten. Is she in here?"

The older lady, who looked like our school librarian with her glasses sitting on the bridge of her nose, met my gaze with a raised brow. "I can't answer any questions until you show your ID and sign up for your Rewind."

"What?" I jerked back and stared down at her.

"You started testing but I don't have your paperwork on file. If you don't want a Rewind, just push through that door there." She pointed to a red metal door.

"Is Rashan here?"

"I can't tell you anything." Her gaze reminded me of mama's when she had the last word in a conversation.

Leaning forward I whispered. "That's not possible, no such thing as rewinding your life."

She shrugged. "You'll never know. There's the door."

Confused by her attitude, by everyone's attitude so far, I looked at the bright red door with the large exit sign above it and then back at her. "What if I take the test and change my mind?"

"What do you think happens?"

"I go home."

"You go home," she said, meeting my gaze.

"Is this some kind of scam?" Based on the expensive security, the equipment and the lay-out, if it was a scam I didn't see how they'd come out ahead.

"No. I wouldn't be here if it was."

Yeah, but I don't know you. "If I sign up for Rewind can I find out what happened to my cousin? Will someone tell me if she's here or not?"

"Probably. I can't tell you what I don't know."

"How long does it take?" I couldn't believe I was considering doing this. But I had six hours before I needed to be home for the boys.

"As long as it takes for you write a new past and answer several questions."

"What happens when I'm done answering?"

"If you pass the test, you'll make a choice, take the rewind or go home."

If Rashan made it this far she might be home by the time I get home or... or what? Rewinding her life, whatever that meant?

"When does the Rewind start?"

"Different times for people, most start right away."

"So she could be…" What was I saying? It wasn't possible to rewrite the past. Chances are my answers would be in review like everyone else's. "Okay, sign me up." Adrenaline rushed through my veins at the idea of playing and winning the game. I flashed my school ID and waited for the next step.

Her brow rose, silent, she turned the keyboard toward me and then her monitor. "I don't sign you up, you do that. Fill out the form, print, read, and then sign it. When you're done, you go into testing. In testing you'll have a computer, food, drinks, music, and a monitor to help prompt with ideas of how you'd like your past. The important thing to remember is nothing from your current life can be a part of the rewind process. Everything comes from your imagination, start at any point, but no later than elementary school. The rewind lasts for 30 days. Any questions?"

I blinked. She'd spewed that information so fast it took me a minute to process and even then I needed more time. "My cousin explained most of it." I looked at the monitor and filled in the blanks. Since I had no intention of going any further than the next room I agreed to everything to move things along. Finished, I stepped back and pushed the keyboard across the desk.

"Did you read everything?" She sounded skeptical.

"Yes, most of it. I'm just doing this to find my cousin."

"Why not wait until she's finished, I'm sure she'll contact you."

I shrugged, not wanting to explain Rashan's situation.

"Okay." The woman clicked a few keys and a few seconds she handed me a pad with a pen. "Sign here."

I watched my signature fill the line on the screen.

She looked at it, pressed a button and said. "Welcome to Rewind." A door I hadn't noticed before opened in the wall behind her.

"Go through there?" I asked.

"Yes."

I walked through the door. This room reminded me of the first. A table sat in the corner loaded with food, drinks, and bottled water. Seven people sat on comfortable chairs or sofas, typing on laptops. One of Taylor Swift's songs played in the background.

"Come in, come, come. I'm Toro and welcome to Rewind." A tall, slender Latino guy with gorgeous dark eyes and nice black hair waved me forward. Suddenly self-conscious of my hoodie and jeans, I moved at a clipped pace to avoid more attention.

The closer I got to this guy, the more I realized how attractive he was, like runway model quality. Clearing my throat, I hoped he could hear my words over my heart beating in my throat and the background music. "I'm looking for my cousin Rashan, have you seen her?"

"Who?"

"Rashan Curten, my cousin. She came here, I need to find her."

Toro frowned and even that was sexy gorgeous. Sexy? OMG where did that come from?

"Today? What time?"

"Yes, and I don't know."

He glanced at his watch. "I've been here for an hour and I haven't met anyone with that name. Let me get you started and I'll check the database, okay?"

"Okay." I shook my head. "No."

He frowned. "No?"

"I'm just looking for her, not the rest of this." I waved to the others sitting and working on their programs.

Toro crossed his arms and looked at me. "Cold feet?"

"Huh?"

"You're afraid to tap into your innermost desires and create a new world for yourself? You think you're betraying your parents? Or is it you can't think of anything you'd like to change?"

The direct challenge stung. Maybe I didn't want to think of a world without my family, that wasn't childish or afraid. "Innermost desires? Where'd that come from?"

His brow rose. "You've evaded my questions so I assume you aren't ready for the challenge. I'll escort you outside."

"What? Wait." I inhaled and then released it. At some point I stopped thinking the whole Rewind thing was a scam, but I wasn't sure it was a game either. But I was curious. What would I change if I could? The question teased and tantalized on so many levels. Could I be honest? Bare my soul to a game?

"Wait?" he asked. "Why? I don't know if your cousin's here or not."

"Can you check the computer? See if she was here?"

He stared at me for a couple seconds and picked up his tablet. "Spell her name."

Looking at the others typing, I rattled off the spelling and waited.

"Yes, she made it to this level and was offered the prize. It doesn't tell me if she accepted or not." The look he gave me clearly said, now what?

Caught up in the energy of the room, plus the knowledge Rashan, a non-gamer, made it this far, I wanted to play. "What do I need to do?"

Toro smiled and at that moment I couldn't wait to write a guy like him into my past to reappear in my future. "Would you like something to eat while I get a laptop prepared for you?" He pointed to the table. My stomach was too jittery to eat, so I grabbed a bottle of water and drank most of it while watching him move around.

"He's a hunk, huh?"

I looked over my shoulder and met the amused gaze of another girl with black spiked hair and pink edges. Pale, and much shorter with a round, pudgy frame, she watched Toro as if he were a tasty side of beef. Dark liner drew out green eyes with a hard edge that said she'd seen more than any child her age should. I wouldn't call the way she twisted her lips a smile, but it made her appear younger, less edgy.

"Yeah." I took another pull of water and watched her fill a plate with fruits and veggies. She filled a cup with punch and headed back to a seat on the sofa without saying anything else.

"Is that all you want?" Toro asked as he approached.

I held up the bottle. "Just thirsty right now. How long will this take?" I needed to pace myself, the walk to the bus stop, the buses back across town could take an hour and a half.

"As long as you need. Answer the questions honestly, and before you know it you'll have a choice to make. Do you want the life you've written or not? It's that simple. But you must be honest with yourself. I'm not sure how the game knows when you aren't, but it does and it locks you out without making the offer."

"The offer?" I didn't bother hiding my skepticism.

He nodded. "Yes, that's the only way to win."

"Win? Win what?" Now he held my interest. Playing to win was my weakness.

He shrugged. "It's different for each person, but nobody who's won has been disappointed."

"Tell me about some of the prizes you know about?" Eager to know what could be mine, I moved closer.

"Get started and see." He turned and headed to a seat not too far from the girl whom I spoken to before.

I looked at her half-eaten plate and the way she concentrated on the screen as her fingers flew over the keys. "One sec." I returned to the table, placed ham, meatballs, a few chunks of cheese and grapes on my plate, grabbed a bottle of water, and returned to Toro, who remained next to my chair.

"Ready?" he asked, smiling as I set things around me and took my seat.

"Yeah." I pulled the rolling table in front of me and tapped the laptop keyboard. The question appeared, "Do You Want to Rewind Your Life?" I clicked "yes" while wondering what would happen if I clicked no. The next screen asked for my first name, age, and location. Answering those took a few seconds and then the first question appeared.

"*Single parent or Both parents?*"

Both

"*Traditional family or non-traditional: Heterosexual or Same sex parents?*"

Traditional. I'd always believed I must look like my dad. It'd be cool to live with someone everyone knew was my parent without asking questions.

"*How many siblings?*"

None. I cringed over how selfish that answer sounded, but in a new life, it'd just be me.

"Would you like to attend day care or remain at home with your parents? Mom or dad, or both?" My initial thought was stay home with mama, but then I remembered the fun I had in daycare with Rashan and the other kids. I'd never had the chance to know my biological dad, what would it be like to stay home with him? I closed my eyes trying to imagine a day with both mama and daddy and couldn't. Even when mama dated and later married my stepdad, I never spent time alone with him that I could recall. My fingers hovered over the keyboard as uncertainty rocked my world. I went to the next question, hoping I could answer that one.

"Listen up everyone, think beyond today, nothing from your past enters your new life. Be creative, share your innermost hopes and dreams. No one will ever know unless you tell them. It's time to recreate your pasts," Toro encouraged.

His words hit a chord in me, challenged me to look into a place I'd been afraid to see before. If I could change anything from my past, things would definitely be different. Intent on releasing secret disappointments from the dark box in my mind, I didn't realize how much was inside. Caught up in the idea of change and seeing a new identity form on-screen based on my past energized me to push to the finish.

I could win this game. I yawned loud and long, but continued fine-tuning high school, and changed many things about home life as my eyelids grew heavy.

"What would you rename yourself?"

I wrote Phoenix and then erased it. Next I typed Serena, after my gaming avatar, imagining the laugh the group would get out of it later. Instead of laughing, I yawned again, longer this time. My eyes itched and I wanted to rest them for just a few minutes. But I hadn't finished the game. I took another sip of water, popped the last grape into my mouth, and pressed the enter key.

"Why do you want to Rewind?"

I groaned. Why can't I get to the end and win this thing?

"Why do I want to Rewind?" I murmured. My first thought was, I don't. But then I thought of everything I'd written, and how good it felt releasing those feelings. A few more seconds passed and I answered honestly. "To have another chance to get it right." The words mocked me. I couldn't mean that.

A wave of tiredness slammed into me. It hurt to hold my head up. My finger hovered over the send key for a second before I hit it.

"Congratulations, you've won!"

Smiling, I leaned back in my chair and closed my eyes.

Chapter Nine

I woke to the smell of bacon and fabric softener. Rolling to the side, I stretched and rubbed my heel against soft sheets as morning light trickled in through the blinds. Not quite ready to leave my dream, I pulled the sheet over my head and tried to pick up where I left off. A good looking guy, dark eyes and hair. I smacked my lips at the memory.

"Ummm." I moaned and stretched again as his face slipped away into that shadowy place all dreams hide, leaving me with a pleased reaction to whoever he'd been. Blurry eyed, I stood and headed to the bathroom. My feet sunk into something thick and warm. Looking down, my toes wiggled in a lovely lavender and cream print rug next to my bed.

Wait, a rug? Wood floors? Jolted awake, I looked around. A bed twice the size of mine sat in the middle of the room. In spite of the comfortable temperature, chills raced across my skin as I turned, slowly eying the large flat screen TV on the wall facing the bed. A picture with colors, not people, hung on another wall. Two chairs with a table between them were in the corner next to a long dresser. A small desk with a laptop were in the other corner. A most unusual digital clock with the number one hung from the corner of the ceiling. *Strange.* I stared at it for a few seconds, then at the clock on the desk, and then back at the number one. One clock told time, the other... a calendar? But today wasn't the 1st of the month. I sat on the side of the bed to give my chaotic thoughts a chance to settle.

Had we gone to a hotel and I slept through the drive? At least no one undressed me, I still wore my jeans, tank, and hoodie. This room was so much bigger than mine at home, I wondered why mama had given it to me instead of grandma or the boys. Curious at the silence, I stood and opened a door that led into a bathroom. "Nice. I won't have to share."

Since I needed to go, I stepped inside. It was a nice size, the glass-enclosed shower spoke to me. An unopened toothbrush lay on the counter. I made quick use of the supplies, slipped into my sneakers, and headed to find mama to see what her room looked like.

"Mom," I yelled, stepping out the room and stopped looking down the hall. This wasn't a hotel, it was a house. Someone else's house. Confused, I tapped on the closed door next to mine. No one answered. I headed down the stairs and hesitated on the last step. I'd never seen a living area and kitchen decorated this nice. Even Uncle Frank's house couldn't compare.

A large beige and cream sectional separated the kitchen from the living room. Two big chairs faced a huge flat screen TV. This place looked like the houses in mama's magazines. Maybe that's what this was about.

"Mom? Dad? Griff? Where's everybody at?" I didn't remember mama saying we had a trip planned, but this house was epic. I opened another door, it led into a half bath near the kitchen. *Awesome and convenient.* Another large table and eight chairs were in another room off the kitchen.

"Must be the real dining room." Four chairs sat beneath the island in the kitchen, and another small table with four chairs sat near the kitchen window.

Several slices of cooked bacon lay on a paper towel next to the stove. I picked up a piece and opened the refrigerator to look for something to drink.

"Hello."

I jumped and dropped my bacon on the floor at the stranger's voice. Holding my chest as my heart tried to knock its way out, I turned and stared. A slender woman who may have been close to mom's age, with short wavy sandy brown hair and blue-grayish eyes, stood a few feet from the kitchen island. Scared, I dismissed the hope and uncertainty in her gaze, and sought to protect myself. Standing on the other side of the kitchen island, I eyed the wooden knife block and then looked back at her.

"Who are you?" I asked, inching toward the knives. "Mama!" I yelled, ending on a higher note than I'd planned.

She held out her hands, palms down. "I'm Terri, Terri Hemper."

"Where's my mom?" Searching for the way out of this place, my gaze darted across the room toward the hall and stairs. My heart continued to slam against my chest. Breathing became hard when mom didn't appear or respond. How did I get in a strange house alone? Something wasn't right.

She swallowed, and reached into her pocket.

When she moved, a chill raced down my back. Certain she had a weapon, I took two quick steps, pulled a knife from the block and held it in front of me. "Stop and tell me where's my parents?" The knife shook in my hand, refusing to remain still until I wrapped the other hand around the first. Holding a weapon didn't comfort me like I thought. She was slightly taller than me but not a whole lot bigger. Still I didn't want to fight, I just wanted mama or answers or to go home.

"Do you remember anything? The last thing you were doing before you woke? Do you remember?" She pulled a piece of paper from her pocket.

"What?" I frowned, wondering what she was talking about.

"Think Serena, what were you doing before you woke up?"

"Serena?" I snorted as tension rolled off me at the mistaken identity. I had no idea how I'd gotten in the wrong house. "You've got me confused with someone else." I moved slowly around the island. She continued to hold her hands out and moved to the side, her gaze flicked from my face to the knife.

"Do you know Linda or Griffin Chesney?" I asked eyeing the front door as I moved toward it.

Her brow furrowed. "No. I've never heard of them. But this --"

I ran, opened the door and kept going. I made it to the middle of the long block. Several homes lined the road, some with cars in the driveway. Bending forward, I took several deep breaths and held my side. *What was I doing in that house?* In a bedroom. Dread rolled down my spine and I did a quick check of my clothes. Nothing ripped or torn, I didn't feel sore or violated. Relieved, I patted my pocket for my phone to call mama.

"Noooo, I left my phone in the room." I looked in the direction I'd come and couldn't tell which house I'd been in, not that I'd ever go back there. But that had been my Christmas gift last year. When mama picked me up, I'd have her call the number and then we'd go get it. First I needed to find a phone to use.

Pleased with a plan of action, I walked to the end of the road and turned left. This area looked more like Uncle Frank's than ours, with big, new looking houses and huge green yards. Large trees cast long shadows on the sidewalks and road. No one was outside, and few cars were on the road. I continued walking until I came to what looked like a community center and hoped someone there had a phone. According to the hours posted on the door, it opened at noon. I had no idea of the time or if there were any shops nearby where I could make a call.

Nothing looked familiar. Holding onto the knife, I sat in the chair on the porch to wait for the center to open. Terri's question barreled into my mind. *What had I been doing?* "Watching the boys or grandma," I murmured and then stopped. No. Yesterday had been different... snapshots of me on the bus, in a large room with food, music... what had I been doing? I couldn't capture any one thing.

"Hey, you okay?"

I looked up. A familiar looking girl watched me from the concrete sidewalk.

"Who are you?" I asked, trying to place her.

"Cricket, who are you?"

"Shelly. Do you have a phone I can borrow, please?"

"Sure." She handed me her phone.

Giddy at the sight of the device, I sagged against the seat for a brief second and then took it. I dialed mama. No answer. I redialed using our area code, still she didn't pick up.

I glanced at Cricket, her dark hair and compact form teased my memories but I couldn't place her. Terri's face flashed across my vision as I dialed daddy's cell. No matter what, he always answered, but not this time. Crazy thoughts of being lost raced through my mind as I dialed Rashan, then Lucy, and Uncle Frank. Throat tight, I called mama again, silently begging her to answer.

Shoulders slumped, I stared at the phone a few seconds before returning it. "That's fucking weird. No one's picking up." How would I get in touch without my phone? Maybe Cricket could tell me something. Dry mouthed, I swallowed and looked at her. "I have no idea where I am. My mom's gonna be pissed."

She frowned and pocketed her phone. "We passed the Rewind test and won 30 days of the life we'd live if the past we wrote were true. I saw you, we drooled over Toro, remember?"

A fuzzy outline of what she said crept into my awareness. Skin tingling, I stood to shake it off. A heaviness filled my stomach as her words penetrated.

"Cool, huh?"

"What?" I said, much louder in my mind than what came out my mouth.

"We won." She looked behind her. "This is epic."

Unable to speak, I took a step forward and looked over her head at the road, the houses, the sign for the community center. How could this be a game?

Her gaze dropped to my hand. "What are you doing with that?"

I looked down as the sun glinted off the blade in my hand and then looked at her.

"You're crazy." She took off running.

I ran a few feet to the edge of the property and looked in the direction she'd gone. "Rewind? The game?" I whispered as memories filtered in, slowly at first, and then picked up speed. *I won the game.* My stomach clenched in remembrance of the crap I'd wrote. Truth, my conscience taunted. Truth or not, I needed to get home before the boys came home from school.

I started walking. There had to be a way to get home. I wasn't Dorothy and this damn well better not be Oz.

Chapter Ten

Unbelievable. Did they rent a town to host their game? Rows of houses, a strip mall with a grocery store, clothing shops, drug store... just like a real town. Was everybody in the game? Every phone I used had the same results. No one answered. Nor could anyone tell me how to get back home. I'd been directed to call the cops, call home, or continue down this road or that.

I walked for hours looking for a way out of town and still hadn't found one. The roads went on forever until I saw a copse of trees at the end. Picking my way through trees, sticky bushes, and some debris, I wasn't sure this was the way out, but I had to try. A fast stream, with wide muddied banks, too deep and wide to cross stopped me cold. This had to be the worst day of my life.

"Mama," I yelled. "Get me out of here." Tears rolled down my cheek as I looked downstream. *Trapped.* This was a hundred times worse than the time mama thought Uncle Frank would pick me up from daycare and he thought mama would pick me up. Being the last kid in daycare sucked, especially when the workers have their purses on their laps and call everyone on your contact list to come get you. Tears prickled her eyes at the memory. I'd been alone, unwanted and abandoned. Mama was two hours late and the director wasn't smiling when she locked the door to the center behind us. Although she nodded at mama's apologies and excuses, she never looked at me the same after that. Strange I should think about that now.

I looked up at the blue sky and tried to remember the rules about talking to God. "Forgive me for I have sinned. I'd like to go home now." Maybe it was my imagination or my empty stomach, but it seemed the stream roared, the water moved faster, and the clouds covered the sun. I took that as a good sign that at least someone was listening, and walked out of the woods.

Tired, thirsty and hungry, I sat on a bench at the park as the sun lowered. Several cars passed, which surprised me. Where were they going? Familiar sounds of a neighborhood at the end of the day flowed around me. *This couldn't be real.* There had to be an answer for all of this. I watched a woman walk her small dog and wondered if she played the game or if she'd got here another way.

A cool breeze rustled the leaves nearby, sending them dancing in the air for a brief moment and then drifting away. Tears pooled in my eyes again. Tired of crying I wiped them away before they fell. Thoughts tumbled over and over in my mind until I wanted to scream the guilt away. Mama would be upset and scared while trying to find me.

Without a doubt this was my fault. But I always played games, how could I know this one was crazy? Where the hell was I anyway? That's what I wanted to know. Someone spent a lot of money making this game real, it was nice, but I didn't want to play anymore.

An anchor sat on my chest, reminding me of the extra stress this placed on mom, my family. Who would watch the boys or grandma? Mama depended on me, I needed to get home to help.

Useless tears flowed, seems I couldn't stop crying. I hadn't felt this alone or desolate since my first day of kindergarten and mom had to come on her lunch break to calm me down. How would I get out of this? I'd messed up, made things worse, and had no idea how to fix it.

How long I sat on that bench I don't know. A hammer beat inside my skull and my stomach growled. Dizzy, I laid down and closed my eyes. *Why did I play that stupid game? Because this isn't supposed to be possible.* All that stuff I wrote about a new past, God's punishing me for being ungrateful.

"Please God, show me how to get home. I won't complain again." I stayed really still, and a few moments later opened my eyes hoping I'd be home. Groaning, I closed my eyes again.

A car stopped. Footsteps came closer.

"Miss?"

"Yes?" I asked, the back of my head lying on my hands.

"Are you alright?"

"No. I want to go home."

"Where do you live?"

I rattled off my address.

"That's not around here. What's your address here?"

I didn't answer.

"Miss?" His voice hardened.

"I don't know."

"How long have you been here?"

"Today."

"Oh, I see. One second."

I peeked and saw the police car. My mouth dropped open as I sat. "They have police? What kind of place is this?"

He spoke on a shoulder microphone, and looked like a real cop. But that was impossible. He headed back toward me with a bottle of water so cold it sweated.

"Here. No doubt you're not feeling well. The body can go without food but not water."

I took the offered water and didn't speak until I'd drank the entire thing. Immediately I felt better.

"Your parents are looking for you."

I nodded. "Damn right they are and they can't find me because I'm here." I met his gaze. "Where are we exactly? I'll let mama know where to pick me up."

"Not that mom. Your mom for the next 30 days."

"Arghh." I screamed, letting it all out. "But my real mom doesn't know where I am, she's going to be looking for me and worried. You're a cop, how can you go along with this. It's almost like kidnapping."

He frowned. "You didn't sign up for Rewind?"

My face twisted into a frown. "Yes, but I'm almost 17, it doesn't count."

"Yes it does. How many times could you have walked away?"

I jumped up. "That doesn't matter, I want to go home now." I stamped my foot in a similar fashion like my younger brother Roger did to get his point across.

"It matters. I can't tell you where we are other than BellaVista. I don't even know what state or country; I just work here."

"So you're not a real cop?"

"Oh yeah, served on the force for five years. I'm real. The jail's real, so's the town. If you have more questions, talk them over with your parents." He held up his hand when I started to correct him. "For the next 30 days they're responsible for you. Take it easy on them, they want to be here and they want you." He waved for me to follow him.

I looked at the all too real-looking gun and handcuffs on his belt. "Do you know where the house is?" I opened the front passenger door, and realized there was no room with all of his equipment. Opening the back door, I slid inside.

"Yeah, I know where it is. Go home, ask questions, and get some rest."

I crossed my arms and looked out the window as we passed another shopping center, larger than the other one, the community center, and then he turned down a road. When the car stopped, I noticed a few people looking out their doors.

"Some things never change," I muttered when I got out and headed to the door.

Chapter Eleven

Terri opened the door before my feet hit the porch and stood back. I must've scared her earlier with the knife, which I'd tossed in the stream, but I refused to apologize. She stepped outside and walked past me. I heard her and the cop talking, but didn't try or care to hear what they were saying. I moved inside without giving them a second thought. Everything I knew was gone. Gone because I'd played that stupid game.

Rashan? Like a ghost, her name floated across my mind.

I stopped and stared at the floor. If Cricket was here, maybe my cousin was as well. Together we'd figure out a way to get home.

But Rashan wanted to start over, like Cricket. Would she help me? Glancing at the nice furniture and the delicious smell of something roasting, I doubted she'd give this up to deal with Aunt Miriam. What would Rashan do after the 30 days? I had no idea. Plus, I needed to deal with my own situation. What was *I* going to do? There had to be a way to get home or get a message to mama so she could come get me.

The front door closed.

Footsteps came from behind and from the side. Not wanting to talk to anybody, I kept my head down. My stomach growled but I refused to acknowledge anyone.

"Serena?" a masculine voice said.

I didn't respond, it wasn't my name.

"Just so you know, we can't call you by any other name. I'm Greg and this is Terri. We're both new to this and have been waiting for a child. If you'd like, we can talk and answer questions. One thing, we'll never lie to you, but we don't know everything. You'd probably say we don't know much."

The deep voice had a nice, kind quality, a cross between daddy and Uncle Frank when he was with Rashan. Greg and Terri took seats across from me. When I looked up, I gasped. Blond, blue-eyed, tall with muscles everywhere, I could easily pass for his kid. I frowned. Where'd that thought come from?

He leaned forward and met my gaze. "Are you hungry? Do you need anything?"

I shook my head to dismiss the gooey feeling his words set off inside. *Stranger. You don't know him.* Crossing my arms, I leaned back. "Is there any way to contact my parents to let them know where I am? That I'm alive and didn't run away?" My gaze flicked from his to Terri.

"No. For the next 30 days none of us have contact with the outside world. Just this community, BellaVista," he said in an even tone.

"So that's it? Just keep me against my will for 30 days? Isn't that illegal?" I snapped as frustration and a healthy dose of fear swamped me.

He looked at me for a few seconds. "When Terri told me you ran away, I asked Admin why our kid didn't want to be here. I was assured you had several opportunities to leave, and that it had been suggested that you leave, but you refused. You said you wanted to Rewind several times. Are they wrong?"

What was fast becoming a permanent emotion, guilt rippled across my chest as I remembered the old lady at the desk, Toro, even Iris, would've showed me the exit. I pressed forward using Rashan as an excuse when it was really the draw of winning, beating the game, that kept me going. And it cost me.

Rather than admit I'd entered the game willingly, I snorted. "No you're not wrong, but I never believed this was possible, so there was no downside to playing the game." I swallowed around the lump in my throat. "A game that takes you from one place to another? In 2016? That's not supposed to happen. What'd they do rent a town? How can they afford this?" I looked around the large house, the good quality furniture, and remembered the large community center. This hadn't happened overnight.

"I was just as surprised when I heard about it," Terri said, her eyes shining. "I had my doubts, but I took a chance and am happy to be here now. One day, I'll share some things from my past with you if I can."

Knowing I wasn't the only one thrust into the game arena eased my fears a little, but raised more questions. "How long have you been here?" I looked at her first and then him.

"I've been here a week," Greg said.

"I got here two days ago," Terri said. "Since I wanted an older child I had to wait longer. The call came last month that there might be an opportunity and I signed on hoping I'd get the chance to start over." She glanced at Greg, who watched her closely. "I can't have kids and didn't want to adopt alone. This was the next best thing."

"Did you play the app?" I asked, caught up in what she said.

"No, I went through a website a couple years ago and applied for a program that matched families. I never thought anything would come of it, but I was happy to hear from them. So far everything's been above board and exactly what was promised," Terri said, looking at me and then Greg.

"So your family knows where you are?" I asked, not quite buying into her story.

"There's just my sister and I haven't talked to her in five years." Her cheeks reddened and I couldn't help but feel bad for her lack of family and strained relationship with her sister.

"Same here," Greg said. "I lost mom two years ago to cancer, dad three years before that in a car accident, and my brother died in Iraq. Seems we have a lot more in common than we first thought," he said, looking at Terri.

Red-cheeked, she nodded.

Holy shit-balls! They really didn't know each other either. We were all strangers, and even though I was the only one wanting to leave, it made things easier knowing everyone knew this was temporary. Talk about weird. "And you're okay with this?" I looked at Terri.

She nodded and bit her lower lip as her gaze slid to the side.

"I'm good at games but not lying, I won't be your daughter. If you moved here for a family and intend to include me, you wasted your time. At the end of 30 days I'm going home, sooner if I can, and I won't call you anything but your name until then." I have no idea where the courage to make such a bold, in-your-face statement came from, especially with Greg being so big, but mentally, I patted myself on the back for setting some ground rules. Besides, I had no place to go, it was warm and clean here, and there was food. Nothing wrong with taking advantage of a few things while I tried to find a way out.

"That's fair and I understand. It's one of the risks I took when I agreed to come," Terri said.

"So there's nothing that can be done about me wanting to go home... being a minor and all..." I gave it one last shot, realized they wouldn't answer and stood. "Can I get something from the kitchen?"

"Of course, anything you'd like. There's a plate of food for you in the microwave," Terri said.

"Thank you." I opened the refrigerator, grabbed an apple, some cheese, and a bottle of water, and headed back upstairs. Nobody tried to stop me. When I glanced over the staircase railing, Greg and Terri were talking. They looked good together. He reminded me of Ken from my old Barbie collection and she'd be Josie from my Pussycat Dolls set.

I continued up the stairs and entered the large bedroom where I'd woken earlier. Placing my food on the desk, I locked the door, and then booted up the laptop to go online. *Interesting.* It looked like the search engine I used at home, but when I tried to log into a few games, an error message appeared. "Won't be contacting anyone that way. Smart." Restricted contact was the only way to make the 30-day thing work. I glanced at the number in the corner. "Will you be "2" tomorrow?"

Within minutes I'd devoured the apple and cheese. I tossed the empty water bottle into the trash. Removing my shoes, I wiggled my toes and looked toward the bathroom. I needed a shower.

A half hour later I was clean and tired from the long day. I sat on the bed with the laptop. *Thirty days.* My heart ached for mama and everybody. They had to be worried and scared, especially if Rashan hadn't gone home. I opened the word processor and wrote her a letter.

Mama, I'm so sorry for leaving without saying anything. At the time I thought I was helping, but I made matters worse. I should've talked to you about everything going on and didn't. I'm not blaming anyone else, well, not completely. I know you're worried and hope you forgive me. Next I told her about the game, how I played, and about BellaVista. I didn't mention Terri and Greg, not yet. Maybe in the next letter. I saved the letter to my flash drive.

Somehow apologizing and explaining what I'd done eased my pain. I stretched out on the bed, looked at the ceiling, and closed my eyes.

Chapter Twelve

Lying on the living room sofa, Linda stared at the wall, unseeing. Five days and Shelly hadn't come home. Life lost its color, a limb had been torn from her body, and she hadn't been aware it was missing until it was too late.

Red-eyed, she wiped her face with the back of her hand as the news droned in the background. A misty haze cavorted on the playing field of her mind. For days she'd gone over every scrap of information, replayed every conversation, regrettably there were too few of those, to figure out what had happened to Shelly. She came up empty each time. Disappearing was so out of character, even with Rashan's influence.

A hard painful lump formed in the back of her throat as more tears formed. Her breathing slowed and a small, sharp pain struck a nerve in her head. Guilt, sticky and toxic, refused to give her any peace. She'd done this. So caught up in her own career, she never thought what dumping so much responsibility did to a young girl. Griffin had begged her to slow down, spend more time at home, assured her they'd make it financially, but she hadn't listened. Ego, an ugly three letter word, had pushed her to the limit of her health and pushed her daughter out the door.

"I'm leaving now," Ms. Angie, the nurse's aide said. "Your mom ate a nice breakfast and lunch. I've got her all cleaned up and took her for a short walk outside." She paused. "Anything I can do for you?"

"No, thanks." The words were pushed through a tight throat and Linda hoped the conversation was over.

"I'm praying for you and your family. Shelly's a nice, helpful girl, always used good manners."

"Thank you." At least Angie didn't refer to Shelly in the past tense like so many others who stopped by. When Angie left, Linda turned off the TV and listened to the silence in the house, seeking solace from the emotional storm. Her fingertips brushed against a poster they'd plastered over the four neighboring counties that lay on the coffee table.

"All I want to know is that you're someplace safe," she murmured, looking at Shelly's face. "Please God, let my baby be safe. Tears continued rolling down her cheeks as she thought of her first born and wondered for the thousandth time, what happened that morning Shelly left for school. She'd last been seen getting on the city bus and getting off downtown near the industrial area. After that she disappeared. The police were just as stumped as she was because that was a nice part of town.

She picked up the flyer and stared at the image. It wasn't that good but Shelly hated taking pictures. Linda traced the outline of her daughters face while staring at her blue eyes. "Why didn't you talk to me?" She sobbed. "Why didn't I make more time for you to talk to me? You didn't want all the responsibility I placed on you, I know it bothered you, but you should've ... what? Told me?" She closed her eyes, remembering all the times Shelly had complained about not being able to do things with her friends, or stay after school for activities and watching the boys all the time. "I kept dumping more and more and more on her... for what?"

Griffin had been right, for months he'd complained she'd placed the job ahead of family and him. Now she had no choice but to step away from the high-pressured position to search for Shelly and care for her mom and the boys.

The house phone rang. She didn't recognize the number and let it go to voice mail. Same number rang again. This time she answered. "Hello?"

"Hi, Mrs. Chesney, my name's Celine. Shelly and I play games together online but she hasn't been answering her phone, is she there? Can I speak to her?"

Linda closed her eyes, cleared her throat, and told Celine that Shelly was missing. Before she finished, Celine was saying no.

"Where's her cousin, Rashan?"

Frowning, Linda wondered if Celine knew about Rashan's disappearance. "She's missing too, happened a day apart. Do you know anything that can help me find Shelly?"

"Only that Rashan wanted Shelly to play a game through an app called Rewind. Shelly was online the night before and hadn't downloaded the app at that time, but Rashan was all about playing the game."

Her stomach dropped in disappointment. "Game? What does that have to do with anything?" All Shelly did was play games.

"Well... Shelly and I didn't believe it, but this app, game, asks a lot of questions and if you win the prize you get to rewrite or rewind your life."

"A what?"

"Hard to believe and I doubt Shelly got involved, but Rashan took her to a party to find out more about it."

"Party? What party? Shelly doesn't go to parties." She sat up and held the phone close.

"Not a party, party, more like a gathering to talk about the game. Lots of kids were there and Rashan knew the guys in charge. They explained how the game worked."

Linda grabbed her pen. "Where was this party? Do you remember what day it was? What time of day?"

"No, I live in Ohio so I don't know where it was but she went one-day last week, either Monday, or Tuesday. No, it may've been Thursday."

Linda closed her eyes and threw the pen down. "I still don't see what this has to do with Shelly not coming home."

"Probably nothing. Shelly's grounded and didn't believe that stuff. I'll ask everybody if she said something to them about leaving."

"And who are you again?" Linda asked as hope deflated. This girl didn't know anything.

"Celine, Shelly and I are good friends."

Linda wrote Celine's name down. "Okay, thanks, and if you find out anything or even think of anything that could help with our search, call me."

"Will do, it's hard to believe... sorry. I'll ask around and call if I find out anything." They disconnected and Linda lay on her side, looking at the poster.

"Where did you go, Shelly? Are you okay?" She closed her eyes. "Please, God, let my baby be okay."

Chapter Thirteen

Two days later, in the quiet early morning hours, I tiptoed downstairs to the kitchen. Both the master bedroom and second bedroom doors were closed. *Perfect.* I'd woke several hours earlier for food and discovered there was no alarm system. Terri and Greg slept in the other two rooms.

Clothed in the same clothes I arrived in, I hefted the small canvas bag I'd found in a closet onto my shoulder and left the house. When I reached the sidewalk, an older woman turned the corner with her dog. Eager to set my plans in action, I pulled the hoodie over my head and jogged in the opposite direction. Over the past two days I'd seen several office buildings and hoped one of them housed the Admin Greg had talked about, or at least a library with public computer terminals so I could get online and send a message to my clan to give to mama. Even if I couldn't tell her where I was, I wanted to let her know I was alive and would be home in thirty days. A long explanation about the game and my role in it was on my flash drive, which I'd upload and send. Wouldn't take long, I should be back before Terri realized I was gone.

After walking several long blocks, I saw Main Street. A car passed and turned a corner. Head down, I jogged across the street to a one-story library. The police station and government office buildings were next to it and took up most of the block. All except the police were closed at this hour. The library opened in fifteen minutes. In the middle of the government building was a large round clock which displayed the time.

Putting mama's mind at ease fueled my determination to get a message to her. I sat on the metal bench near the library entrance and pulled out the laptop. A few seconds later, several possible connections illuminated, but without the passwords I couldn't log on.

I took the apple from my bag and bit into it. Tasty juices ran down my chin before I wiped them away with the back of my hand, making them sticky. Cars pulled into the parking lot, people walked inside various doors, laughing and talking as if all of this were real. I poured water from the bottle over my fingers and then took a sip as I watched the hands on the clock. The moment it struck nine, I tossed the empty bottle and apple core into the trash bin, hefted my bag on my shoulder, and walked into the library.

"Good morning," an older woman with gray strands mixed in her dark hair said, smiling.

"Morning," I murmured, and followed the signs for the computer section. It didn't take long to determine the library was as limited as the connection in the house. Fist balled, I slammed it down on the desk as I watched the monitor deny me the connections I needed.

"Can I help you, Dear?" the librarian asked from behind me.

"Yes, I can't connect to the internet."

"You're on the internet." She pointed to the screen which showed several connections, just not the one I wanted.

"But I can't use my email account," I gritted out while staring at the screen.

"Calm down, let's try mine over here." She moved toward her desk and I followed.

"What's the address?"

I gave it to her.

"It's not a good one, do you have another?" She frowned, touching keys.

"How can it not be good? I've used it every day for the past three years," I yelled.

"Control yourself or leave," she snapped, her eyes frosty.

"I want to go home," I said, my voice ending on a whine. "I made a mistake, I don't want rewind."

She looked at me for a few seconds and then typed something. "You changed your mind?"

I nodded, hoping she'd let me use her phone or internet to contact mama.

The door opened and the same policeman who'd taken me home the first day strode forward with his hand on the butt of his gun. "Did she damage anything?"

"No, just yelling and slamming her fist down." The librarian glanced at me and then looked at the police. "This cannot continue."

He touched my arm.

I yanked it away, spinning on him.

"Easy. You'll have to come with me," he said, moving close.

"No, I don't. I want to go home. I can change my mind, the lady said I could change my mind," I yelled, trying to avoid him.

He grabbed me around the waist, lifted and turned me around. Plastic bit into my flesh as he wrapped it around my wrists and tightly bound them behind my back. A slight shove pushed me through the front door. A few people stopped and watched as I was put in the back of the patrol car.

"Why can't I just go home?"

Instead of answering, he pulled out and drove a few blocks to what appeared to be a large warehouse. As we went through a security gate, my heart raced, throat tightened to the point it was hard to swallow. He opened the door and helped me out of the car. Too scared to speak, I thought of Terri and Greg, wishing they would help me as we walked up a ramp and through a double set of doors.

A woman behind a tall desk looked up, waved him in, and met us in a room. This smell of the place reminded me of the hospital when mama gave birth to Roger. I didn't see the other woman in the room until after she gave me a shot.

"Ow!" I tried to move out the way but couldn't. A few seconds later my world darkened and I passed out.

Chapter Fourteen

The past few days were fuzzy. I wasn't sure what happened after the library, only that I hadn't been successful in contacting mama. Terri and Greg explained the cop brought me home, claiming I'd been disturbing the peace and if I were caught doing it again, I'd be sent to some sort of detention.

I'd begged them to help me go home, and slammed the door in my room when they couldn't.

The soft tap on my bedroom could only be Terri to let me know breakfast was ready.

"Foods ready, hon."

Poor woman, no matter what I did or said, she never gave up. Never stopped being nice or understanding, a perfect match for the type mom I'd written in my Rewind description. I had to admit it was nice having someone doing the cooking, trying new recipes, and having me as taster. Terri wasn't a great baker, not like mama, but she got an A for effort.

"Thanks, be down in a bit," I said rolling out of bed, turned off my laptop and headed to the bathroom. Every day of my captivity, yes, that's what I called it since I wanted to go home and couldn't, I wrote letters. This morning I struggled with remembering names and faces of classmates and grandma, so I printed a letter introducing myself, and put it in an old water bottle. Later, I'd head to the stream and bury it. *Dramatic*? Yeah, but I was getting the feeling that people watched me. I now carried my flash drive containing mama's letters with me all the time. Stomach growling, I showered quickly and went downstairs, hoping to catch Greg before he left for work at the bank. Seeing him at the table in the mornings made all of this seem better for some reason. Terri had breakfast laid out, and I took the same seat I'd taken the past few days.

Pancakes, sausage, and cheesy eggs. My mouth watered but I waited for Terri, it seemed rude to eat while she puttered around the kitchen. Smiling, she placed blueberry and maple syrup on the table and then took a seat. After she blessed the table, I placed three pancakes on my plate, a couple sausages, and a heaping of eggs. Greg walked in with a large smile directed at Terri first and then me, just as I cut into my meat. He placed a kiss on her cheek and then kissed mine before sitting down.

That was new, I stared at him. "Well, good morning to you," I said, wondering what was going on.

"It's a really good morning." He winked.

Terri's cheeks reddened as she chewed her food.

"Anybody interested in going to the movies this weekend?" he asked, looking at me and then Terri.

Weekend? I hadn't thought that far.

"Ooo, sounds like fun." Terri looked at me, her eyes bright and happy. "What do you say?"

I didn't know what to say or think, movies weren't something we normally did as a family back home, but it would get me out of the house. Maybe I could find another way to leave a message or make outside contact. "If you want to."

"Great." He smiled and I could tell he meant it. He wanted to take us to a movie instead of watching sports or hanging with friends. He pushed back and stood. I glanced at his cleaned plate. How'd he eat so fast?

"I'll see you both later." He grabbed his keys from the hook and looked back. "Are you going swimming today?"

Since I thought he was talking to Terri, I didn't say anything.

"We might," Terri said. "It gets so hot during the day, going for a swim might not be a bad idea. Plus, I have some shopping I need to get done."

"Okay, have fun." He left.

Terri and I finished breakfast in silence. I'd forgotten about the community center and the pool. In my mind, participating in anything meant I accepted my fate. Non-participation had been my silent protest and proof of loyalty to my real family. But what if I'd missed opportunities to make vital connections? I couldn't be the only person unhappy here who wanted to go home.

"What do you think, want to go swimming? I'd love a few laps." Terri looked at me, her big eyes hopeful.

I'd have to be a real douche to say no when I wanted it just as much. "Sure. Wait." I frowned. "I don't have a swimsuit." I'd been doggedly wearing the same clothes I'd arrived in for the past few days, washing them at night, of course.

"We can fix that. If you can't wear one of mine, I'll buy you one." Clapping her hands, she smiled as if I'd granted her fondest wish. "I'm so excited." She reached over, kissed me on the cheek, and stood to clear the table.

"No, you go get started. You cooked, I'll clear this." I picked up our plates to scrape and place in the dishwasher.

"Thank you, I appreciate that." The look of surprise and then gratitude touched me.

I shrugged. "I did a whole lot more than this before."

She squeezed my shoulder and walked out. The room seemed a little brighter as I wiped down the island and ran the dishwasher. In twenty-five days, preferably sooner, I'd be home with stories to tell, and going swimming would just be another chapter.

Three hours later, Terri and I walked into the community center, which from the outside didn't look big enough to house the large air conditioned area with tables and chairs, large screen TV, and a small food court. On our way to the pool, Terri waved at a few of the ladies sitting with smaller children. How she thought I could fit into her size three bathing suit baffled me. Sure I was slim but not that small. I hadn't been that size since middle school. We'd had fun in the shops buying summer clothes, and even drove by the bank Greg managed. I snagged two chairs and laid our towels on top while she placed the cooler with our drinks and snacks between them.

The sounds of laughter and children squealing in the water erased everything from my mind. Eager to swim, I headed to the lap section and dove in. The cool water kissed my heated skin. Back and forth I swam until my muscles demanded I take a break or else. Not wanting to ever go with the 'or else' option, I reached the ladder and climbed out. Great. Terri, my towel, and chair were on the other side.

"Hey."

I turned to see Cricket sitting nearby with a guy who looked familiar.

"Hey." I waved and kept moving. My cheeks warmed in remembrance of the last time I saw her.

"Serena?"

Something about the way he said that name made me stop and look.

A guy my height, with brown eyes, stood and walked toward me. Strands of brown hair blew across his oval face as he leaned close and whispered. "It's me, Pete."

I stared a few seconds until his name clicked and wrapped my arms around his neck. "Oh my God, Pete, I can't believe it. How long you been here?" Over the years I'd seen my clan leader on Skype a few times, but his dark eyes, short dark hair and medium build were the same.

"Been here four days. You?" He stood back, staring up at me. I never realized how short he was.

"Five. This is my first time out." I glanced at Cricket. "Other than the first day when I freaked. Have you been able to get online?"

"No, but I haven't tried. Call me Max," he said, drawing my gaze. "That's my name now."

I jerked back and stared into his eyes. He was serious. "Okay, you're Max and you haven't tried to get online?" As clan leader, Pete all but lived online, his comment made no sense.

He shrugged. "New life, I wanted this chance to do things different."

I looked at Cricket and then at Max. "We need to talk. Hold on, let me tell Terri I plan to hang with you guys."

"Let's all hook up later this evening. I've got some things to do right now." He stepped back and even though I knew he didn't mean to be dismissive, that's how I felt.

"What time? Where?" Pete was good with computers, maybe he could find a way to help me contact my mom, and find out about Rashan.

"Park around seven, after dinner," Cricket said, her cool gaze watching me.

Shoulders slumped with the knowledge she'd be there and Pete hadn't objected, I nodded and walked off.

"You know her?" Terri nodded toward Cricket.

"Met her that first day while holding the knife." I frowned in remembrance.

Terri's brow rose and then she chuckled. "Seems you made an impression."

I shrugged and lay down.

"Want me to put sunscreen on your back?"

"Oh yeah, that'd be great, thanks." Unsure how all this family stuff worked, I looked back at her. "She asked if I wanted to hang out at the park around seven this evening. I figured it's after dinner and should be cool, right?"

"Sounds good to me, was that her boyfriend?"

"I don't know her well enough to know that." For some reason I didn't want to share I'd known Pete before. For one thing I wasn't sure he was the Pete I'd known, and I wanted to get his take on this game.

"Dinner won't take long, just have to pop the meat in the oven when we get home and whip up a few things. Should be plenty of time for you to get together with your friends."

"Don't know if we'll be friends yet, but I'd like to meet people my age." Cricket had been in my group when I started, which probably meant she was from the same area. Maybe we had a few things in common. I'd find out tonight.

Chapter Fifteen

Based on the looks Greg had been giving Terri since he arrived home, I'm sure he appreciated the alone time with his wife while I'd be at the park. Seems they'd made progress in their relationship, which could either be a good thing or cause problems after the 30 days. Wasn't my business so I kept quiet and headed out.

It didn't take long to reach the park, which was two blocks in the opposite direction from the community center. When I arrived, Pete or Max, Cricket, and another guy all sat on the bench or the ground. The closer I got to them, I recognized Red from the game.

He waved, but that light of recognition wasn't there. Cool. If he wanted to play strangers, so be it. I gave a general wave but headed to Pete. I had questions.

"Max?"

Pete looked at me, so did the others.

"You're happy you're here?" I allowed doubt to enter my tone.

"Yeah, I signed up for it."

"You knew about this?" I waved my hand around, glancing at the houses.

He grinned wide as if he'd won the lottery. "No. I never dreamed anything like this could happen. I thought it'd be on a smaller scale, but this is so much better."

"How'd they do this? I mean, do you have any idea how big this fricking place is? I couldn't find my way out."

"It's a real town, not sure how they did it, though," he said, sounding unconcerned.

"Some people claim they've been here since they were born," Red said. "I can't remember back that far."

"Most people don't," Cricket said.

I didn't care about people born in this place. "Did you get new parents?" I asked Pete.

He chuckled. "No, twenty is too old to be adopted. I'm waiting for my partner; he should be here later today."

Partner? I didn't care he wanted a guy, I just had no idea.

"Cool," Cricket said. "A noob?"

Pete shrugged. "Don't know yet, have to wait and see." He glanced at me.

"My new parents rock, total upgrade from before, not that it'd be hard to do," Red muttered.

"Same here," Cricket said. "Nice house, plenty of food, nice clothes, no yelling or cursing at me all the time." She held up her hands and looked at her nails. "This time I wanted civilized people who talked to me and each other rather than disappear for days at a time."

Her comments reminded me of the time I'd first seen her. The pink tipped hair, heavy make-up and black polish was gone. She looked much younger, homely was the word that came to mind, but content.

"Tell me about it," Red scoffed as he stretched. "Past few days, I slept in a comfortable bed in a room by myself, haven't done that... hell, I can't remember ever doing that. Are you sure this is only for thirty days? I wish it'd go longer."

"So nobody thinks it's strange we woke up in a new town and have no contact with the outside world?" I asked, looking at Pete and then Cricket.

"Strange? Yeah," Cricket said. "Does it bother me? Am I scared? No. I plan to enjoy the hell out of the next few weeks and store a lifetime of memories for when I return to the other world. I'll need them when times get rough."

"Or we could leave here together, start over someplace else," Red said, staring at Cricket.

She smiled. "That'd be nice."

No, no it wouldn't. My gaze lit on Cricket and then Pete.

"I want to be here. All of us do," he said.

"Except her." Cricket pointed at me.

Pissed that I needed to defend myself, I leaned toward her finger. "Excuse the hell out of me if I'm worried about my parents wondering what happened to me. What happens to the life I had before? I left for school and never went back home. They probably think --"

"You ran away?" Cricket said, standing and moving toward me. "That you're one of the thousands of teenagers who disappear and are never heard from again? Sold into prostitution? Or dead?"

I jerked back from her cold tone and then met her icy stare. "All of those are bad."

"You have 25 more days, three weeks, and then just tell them you took a wrong turn in Kansas," Red said.

Cricket laughed.

"This isn't funny," I snapped.

"No, it's not, but you have to see it from our perspectives," Pete said. "I spent hours recreating a new life. No one from my past crossed over and yet here you are. I'm not gaming anymore. I'm in grad school with a great relationship that I couldn't have in the small town where I lived in Georgia. Sure my family knows I left, but not where I am. My future means everything to me, not my past."

"But--"

He raised his hands. "Wait, hear me out. In order to be here we all agreed, signed several papers, passed all kinds of tests. You took those as well and now you're upset, why? Because you didn't believe it could happen? It happened. You wrote such a compelling new life, that for the next thirty days you experience what your life would've been if that were indeed real. You did that, Serena. You told them that name. You filled out the forms and signed off on it. No one but you." He exhaled. "Don't hate on everyone else because you're too scared to own up to your actions.

The only reason you're here is because you wrote a better past for yourself than the one you had."

Our gazes clashed.

I couldn't believe he blasted me like that. We'd all shared parts of our lives with the clan, but to throw it in my face...to be so mean. I couldn't believe it. I took a step back, turned and headed down the road. His hateful words replayed in my mind. *A better past than the one I had...* By the time I reached the house tears ran down my cheek. Terri and Greg sat in the living room and turned off the TV when I walked in.

"What happened?" Greg asked. Standing up, he looked more like a nightclub bouncer than a bank manager.

Embarrassed that I'd allowed Pete's words to get to me, I shook my head and headed toward the stairs.

"Shelly?" The sincere compassion in his voice and his use of my real name stopped me.

I wiped my face with the back of my hand and turned to face them. I hadn't been horrible with them, at least I didn't think I had, but I wasn't ready to see or hear them agree with Pete, Max be damned.

"Did your friends?" Terri waved her hand, her voice stronger as she moved to me. "Did anyone say something to upset you?"

"What was said..." I picked my words carefully. No matter what happened I wasn't a snitch. "It hurt, but I think it did because it's true."

Neither said anything, which was a good thing. I needed to process things myself, get beyond the snark and BS to deal with everything. "I screwed up even though I thought I was doing the right thing. When my cousin asked me to download the game, I was afraid. I didn't want to look or see anything different." I looked at Terri, hoping she'd understand.

"It's okay, don't beat yourself up about it." She placed her hand on my shoulder.

"No, it's not. I haven't accepted the consequences of what I did, writing a new past. Not yet. Worse, I really wrote a different past." I swallowed hard as tears rolled down my cheeks. "That's what I got called out on. I submitted a detailed past and won the game. On some level I wanted this," I whispered, ashamed to say it aloud.

Goosebumps rippled across my skin as Terri pulled me close and held me as guilt slammed through me. I shouldn't like this place or these people, not while mama and everyone searched for me, but it *was* nice being the center of their attention, with limited responsibilities. I could see myself living this life and that scared the hell out of me.

"Shhh, it's okay. In your own time, you'll figure out how this works for you," Terri said.

Greg handed me a bottle of water.

"Thanks." I took it and stepped back. "How could I have done this to her, she doesn't deserve it. She works hard, too hard I think, and now she's got to handle my disappearance on top of everything." I drank down the bottle and wiped my mouth. "But that doesn't change what I did."

"Or what was in your heart or mind," Greg said, placing his hand on my shoulder and squeezing. "Watch TV with us, it's a silly show but it'll take your mind off everything." He pressed the remote and the screen flared to life.

I sat on the sofa next to Greg. He placed a blanket over me as I stretched out. Terri smiled and sat in the chair. Greg was right, it was a silly program and I didn't think about anything.

Chapter Sixteen

The first week rolled into the next with me no closer to finding a way home. Worse, each morning became a struggle to recall specifics from my life with mom and everybody. Since then, I re-read every letter I'd written from the week before to try to keep my memories intact. A lot of what I read seemed like someone else's life which terrified me. Something weird was happening and I had no idea what or how to stop it.

When I asked Terri if she'd lost any memories, she said she didn't think so and left it at that. The next few days, Terri and I went to the pool earlier in the day to swim laps. I didn't want to see Red, Pete, or Cricket. Even though they were right to a point, I didn't appreciate the way they'd ganged up on me that night. Almost as if they'd rehearsed what to say.

Terri placed our cooler between our chairs and sat. "Nice day to get some sun," she said.

"The weather's pretty good here, wonder what part of the country we're in?" I asked, leaning forward so she could rub sunscreen on my back.

"South?"

I shrugged. "Maybe or west, like Nevada." I'd never been anywhere outside Kentucky, so I had no point of reference.

"Think it's dry enough here for Nevada?" She finished my back, handed me the bottle and turned around.

"I don't know, just a thought." I returned the favor and rubbed the sunscreen on her back.

"Don't forget we're going to the movies with daddy tomorrow."

My hand stilled. I frowned. Her comment sounded off, but I couldn't place my finger on what was wrong with it. An image of a tall man with brown, not blond, hair flashed across my mind so quick I couldn't process it. "What are we going to see?"

"Don't know." She laughed. "We'll go to dinner first, so I get the night off for our family date."

Family date? Once again it sounded off, but I couldn't think why and let it go. I finished her back in silence, and then went to swim laps. Laps done, I headed toward Terri on the other side of the patio.

"You should've seen it, they attacked the guy just because he made a lame comment about people's sexuality," a masculine voice I hadn't heard before said.

"Did you say something?" a much younger male voice asked.

"Just that we should agree to disagree."

The comment sounded familiar enough that I looked over my shoulder to see who was talking, and met the piercing dark gaze of a tall, black guy with one of those haircuts with more hair on top and close-shaved on the sides and back. A small diamond stud in his ear sparkled in the sun. My glaze flicked over his angular face with a pointed chin and thick lashes. No male should have natural eyelashes that long when it took most women several coats of mascara to get close to that look.

"Hey," he said, standing and walking with a loose limbered stride toward to me.

Looking up, my gaze swept across his muscular chest and then at his white-toothed smile.

I swallowed to loosen my tongue and fought to remain still while he checked me out. "Hey."

"Reginald Thomas, Reggie, or Chip here." He waved around the pool. "I've been here four days, haven't seen you before. What's your name?"

I pulled my eyes from his gorgeous smile and met his gaze. "Um... Serena." I shook my head. "Shelly. Serena here." How'd that happen? I never used my avatar's name, but it flowed from my tongue naturally.

"Serena?"

I nodded.

"I like that. How long you been here?"

Another Rewind gamer, my spirits sank a bit. Everyone I'd met so far seemed content, as if they were on a thirty-day vacation. Each day it seemed I'd joined them and that bugged me. "Ten days, twice as long as you."

Rather than comment, he looked around the pool with an easy-going smile, giving me another chance to check him out. He had the height of a man and muscles beneath his tee, but not the bulky kind you get from weight lifting. I watched him move, there was something of the urban warrior in him, combined with a gentleness that made my heart reach out.

"Is that your new mom?" He tipped his head and I followed his gaze to where Terri lay on the chair with headphones listening to an audio book.

"Yeah, Terri. You?" I looked around and didn't see anyone.

"She's at work. That's my new younger brother, Carlton." He pointed to the younger Latino boy sitting in the chair watching us.

I waved.

Carlton nodded and then looked away.

Oh boy, that one's got attitude.

"Is that what you wanted? Brothers and sisters?" The moment I asked that question, I frowned. *Brothers?* Two smiling faces flashed across my mind like slippery eels. A few more families with smaller children arrived.

He nodded. "Yeah. I didn't have any before, just an uncle who I hardly saw. This time I wanted a real family with a dad who works and comes home every night, and talks like he's got some sense. It's cool, seriously different."

Neither of us said anything for a few seconds. "I think we were in the same class." The words slipped past my lips without my consent. Heat flooded my cheeks and I lowered my gaze to watch the action in the pool.

"Huh?"

I shook my head trying to line up my thoughts. "I heard you tell Carlton about something, it sounded like a situation I had in Sociology 101 last semester." The moment I said the class, I recalled the fast-paced discussion on LGBT rights, and then it started to fade.

His eyes widened and then he smiled. "I took that class to finish my electives for graduation."

"You graduated?" He sounded older than he looked. I pegged him for 16 or 17.

"Yeah, that's why I got here later than everybody else. They said I was the last one from Kentucky." He looked around and took a step closer. "Where are we? Do you know?"

The curious look in his eyes mirrored the one I'd seen in the mirror just this morning. It'd be great to have someone other than me asking questions. "No, I've asked and nobody knows anything." I swallowed a shout of joy, wishing we could go to a corner and talk about how weird things became after winning the game.

Reggie smiled but it didn't reach his eyes. "Gotta admit it's a sweet deal, thing that worries me is who's paying for all of this? What's it going to cost me in the end? No one's taking pictures, so this isn't a promotional gimmick like I thought," he said in a lowered voice, his gaze flicked around before returning to me. "Don't get me wrong, I'm happy to be here. I've got the summer free before starting at State in the fall, full academic scholarship, but a brother's got questions, know what I mean?"

Lightheaded with excitement, I wanted to scream thank you to the heavens but controlled myself and nodded. "Me too."

"Good, maybe we could get together, talk and hang-out sometimes?"

Unable to restrain the joy bubbling from my chest, I grinned. Not only was he cute and didn't buy into this Rewind crap, he wanted to hang out. With me, I couldn't believe it.

"You have a nice smile, I like it," he said.

I couldn't stop smiling if I tried. "Come with me for a sec, I'll give you my number."

He looked at Carlton. "Be right back."

We headed to Terri in silence. I touched her shoulder. She sat up, pulled off her sunglasses and smiled at both of us.

"This is Reggie, a new friend. I don't remember our phone number, do you?" I glanced at him and met his direct gaze. The questions he asked made a lot of sense, if this wasn't a marketing campaign for the App, then what was it all about? I hadn't thought beyond going home, but his comments were on point. Maybe we could find answers together.

"What? Oh yes." She dug into her bag, pulled out a cell phone and rattled off the number.

I tore off a piece of paper, wrote the number down, and handed it to him.

He looked at it and pointed to Terri's phone. "I need one of those."

"Me too, don't know why I don't have one." I looked pointedly at Terri.

She laughed. "I'll talk to Greg, or better yet, you talk to him when he comes home."

"Can you walk with me for a minute?" he asked.

I looked at Terri.

"Go ahead, this story's just getting good." She placed the earplugs in her ears and lay back down.

I grabbed two bottles of water from the cooler as we walked toward the doors leading inside the center. He looked at Carlton playing in the pool with some other kids. "Hold on, let me tell him where we're going."

I nodded and watched him walk away. Something about the way he moved, smooth, and how he held his head high with confidence made him stand out, to me at least. Not that I had a lot of experience with guys. I didn't. But I knew enough to recognize he was the kind of guy girls liked. When he returned, we headed inside to a small table. "You want something else to drink? Eat?"

Considering Terri always brought a cooler with snacks, I wasn't hungry and held up the bottled water.

He took the seat next to me. "Tell me about you, Serena. Why are you here?"

The reaction I'd received the other night from Pete, a person I thought was a friend, made me cautious. Granted, I hadn't been arrested again for seeking answers, but I knew it was wrong to keep me here when I wanted to leave. "You first. What made you rewrite your past?"

His smile slipped a notch. Had I overstepped? I'd asked the same question he asked me, so there shouldn't be a problem.

"My dad was killed in an accident on the job when I was ten. I went to live with Uncle Ponce. He was a player, loved the ladies, and made it clear from the start he didn't want to deal with a kid, and for the most part, didn't. Most of my care came from the women he dated who thought being a mother to me would tie him down. It never worked." He looked at the opposite wall and then at me.

"You should see your face." He pointed at me. "It wasn't that bad, he never beat me or didn't feed me or buy me clothes. Never been on welfare or no shit like that." He sucked his teeth, leaned back, and crossed his arms over his chest. For a few seconds neither of us spoke.

What could I say after the welfare comment? He didn't seem offended *or* act like he was joking. Besides, welfare never entered my mind. What would make him say that?

"It was lonely though. I lived through books, games, sports," he said into the silence. "When I turned fifteen, he opened a bank account for direct deposit of the social security check from my old man so I could buy clothes and food. I sold my car just before I graduated, and put it with the lump sum from my old man's estate into an offshore account."

I frowned, no one I knew used the words offshore account. "How old are you?"

"Turned 19 the day I graduated, late birthday. How old are you?"

"Seventeen." I frowned. "Or I will be on my birthday, should be soon. I have one more year of school." The words tumbled over each other not making a lot of sense. I took a long drink of water to keep from saying anything. *Let him talk, listen and don't try to be funny, that never works.*

He stared at me for several seconds.

Certain something weird hung on my lips; I itched to wipe my mouth with the back of my hand, but maintained my cool.

"Hard to believe you and I were in the same class. Did you say anything during that BS?" he asked.

One thing I noticed, he didn't rush, not his words or his movements. I got the feeling we would be talking for a while and wasn't sure how I felt about that. What if I said something awkward or insensitive and he'd be like Cricket or Pete and embarrass me? I would die, right here ... on the floor.

Determined to relax and stay focused, I cleared my throat. "My comment started everything, well, his response to my comment. When you said agree to disagree, I wrote, agreed."

"That was ugly." He looked down at the table and then glanced at me with a half-smile. "But I made an A."

"I don't know what I made last semester, not yet anyway. I came here a day before the last day of school."

He nodded.

"What's the deal with the offshore thing?" I asked, preferring to hear him talk.

He waved. "Just some things I read about protecting money." He paused and inched closer. I leaned into him hoping we'd get around to dissecting this Rewind situation.

"When I first checked out Rewind, I overheard one of the ladies say when we go back in thirty days we won't remember anything from this time. So I figure there may be other things we forget, like my money. So I sold my stuff, put the money away and left a string of clues so I can find it later." He tapped his arm.

I envied his planning. "So you knew this would happen?"

"Not this." He looked around. "Never anything this ... this well put-together, but I figured they had to have a place to carry out the new life."

"And that didn't bother you?"

"Yes and no. I hated selling my mustang, that baby flies on the road, handles like a dream. It took longer than I thought to open the accounts, lots of channels to go through, plus closing out my dad's estate. Doing all of that in a short window of time was hard. I say no because no one, other than a few classmates, will know I'm gone." His hand covered mine. I stared at the long, brown, fingers, intrigued by the contrast. "What happened with you?"

Exhaling, I told him everything I remembered, it surprised me how much I forgot until he'd ask questions to explain answers. When I finished, I dreaded looking at him. Would he condemn me like Pete and the others had?

"I see your point."

Sympathy filled his gaze. "You didn't come from a bad or abusive home like a lot of us. Knowing your parents are going through hell wondering what's happened to you... I can only imagine. It sucks. I can't believe they wouldn't release you."

Happy to have someone see it from my side, the tension flowed from my shoulders. "They said I agreed, so I go home after thirty days."

His dark eyes stared with burning intensity into mine. "At thirty days you're offered a choice to return home or continue. Nothing's automatic, gotta know the fine print."

I regretted not taking the time to read. "I didn't know that."

He shrugged, it was a small movement that he used often. "I went over the contract, asked questions several times before signing."

At nineteen the contract was legally binding in his case, but since they treated us the same, I didn't point that out. "That was smart."

Not wanting to sound like a whiner, I tried to go with a mature, upbeat tone of someone who accepted responsibility for her actions. "Each day is better, Terri and Greg are nice, and getting more into each other each day."

"Yeah?"

Pleased with his response, I perked up. "They haven't been here that much longer than me and didn't know each other when they arrived." Thinking of the kiss Greg planted on Terri this morning, I assumed they knew each other a lot better now.

"Epic. How's that working?"

"They seem happy." I hadn't paid them that much attention, something I planned to change.

"Robert and Jill Thomas, my new parents, have lived here for years," Reggie said, rubbing his chin. I noticed a light mustache above his lip. "He runs the big grocery store on Main Street and she works there part-time. She's been coming home at noon all this week, seems nice, but I haven't been there long. I think Carlton's their biological kid, he doesn't recall when he arrived and doesn't seem to realize this is a game. Nice kid though."

This time the silence was comfortable and I didn't feel the need to talk right away. "Thanks," I said, holding the top of the empty bottle between my fingers and looked at him.

He finished his bottle of water and tossed it in the wastebasket. "For?"

"For not thinking I was weird for how I got here and then wanting to go home. Everyone hasn't been that understanding." *And the prize for the understatement of the year goes to me.*

"Sounds like things weren't perfect back home, but they worked for you. Don't waste time defending how you feel, my uncle broke me out of that a long time ago." He glanced at his watch and stood. "I'm meeting some guys at the park to shoot hoops, wanna come?"

The park? Hell, no. "Not today, maybe some other time. Terri and I are going shopping later."

"Next time then, I'll call you." Headed back to the pool, he waved and disappeared through the door.

Inexplicably drawn to him, again I watched him move. He reminded me of some of the jocks at my school, but without the huge egos or cockiness. The gentle way he spoke to his brother and teased the other kids, tugged on my heart.

In that instant, he turned and caught my eye before I could duck away. Instead of teasing me, his lips curled into a genuine smile. Snared, I couldn't look away, and soon an echoing smile blossomed across my face. He was someone I wanted to know, not just what he liked to eat or his favorite color. Those were appetizers. The guy behind the smile made my heart flutter and I wanted him. For the first time in my life I wanted a real, flesh and blood, I can touch him, guy.

He winked as he and Carlton walked by, and waved before closing the door.

I remained in my seat going over our conversation. Did I sound mature or make a mess of it? He seemed to be interested and I didn't push. Pleased I hadn't sounded like a dork or a skanky whore, I basked in the warm glow of his attention. It had been nice.

Sometime later Terri found me in that same spot day dreaming about a date with Reggie, and our first kiss.

"I know that look, I've seen it on my face a few times this week," she said, snapping me out of my reverie.

"That's too much information," I said, matching her smile as we left the building arm in arm.

"Feels good though, doesn't it?" She said as we crossed the parking lot.

"Yeah, it does. I hope he likes me."

Terri snorted. "He'd be a fool if he didn't and my daughter don't date fools."

My heart swelled and I hugged her briefly for the vote of confidence. "He may be a fool but a lot of girls will want him cause he's so cute." I closed the door and looked at my personal cheerleader for more words of comfort.

"Yeah, I saw quite a few of them at the pool watching him. But he didn't talk to them, he talked to you." Terri turned and placed her palm on my cheek. "Someone will always want the good ones; you can't let that bother you. It's what he does that's important. A good man will respectfully ignore other women who want his attention while making sure they know he's with you. That you're his choice, his girlfriend." She touched the tip of my nose and started the car.

"What about me? What am I supposed to do?" I hated not knowing this stuff.

"Let him do his job. Never answer a woman who thinks she has a claim on your guy, just pass the information onto him, let him handle it. If he doesn't step up to the plate and correct things, he's not your guy. See? Simple."

Yeah, simple.

Chapter Seventeen

Aldrik Sigman sat at the table reading something on his tablet. He looked up at Remi Karo - Project manager, and Dr. Kenn Berkhorn - lead scientist, seated at the small conference table. "Where are we with testing?"

Berkhorn patted a huge stack of papers. "All of the test results are here and have been sent to you electronically. I'll give highlights."

Sigman nodded.

"As you know Siggost is odorless and tasteless, very easy to digest, so the new formula mixes well in water, it's primary form of delivery. Test subjects ingest the drug every day with no real side effects other than the slow loss of their old memories and solidification of the new ones. Once a subject drink their first bottle of water, the drug is introduced to their system. Within 24 hours a craving for the Siggost water develops. Within five days the subject experiences memory loss, it could be their oldest memories or more recent," Berkhorn said.

"What about their skillsets? We've gone over this before; it always concerns me that the drug might go too far. This does no good if they forget how to read or write," Sigman stressed. That had been a problem noted from previous programs in MK Ultra, in the 50's and 60's.

Berkhorn nodded and pushed his glasses up his nose. "Understood and is the reason for 30 days to allow full integration of the created past and present. The subjects are required to remain active, reading, writing, working, basically doing whatever they've recreated for their new lives so that their skillsets remain unaffected. If a person does nothing, refuses to live in their new environment, they run the risk of losing their past with a limited future. It's critical not only to know what you want going forward, but also to flow into the newly created reality daily. In other words, whatever past has been written must be enacted; new names, new family, friends, discussion of new pasts, that type of thing to replace the old memories with the new. It's a wonderful thing--"

Sigman waved his hand and tapped on his tablet. "What percentage have negative reactions from the drug?"

"Right now, twenty-two percent, which is significantly lower than this time last year," Berkhorn said.

"Yes, but not as low as you promised the last time we met. After Ted Kazinsky and that unabomber shit, and Mark Chapman shot Lennon, and Sirhan shot Kennedy were identified as participants in MK Ultra, the government raised competency thresholds for these drugs." He shrugged. "Can't blame them for that after paying millions in lawsuits. What is the bar our government contact requires before we can pitch to a committee?"

"Between eight and ten."

Sigman leaned back in his chair, staring at the doctor. "You see the problem here?"

"Yes, we will get there, but it will take time," Berkhorn said, meeting Sigman's gaze slowly.

"If memory serves me correctly, you've been perfecting this for twenty years already. My father died before he saw it go mainstream, you can bet your ass I'm not waiting that long. I want these numbers down." The pen jumped when he slammed his palm on the table.

"We are dealing with memories, the mind." Berkhorn leaned forward, his tone pleading. "To erase a person's memory and allow their new existence to become their reality is a delicate balance, it must be done correctly or the consequences could be deadly."

"I want the percentage down. How long before that happens?" Sigman demanded.

Berkhorn looked at his notes, his shoulders drooped.

"How long?"

"I cannot answer with certainty, testing takes time. Resources are limited." His gaze lit on both men, seeking their understanding.

"Resources? How is that a problem? We've spent millions on this project." Sigman looked at Karo. "Is there a problem getting test subjects? Seems we had a waiting list before."

"With adults. He's referring to kids and teens."

"What about the game? The app you designed, it's been downloaded over a million times. Don't tell me we can't find qualified candidates. There's got to be several kids living on the streets who want a family, a home, food, clothes."

"Yes, but they remain in the game after 30 days and eventually mainstream near one of our towns. What the professor needs to test is those who leave the game, or have patches of memory loss to test different variations of the serum," Karo said.

"Exactly," Berkhorn said, animated. "The complete loss of memories happens quickly using the serum, but sometimes ghosts reappear."

"Ghosts? Holes? Patches?" Sigman asked looking at each man briefly.

"Yes. You see or hear something and it evokes a memory you can't grasp or recall. It's there one second, gone the next. Patches are holes in the memory. Much different than ghosts. If there is a hole in the memory a person is stuck between the two, old and new. Terribly confusing. Most will try to find a bridge to connect the two and won't be successful." He shook his head. "It's not good."

"No, it's not," Sigman said.

"I must test the patching serum, it removes the holes, erases the bridges. That's where I need to bring up the numbers, but it's difficult without test subjects," Berkhorn said.

Sigman looked at Remi Karo. "What do you need to make that happen?"

"Incompatible assignments would force the subject to leave at 30 days. But there'd be some mental issues accompanying that." He looked at the doctor.

"We can ease that, in some cases, fix it," Berkhorn said eagerly.

Karo tapped his keyboard. "I'll run Rewind again, different state this time, maybe in the mid-west. I have a few openings in BellaVista, but Coronado is closer to your main lab, will that work better for you?" He looked at the doctor.

"Yes. Cheaper too, everything's already there in place. On the thirty-first day, I'd need to monitor the injection they received the day before and begin treatment."

"Alright, I'll have a team relocate and work the area for the subjects we need," Karo said.

"Let's make this happen, and remember, the last thing we want is to have agencies investigating our testing methods. My father almost lost his company behind the MK-Ultra witch-hunt two decades ago, that will not be happening to me. Although the military and other government agencies are showing interest in MERP, they've been burned before and made their requirements clear. They will be our largest client or we scrap the program. I refuse to allow that to happen," Sigman said, his eyes alight with zealous fire.

"Yes, yes, exactly," Berkhorn said finger pointed, poised to continue.

Sigman waved his hand dismissively at Berkhorn and looked at Karo. "What are you doing about that family in Kentucky? I saw on the news they've launched a massive manhunt for two girls, Rashan Curten and Shelly Bryson? Related I believe. Both parents were on the news asking for help."

Karo nodded. "My people are on top of it. Seems Bryson went looking for her cousin Curten, who signed up before her. I've watched our tapes of both females during intake. Curten went through with no problem, eager for the change. Bryson was hesitant at first. Several times she was given the opportunity to discontinue the game and leave, she refused." He slid a flash drive to Sigman. "That's her Rewind. She wrote a very detailed new life without mentioning anyone or anything from her past. She wanted to be an only child, have a strong, loving relationship with both parents, especially the dad, wanted to be involved with school activities, have friends to hang-out with, meet a nice guy, basic stuff." He shook his head. "On some level this young lady wanted a different life even though she claimed to look for her cousin."

Sigman looked at the information on his tablet and snorted. "Seems that way. So many think they are happy or wouldn't change their lives and then they play the game on the app. Thousands recreated new pasts."

"Choosing the right candidates is the main thing, so many wanted a chance to do something different," Karo said leaning back in his seat. "Especially the older ones. It surprised me how many wanted to start over with families, kids, parents. Whenever we get this right, it'll be big."

Sigman waved away Karo's comment as if it weren't important or premature. "How soon did she drink the water?"

"Two bottles when she reached the first phase. There were no problems with the serum. The deeper she tapped into her subconscious to create a new past, the more it imprinted. At the end, she accepted her new identity and the serum kicked in.

"No problem inserting her tracking device?"

"None at all, just like the others, it's embedded beneath her skin."

"How's she integrating in the community? Problems?" Sigman asked.

"Once she arrived in BellaVista, we switched her to a stronger dose of Siggost. At first, she wanted to leave and was given a more concentrated dose of the serum to calm her. Watching the tapes, I got the feeling it was guilt more than anything else. With the combination of the drug and new environment, she's now integrating nicely. In a few weeks, she won't remember anyone from her past, and the past she created will be irrevocably imprinted. The team monitoring that community doesn't see any problems at this time," Karo said.

"And the other one?"

"Rashan Curten's the one Bryson was searching for. She's been assigned to Coronado." He looked at his tablet and then at Sigman. "She entered the program with no problems, had an accident, a fall I believe." He looked at the doctor who nodded. "We discovered she was pregnant. First time we've had a pregnant person drink the water. We bought in an obstetrician, and he's monitoring the situation so we can follow the results."

Sigman leaned back in his chair. "Yes, I remember now. She lied about her condition?"

Karo looked at Berkhorn. "We never asked if she was pregnant. From now on we will. We're monitoring her and the fetus. We've had to implement unusual actions on this one. I sent a report to you a few days ago. Things are working out."

"Good. I told you to handle this personally. It could blow up in our faces." He shook his head. "A fetus ingesting Siggost. Let's hope for the best, record everything and cover our asses," Sigman said, making notes.

"On it," Karo said.

"Good. I received a call when the story of the missing girls went regional and had to assure the Counsel. Great idea with the app by the way, seems this group of students are better than before," Sigman said.

"Yes, we chose students between the ages of ten and twenty from Kentucky and Georgia. They were vetted, tested, and placed with adults who'd joined the program earlier. Teams are monitoring their progress with a ninety-two percent success rate," Karo said.

"Those who don't handle the formula well?"

"Are removed."

"Good, let's go over the stats before I meet with the Counsel, they want more answers," Sigman said.

Chapter Eighteen

The next day I spent over an hour trying on new outfits and finally settled on a pair of jean shorts and a peach colored sleeveless tank top. Terri helped me with my hair and make-up. Looking at the finished results I wondered why I hadn't bothered before. My eyes looked larger, pretty and my hair lay really nice against my face and down my back.

"You're so beautiful," Terri said as she combed my hair and looked at me in the mirror.

For some reason I couldn't buy into that and had a difficult time accepting her compliment. She must have noticed my struggle.

"Repeat after me." She took my hands into hers as I faced her. "I'm beautiful."

Heat scorched my cheeks. "I can't say that."

Terri frowned. "Why not? It's true."

"It's vain, plus beauty's in the eye of the beholder," I said repeating something I'd heard before.

"True." She turned me to face the mirror where I stared at my face. That couldn't be me, but it was. I didn't look right, something was different.

"If you don't think you're beautiful, why should anyone else?"

"Oh. No one has to think I'm beautiful," I said quickly.

"No one? Not even Reggie?" She did a deliberate slow turn to look at all the clothes scattered around my room.

Maybe I did want him to think I looked okay, but beautiful might be stretching it.

"Now repeat after me. I am beautiful."

I cleared my throat and repeated the words. Nothing happened. I said them again and added, but not conceited. Terri laughed and hugged me. For a few seconds we stared at our images in the mirror, her arms were around my chest and it felt good.

"Reggie's here," Greg called from downstairs.

"Be right down," Terri said and released me.

For a brief second I wished we could go back to that moment, revel in it a little longer. But I really wanted to see Reggie. Last night he called and we talked for hours. Both of us were surprised by how easy conversation flowed and made plans to continue getting to know each other.

Seeing him downstairs dressed in a fitted short sleeve checkered shirt and jeans reminded me how good this guy looked. "Hey," I said, glad Terri and I spent a little time on my appearance.

"Hey," he said with a look of appreciation as he moved close and surprised me with a one armed hug. The crisp, clean fragrance of his cologne and the hardness of his chest made me want to remain in his arm longer.

"I'm Terri."

Reggie released me and turned. "Hi we met at the pool, right?"

"Yes, but I'm not sure I told you my name," she said stepping back near Greg.

"Okay," Reggie said and then looked at me.

"We're going to the park, be back in a little bit," I said, my gaze flicked from Reggie to Terri to Greg and back to Reggie.

"Sounds good," Greg said as we headed to the door and left.

"They seemed cool. Your dad likes sports. Did he ever play?" Reggie asked taking my hand as we walked.

Stoked by his display of affection and fighting to keep from jumping into his arms, it took me a few moments to respond. "I don't know. Could be, I'll ask." Hearing my response shamed me on some level. Greg and Terri were great. I couldn't ask for better parents but I kept them at a distance, afraid to really know them. A part of me wanted to share my fears about forgetting everything, but Reggie hadn't been here that long. His memories were still intact, which made me wonder if there was more going on.

"You said after thirty days we won't remember what happened here?" I glanced at him as we continued down the block. Last night we'd stayed away from talking about the game in case the parents were listening, and planned to get deep today.

"That's what I heard," he said as we crossed another street.

"I'm forgetting things now."

He looked down at me. "Yeah? Like what?"

I told him about the letters and that I couldn't recall how my mom, brothers, or grandma looked anymore. "What do you think that means?"

Frowning, he looked down at me. "I have no fucking clue. But that's a damn good idea to write down what you know so you don't forget."

"But it hurts." I rubbed my forehead.

"Huh? What hurts?" He placed his finger beneath my chin and stared into my eyes.

Seeing his sincerity, and envying his incredibly thick and long lashes, I lost my train of thought.

"It hurts now?" he asked.

"What?"

"You said something hurts?" He steered us toward the park bench.

"Oh, yeah." I cleared my throat. "When I read the letters, if I don't focus really hard, I can't remember. But when I do that it hurts."

"Seriously?"

I nodded and looked around at the playground equipment. At the other end of the park a couple guys were shooting basketballs.

"In case that happens to me when I get home I'll start writing down stuff, too. It's important to remember." He squeezed my hand.

"We can do it at my house if you want," I offered.

He looked at me and then smiled. "Cool and thanks for the heads up on the memory loss thing. I thought it'd come at the end, not now. There are some things I can forget, but not everything. Uncle Ponce's getting older and I need to make sure he's okay." He pointed at me. "You need to make sure your family's okay."

I nodded, happy someone finally understood.

He stared at me a few seconds and then frowned. "But why? Why take our memories? How are we supposed to manage when we go home?"

That was a great question. "Maybe they don't want people like mama to come after them? Lawsuits. I'm underage and nothing I signed would hold up in court."

He nodded slowly. "Which is strange. Why run that risk? Why not use older gamers?" A frown marred his forehead. "That makes no sense."

I agreed. "I want to go home." The statement lacked fire and conviction. I couldn't rouse my anger or fear to infuse those words.

Reggie's large hand covered mine. "You will. Everything will work out, you'll see."

Dots I'd never connected before snapped into place. "What if the reason I'm forgetting the past is to make it harder for me to decide to leave on the thirtieth day? Think about it. If I don't remember home, or my family, why would I leave Terri and Greg?" I dropped my head back and stared at the blue sky. "Sometimes I think of them as my parents, things get all confused and I believe they love me, care for me as parents should." An image of Terri combing my hair, and then us sitting on the bed talking about boys and school, Greg at breakfast telling us how lucky he was that we were in his life… all of it was just so perfect. I loved it and that was wrong.

"You don't think it's part of the game?"

I released a long stream of air and shook my head slowly. "Most of the time I forget the rewind crap. I'm just living and things are good. What if that's the deal?"

"Same question, what do they get out of it?" Reggie asked, meeting my gaze.

"Hell if I know." I looked around. "All of this has to cost a fortune, so that knocks out a lot of gaming companies."

"The game could be a way to get players, and maybe they're not a real gaming company," Reggie said his voice dropping. "That'd be fucked."

I wanted to smack him for voicing my fears.

"What kind of company would spend millions of dollars for this kind of setup? It's not marketing unless that comes at the end or they're taping everything we do," he said.

I shuddered. "Creepy."

"Just thinking out loud. No one does all of this without a reason or expectation of a return on their investment. I took an online business class," he said when I looked at him.

"Thirty days means something," I said. "Something happens on that day? What?" I looked at him.

Reggie shrugged. "I don't know, but I'll do some research, see what I can find." He shook his head. "Knew this was too good to be free. Not sure what it'll cost, but I suspect it'll be expensive."

"Agreed."

Chapter Nineteen

Later that week…

"Want to go bowling tonight?" Reggie asked as we walked
from the park to my house to eat a late lunch. I'd met a few of his
friends and their girlfriends, Amazing, Kelly, and Patricia.
Amazing was a short Latina with a quick smile, loud laugh, and
super tight lycra outfits. We hit it off right away. Anyone with the
confidence to re-name herself Amazing was a keeper. She dated
Mark, a tall, unassuming white dude who wore glasses and played
decent basketball.

"Why? So you can laugh at me like you did last time?" I
pushed against his shoulder, remembering how bad I'd played the
other day. His parents and Carlton were there, and they'd gone out
of their way to make me feel comfortable. Well, not Carlton. I got
the feeling he didn't like me or the time Reggie spent with me,
which was every day since we met.

"No laughing. I promise." He held up his hand and then laid it
on his chest, but the devilment in his eyes remained.

"Did you finish writing in your journal?" I asked to buy time.
It wasn't that I didn't want to bowl, or go out, I enjoyed every
minute we spent together. But that didn't change what we'd both
discovered. We were losing our memories and the new past we'd
written was replacing them.

"Yeah, but the past and present got mixed up again. If I didn't
have the old notes from that first day we started, I'd have been
confused as hell. Did you mention it to your mom? Terri, I mean?"

I nodded. "She can't tell the past from the present either and
doesn't care. Can't blame her though. From what she told me in the
beginning, right now is better than she's ever had it before." Terri
had been in a physically abusive marriage. One barbaric fight with

her ex had left her unable to have children, something that still bothered her.

Reggie took my hand as we moved across the street and flashed a smile that got me tied up inside. I'd grown accustomed to his public displays of affection after he'd kissed me in front of his parents on our first real, he picked me up in a car, date. We'd never discussed being a couple or how we felt about each other or the future. Things just evolved and I liked that best. But he was the one. I knew it. Reggie filled my mind constantly, my days were scheduled with him in mind; he quickly became my everything.

"Most people I've talked to feel the same. Some of the guys I play ball with are from gangs, juvenile hall, and jail. They used the game to get a fresh start or experience a different life. When I asked what they'd do after thirty days, they didn't have answers, preferred to live in the present."

"What if they meet people from their pasts and don't remember them or the dangers?" I asked.

He shrugged. "If we didn't read our journals every morning we wouldn't be having this conversation. It's the only thing that reminds me this isn't real." His fingertip touched the tip of my nose. "Glad you're real and that's the only thing that matters."

My heart clenched at his declaration, I felt giddy inside. "Same here."

We lapsed into silence. I'd read my journal this morning but couldn't finish because of the pain. Each time I searched for remnants off my past, sharp pins went through my skull. Sometimes it hurt so bad I wanted to throw up, or dots floated in front of my eyes. How much longer could I keep doing it? I wasn't sure it was worth it.

He squeezed my hand as we turned the corner. Greg's car was in the drive and I smiled.

"Your dad's home?"

I nodded without correcting him this time. Each day, Terri and I grew closer, especially after she and Greg had met Reggie.

They both liked him and welcomed him into our home. "Must be lunch time. He's started coming home for a quickie."

Reggie looked at me and then laughed. "I know you meant lunch."

I nodded and bit my lip to stop from grinning. Food had little to do with Terri rushing to be home this time of day lately or their closed bedroom door. I glanced at my watch. They should be done since Greg's lunch break was over in ten minutes. Still, I didn't want to intrude and slowed our walk. Reggie adjusted his pace to match mine.

We both looked up as a car slowed on the road and stopped.

"Hi guys," Cricket called out.

Red sat in the passenger seat staring at us. His beige baseball cap sat crooked on his head and he nodded a few times before opening his door.

Reggie looked at Cricket. "Hey."

"Hi." I watched her carefully.

"Haven't seen you around," Cricket said. She stepped out the car and walked around to lean on the fender. "Are you still angry about that night?"

Red stood next to her.

"No, haven't thought about it." Reggie and I spent a lot of time together, I didn't have the time to think of Pete or the others.

"You stopped going to the pool?" she asked, her gaze flicked over Reggie and then me.

"No, I still go, why?"

She shrugged. "Nobody's seen you around. Pete thought you were sulking or something."

I laughed at her attempt to put me down. Reggie looked at me and smiled.

"Not at all, just busy." I'd been playing with the idea of taking martial arts classes and drama. Somewhere in my mind I had this idea I'd like to fight and act. As always my biggest supporter, Terri, had taken me to sign up at the academy and theater. She insisted I give them both a try. It cut into my late afternoons which worked well because Reggie spent time with Carlton or his friends playing sports.

"Several people have seen her around," Reggie added.

Cricket nodded. "You're Carlton's brother?"

"Yeah."

"Nice kid. You should spend more time with him, help him get acclimated to everything," she said.

Reggie's hand tightened around mine. "And you are?"

"Cricket. This is my boyfriend, Red." She looked at me and then Reggie.

I had no intention of introducing Reggie and looked up the street. Greg walked out the front door, fixing his tie.

Reggie followed my gaze and chuckled. "Timing is everything."

"What?" Cricket asked, looking toward the house.

"Nothing," I said, taking a step backward from the car. "Good seeing you, we've got to get going."

"We're going to be hanging out at the park this evening if you guys want to come," Red said.

"Can't, we're going bowling. Maybe some other time," I said.

"Sure," Red said, opening his door and sliding in the front seat.

Cricket returned to the driver's side and looked at me. "It wasn't personal that other night, honest. Let's hang out some time."

I nodded and tried to smile rather than say I'd prefer to have my teeth extracted without anesthesia first. Pulling Reggie's hand, we headed to the house and waved at Greg as he drove past us on his way back to work.

When we reached the porch, Reggie pulled me close and glanced over his shoulder. "What happened with those guys?"

I told him about seeing Pete at the pool and what happened at the park. By the time I finished, a deep frown marred his forehead.

"That's fucked up. Nobody should judge anybody here, especially friends."

Pleased he was riled for my sake, I played peacemaker. "In a way I judged them first. Strange, I remember what happened that night so clearly, but not the reason I was so angry. I mean I know why I was angry, but I can't recall my feelings behind it. Does that make sense?"

He shrugged. "I guess it's because you've been here fifteen days, halfway done, maybe that's why you're not as mad."

That made sense. I'd never been one to hold a grudge and didn't plan to start now. Inside, we made our way to the kitchen.

Reggie's cell rang. He looked at the caller ID, his brow rose. "What's up man?" The entire time he listened, he watched me pull out cold chicken, coleslaw and rolls. He pressed a button. "Can Carlton come over? He hasn't been feeling good lately and is home alone."

I nodded, hoping the young boy would be friendlier here than he been when I was at their house.

Terri walked downstairs, dressed differently than she'd been this morning. I smiled at her pink cheeks and took out another two plates. "Is it okay if we eat this for lunch?" I asked, waving at the food.

"That's fine. I made extra for that reason. Hi Reggie, how are you?" She gave him a one-arm hug.

"I'm fine, thank you." He looked at me and then at her again. "Carlton, my brother, is coming over so he won't be home alone, is that okay?"

"Of course. You and your family are always welcome," Terri said, placing the chicken in the microwave. "How's your mother?"

"Good. She's running late today, that's why he's alone. He'll be here soon."

"We're going bowling tonight," I said.

Terri chuckled and I joined in. "I know I said I'd never go again, but Reggie promised not to laugh this time."

"I did?"

I shoved his shoulder.

He took my hands, pulled me close, and wrapped them around his waist. "Why you always pushing me away?"

Heat rose to my cheeks in a flash. I couldn't turn away from his gaze, but I couldn't do this in front of mom. Instead of kissing me the way he'd done every night we left each other, he hugged me tight. I wasn't sure if disappointment or relief filled my chest. "I don't," I whispered, feeling warm and safe in his arms.

The microwave pinged.

We separated, but not before I felt the hard bulge in his pants. Without looking down I headed to the other side of the kitchen island to fix plates. We'd played with the idea of taking our kisses further. Amazing and I had gone to the clinic and got birth control pills, but I wasn't ready to make that step. He never pushed or hid the fact he wanted me sexually, which worked just fine. Amazing convinced me to buy a few things he'd appreciate seeing me in whenever we finally came together that way. I hoped he liked the small pieces of material Amazing swore would make him forget his name.

The doorbell rang. Reggie left to open it.

"Seems like the two of you are getting close," Terri whispered moving close. "His eyes says it all, he really likes you." She lifted a few strands of my hair and looked at the ends. It was time to get it done. I'd call Amazing later, see if she'd go with me to the hairdresser, and then get our nails done. Maybe do a little shopping or something fun like that.

"I hope so, because I'm falling for him too and I don't want to get hurt." I glanced at him and Carlton talking softly in the foyer.

"Pain's a part of life, Sweetie. Sometimes you just have to take a chance, see what life's about."

The satisfaction in her voice grabbed my attention. "You seem happier these days, especially after lunch."

She giggled. "Isn't that wild? He asks to come home for lunch and bypasses the kitchen every time. I love it though, never dreamed I could be this happy." She placed her warm palm on my cheek and stared into my eyes. At that moment we connected as if an arc or bridge of some sort linked us together.

"God gives us one life on this earth, make it the best you can. Whenever you have a chance at happiness, go for it. Pain has its own calling card and sometimes there's not a lot we can do about it. Choices today affect tomorrow, so be happy. Love, live and laugh." She smiled with a slight frown. "That sounded like something I read from a book, can't recall now, but you get my meaning, right?"

"Yes, I do." My gaze slid to Reggie, who had his arm around Carlton's shoulder as they entered the kitchen and sat at the island.

"Hi Carlton," I said, since he hadn't spoken.

"Hi."

"This is my mom, Terri." I pointed at her as she fixed plates.

Her eyes widened as she cleared her throat. "Hi, Carlton. What piece of chicken do you like?"

Carlton's cheeks reddened. "I like them all... thank you." He added the last as if it were an after-thought.

I gave Reggie his plate and sat on the other side of him. Terri slid Carlton his plate and then ruffled his curly black hair before taking a seat.

I remembered Cricket's comment to Reggie. "Carlton, do you know Cricket or Red?" I asked.

"Yeah, seen them at the pool."

"She told me to help you get acclimated, but you've been here longer than me," Reggie said. "What did she mean by that?"

Carlton shrugged. "She's nosy. Always asking questions, getting in everyone's business. She asked about you, what you liked to do, where you go and stuff. I told mama. Would'a told you but I forgot."

"No problem, my man." Reggie glanced at me and I knew he didn't like or understand Cricket's probing.

Chapter Twenty

Bowling that night was a blast. Greg and Terri came and played with friends. Reggie's parents and Carlton showed up. One of Reggie's friends Josh was Pete's significant other. I returned Pete's wave and looked away. Maybe we'd be friends again one day or not. The other guys he played ball with arrived and left after Reggie introduced me. An hour or so later they returned with dates.

Thrilled to meet the other teenage girls, Patricia, Kelly, and Brenda, as well as seeing Amazing again, I grabbed a table and the four of us sat talking and cheering on our guys. All four had been here a few days longer than me, were still in high school, and loved everything in their lives so far. Amazing made no excuses for her tight dress pushing her breasts almost to her chin. I loved the way her dark eyes sparkled as she talked and watched Mark. Tall, almost gaunt with short blonde hair and thick glasses, you'd think he was a Brad Pitt clone the way she said his name.

"Mark say we come to bowl first and then we go to my home and watch TV." Her brows wiggled a bit.

We all laughed.

"Yeah, I was surprised when Steven's basketball game changed to bowling," Brenda a petite, girl with a cute pixie haircut said. "One thing I never intend to do again is be taken for granted. I told him if he ever pulls this shit again, say he's doing one thing and then turns out it's another, we're done." I met her dark gaze and nodded in agreement. Reggie's my first in the flesh boyfriend and I'd hate it if he lied to me like that.

"I know that's right," Amazing and Kelly said, high-fiving each other.

Patricia, remained silent and hadn't said much since Tommy, another of Reggie's friends walked in and pointed her in our direction. She'd taken a seat and remained quiet.

"Russ didn't bother lying, just told me he and his boys were hanging out and he'd let me know if anyone brought dates," Kelly, a Hallie Berry clone with light brown eyes and chin length straight hair, said. Her tone lowered as she glanced over her shoulder at the short, muscular white guy bowling. Reggie had mentioned Russell had been in a gang, got shot and took Rewind for a different life. Things started rough but Russell was doing better, especially after meeting his girlfriend. Supposedly Kelly had been super-smart in school but had been in a bad environment.

Brenda looked at them and smiled. "I live past the shopping center on Main and never see anybody except young kids. When he told me there were girls here our age, I got over being pissed, got dressed and came over. Have any of you been swimming at the community center?"

"That's where I met Reggie," I said. We looked at the guys laughing and bowling.

"Good deal. I haven't been, it's far from our house," Brenda said. Her darker complexion glowing beneath the overhead lights.

"Me neither," Amazing said. "Anybody got a car?"

"No," I said, wishing I had a license.

"No." Kelly and Brenda said.

"But I think my mom would drop me off," Brenda said. "Depending on where you live, we might be able to pick you up."

While the three of them discussed addresses I looked at Patricia. She wore very little make-up but she didn't need much to accent her large green eyes or long lashes. She and Amazing were both heavy for their height, but Patricia lacked the confidence Amazing had in spades. Rather than hide her curves, Amazing accentuated and celebrated her lushness. Patricia gave me the impression she'd hide in a corner if she could. How did she attract an athlete like Tommy? He and Reggie were the only two black guys on the team but Tommy had an edginess Reggie lacked. Wherever Tommy came from, it left a mark.

"Good, we live close enough to each other that we can carpool," Kelly said. Her light brown eyes glowed with pleasure. "We can pick a day and all meet there."

"I go in the mornings, it's not as crowded," I said, unsure I wanted to change the time Reggie and I went swimming.

"That might work best for mama," Brenda said.

Her use of that word triggered an image that flew across my mind so fast I couldn't catch it. *"Mama?"* I let the word stay in my mind a few seconds, nothing happened.

"Okay Chicas, what about Saturday morning we go swimming and then head over to the park? It's on that side of town," Amazing said her dark gaze sparkling. "Mark says they just play ball but I'd like to see this place myself. It is close to walk, right?" She looked at me.

"Not too far. A few long blocks," I said. Reggie and I walked it several times.

She waved her hand. "We can do it."

Brenda and Kelly nodded.

Patricia didn't say anything and no one pushed. Plans made, we talked about school in the fall, and the rest of the summer.

"Is it just me or have you forgotten the name of your old high school?" Kelly asked leaning forward and looking at us. "I know I have one more year to graduate high school, I love chemistry and math. One day I'll be a doctor. But I couldn't tell you the name of my elementary school to save my life."

"I went to Frank C. Martin elementary," Amazing said with a half grin.

"I attended St. Frances Catholic school," I said and then frowned because I wasn't Catholic.

"I don't remember either," Brenda said and looked at Patricia who looked down at the table. "What about you Patricia? Do you remember?"

Patricia nodded, cleared her throat and lifted her head. "Jurgens Elementary in New York, private school."

"Is that where you're from?" Kelly asked.

"Yes. We had a Brownstone in Manhattan." She didn't look at any of us, I'm not sure what she focused on but she looked far away.

"Sounds like fun," Amazing said. Her glance flicked from us and back to Patricia. "I've always wanted to visit there, maybe we could get together sometime and you can share stories."

Patricia's gaze slowly landed on Amazing, and rested there for a few seconds. "Okay."

Reggie walked over to the table, placed his hand on my shoulder and nodded to everybody. "Hey."

"Hey," Brenda and Kelly said looking him over. He left and returned with my favorites.

"Who's winning?" Amazing asked as Reggie gave me a can of soft-drink and placed an order of chili-cheese fries on the table in front of me.

"Tommy, he's a demon," Reggie said looking over his shoulder and then back down at me. "I'm running third, feels awkward." He took a fry and popped it in his mouth.

"Considering how much you laughed at me the first time I played, I'm happy you're not winning," I said and took a sip of soda.

Reggie grabbed my hand and pulled me up. My chest pressed into his. Looking up into his incredibly warm, dark eyes I saw flecks of light and my reflection. "Happy I'm losing? How does that work?" He asked the words softly close enough to my mouth I could feel his lips move.

My heart slammed into my chest as he brushed his lips against mine. I thought I'd pass out by how gently he held me.

"I've always got your back." His palms spanned my back. "Do you have mine?" He asked in a soft voice near my ear.

"Yeah, you know I do. But you're arrogant sometimes and losing won't hurt."

He laughed and squeezed me tight before releasing me. One of his arms remained around my waist as he turned to look at the guys bowling. "You know I offered to watch movies with you tonight. Just think, we could be all hugged up on the sofa." He spoke near my ear.

Smiling I looked up at him. I'd accepted his touchy-feely-ness the first week we dated. This was a part of who he wanted to be, he couldn't recall everything about how he'd been before. I really liked he didn't mind showing his feelings for me anywhere. "But I made some new friends, we're going swimming at the pool."

Reggie's brow rose as he looked past me to the table. They looked at him and waved. He sat in my chair and pulled me on his lap.

Amazing laughed as Reggie ate my fries. I slapped his hand to keep him from eating them all.

"Bowling's hard work, you need to feed me girl," he said.

I placed a fry in his mouth. "There, is that good?"

The look he gave me required no answer. I fed him a couple more and ate a few in between.

"You want something?" Steven asked Brenda.

She shook her head and stood. "No, just take me home. There's some things I need to take care of."

"Now?" He frowned.

"Are you finished bowling?"

"I think we're going to play another round." He looked at Reggie.

"Not me, man. I'm done for the night." He placed his hand around my waist.

Steven nodded slowly and looked at Brenda. "Alright, give me a minute."

Brenda looked at me and rolled her eyes. "Tired ass," she said softly after he'd walked off.

I didn't know how to respond. At least Brenda's date asked if she wanted anything, none of the others had done that yet.

"Here's my number, don't forget we're meeting at the pool Saturday." Brenda wrote her number on four pieces of paper.

"Everybody put your numbers on that paper so we can stay in touch," Kelly said.

"Good idea, I have Serena's number, just need everyone else," Amazing said taking the small stack, writing her information and passing it to the next person. Steven waited until Brenda received her paper, they waved goodnight and left.

Mark and Russell had arrived with drinks and food for Amazing and Kelly before Brenda left. They'd pulled another table together so we'd have more room. I tried to move and sit on a chair but Reggie's arm tightened around my waist.

"I like you right where you are," he murmured.

"We're out of food," I said looking at him.

"Hungry?"

"Yes, maybe a slice of pizza this time."

Smiling he lifted me and stood. "Yes, Ma'am."

I watched him walk toward the concession stand. Carlton broke off from their parents to meet him. They talked and Reggie ran his hand over Carlton's head. The two were close.

"Nice guy," Kelly said.

Tommy placed a diet drink and nachos in front of Patricia. "Thanks," she murmured opening the can and taking a drink.

"Yes he is," I said my gaze sliding from Patricia to Reggie again. He stood talking to Josh and Pete. When he pointed toward our table and Josh nodded, I hoped Reggie didn't realize Pete was the person I'd mentioned from the park.

Tommy sat next to Patricia, placed his arm around the back of her chair and ate a nacho.

Reggie returned with three slices of pizza and another drink. I wondered just how much he'd watched his single uncle around women. Confidence was sexy and Reggie had a boatload of it. Not in a bad way though. He was polite to everyone but it was obvious he wouldn't allow anyone to make a fool out of him. He placed our plates on the table and sat in the chair next to me.

"Got you a bottle of water." He pulled it from his pocket and placed it next to the plate with the slice of pepperoni pizza.

"Thanks."

"Hi everyone," Josh said holding his plate in one hand and drink in the other.

A chorus of greetings responded.

"This is Max, my mate." He pointed to Pete who smiled at everyone, including me as they sat down.

I finished my food in silence, half-listening to the conversation flowing around me. Reggie placed his hand on my leg, I looked at him and smiled.

He winked and continued talking with his friends.

Terri and Greg came over to say good-night, Carlton didn't feel well and Reggie's parents left soon after.

Carlton looked back at Reggie with tears in his eyes.

Chapter Twenty-One

"Reggie my stomach hurts," Carlton said from the sidelines where he watched me and the guys play ball the next day.

I tossed Mark the ball and walked to the sideline to check on him. He was burning up. "Gotta go, later," I told the everyone as I picked Carlton up and walked the few blocks to the house. By the time we reached home, sweat ran down his small face like a leaky faucet. Concerned, I ushered him to his room, passing mine on the way.

"Sorry," he said as soon as I noticed my bedroom door was cracked open. I'd left it closed earlier so mom wouldn't see the clothes on the floor or my unmade bed.

I pushed open my door, took a quick sweep of everything, and looked at him. "Why'd you go snooping in my room and break into my desk?"

His small face reddened, reminding me he was young and not feeling the best. "I wanted to see what you and Serena did in your room, you laugh and sound happy when she's around."

I crossed my arms and looked down. This time his sad face wouldn't save him. "Bullshit. You broke into my desk. I'm going to ask one more time, why?"

Carlton's mouth opened and closed. "I wanted to know what was inside. You mad?"

"Very, you little shit. You broke into my stuff and read my personal information. Why the fuck did you do something like that?"

His eyes watered and he hung his head low. I stared at him a few seconds, walked into my room, slammed the door shut, and closed the desk drawer. I booted up the laptop, found my journal, and read. Killed in the line of duty as a firefighter, my dad had been larger than life to me when I was younger. My grandma had lived with us, but she'd died two weeks before daddy. It'd taken years of therapy for me to work through all the changes happening in such a short time. Uncle Ponce had been my only family left. Those years with my uncle hadn't been nearly as good as with grandma and daddy, but we'd made do. The more I read, the more violated I felt that Carlton had a glimpse of my personal, private hell.

There was a tap on the door.

I ignored it and backed up a copy to give Serena later tonight.

Another tap. "Reggie?"

I closed my eyes and released a stream of air.

"I don't feel good," Carlton said.

"Go lay down."

"I don't think that helps, call mom."

I pocketed the flash drives and opened the door. Carlton lay on the floor holding his stomach. At the sight of him holding his stomach, crying on the floor, my heart dropped. Without thinking, I pulled out the phone and punched in mom's number. She didn't pick up. I dialed 911 and gave them the information.

Kneeling next to him on the floor, I placed my palm on his forehead and lifted it immediately. "You're burning up."

Carlton didn't open his eyes or stop moaning.

Sirens blared in the distance and then stopped out front. I ran to the front door and waved to the two men exiting the truck. They grabbed some equipment and ran into the house. Kneeling next to Carlton, they asked him a lot of questions as they did a quick exam. Less than ten minutes later, they'd placed him in the back of the ambulance and we were off to the hospital. I tried unsuccessfully to reach mom or dad a couple more times until we stopped. Once inside, they took Carlton to the back while I remained out front speaking to admissions.

The nurse asked questions regarding Carlton's eating habits. She wanted the brand of water he drank; the last time he drank or ate. I couldn't answer any of the questions other than tell her about the dark blue color of the label on the water bottle and the tuna salad mom eft us for lunch.

Sitting in the waiting room, I contacted Serena to cancel our date tonight and then tried to reach mom or dad. Dad answered, and after I explained the situation, said they were on their way. Relieved to turn the responsibility over to someone else, I closed my eyes for a moment and uttered a word of prayer.

Serena and her mom walked in a few minutes later. "Have you heard anything?" Serena asked, taking the seat next to me.

"Not yet." She took my hand while Terri walked to the nurse station, spoke softly, and then returned to sit near us.

"They're still running tests, were you able to contact your mom?" Terri asked.

I nodded. "They're on their way." We sat in silence as I went over everything that happened since Carlton said he didn't feel well. We'd eaten the same meal, so that couldn't be what set him off, plus he'd been uncomfortable before lunch.

The outer door opened. Bob and Jill Thomas strode inside, concern and fear etched on their faces as they headed toward the information desk. I debated whether or not to call out, or allow them to speak to the lady. A few minutes later, they turned in our direction and headed toward us.

"What happened?" mom asked.

"After the pool we went home, had lunch and then hung out at the basketball court. He'd mentioned a stomach ache yesterday, and when I asked him about it, he said he felt better."

"Did he eat anything different?" dad asked, taking the seat next to me.

I looked at him, noticed the frown marring his brow and his pinched nostrils. "Not that I noticed. We both ate the same lunch."

"We'll know what's wrong soon enough," mom said, looking at dad until he turned away.

"Has he been going in your room?" Dad asked.

"Yeah, just found out today he's been going through my things." I looked at him. "You knew about that?"

"No. But I know he looks up to you, wants to be you, so it doesn't surprise me. Why? Did he get into something? If he ate your stash of snacks or drinks, I'll replace them."

I'd been so busy checking my journal I hadn't checked anything else. "Why would he eat the stuff in my room? He has his own snacks."

Mom shrugged. A doctor walked through the swinging doors, stopped at the nurses' station to speak with one of them, and then headed in our direction. Everybody stood in anticipation.

"Are you Carlton's parents?"

"Yes," Mom said, looking at dad, who also stepped forward.

"Come with me." He turned and walked away. The woman at the nurses' desk left through another door.

Serena wrapped her arm around my waist as we returned to our seats.

Terri walked back to the nurses' desk and leaned over the counter.

"Carlton read my journal." I told Serena everything that'd happened since I saw her earlier at the pool. We both agreed not to trust anyone else with our journals. She took the second flash drive and promised to hide it for me. Terri returned just as Serena zipped her small pocket on her jogging pants closed, securing my memories.

"They pumped his stomach. He took a high dose of some kind of drug and it made him real sick," Terri said, sitting next to Serena.

"Drug?" I asked, frowning. "What kind of drug?"

"I didn't see the name of it, but whatever it was, he took more than his system could handle."

Mom walked through the swinging doors toward us. Her gray eyes darkened and her face tight. Short with a slender build, she quickly crossed the hall. "He's... he's resting." After repeating what Terri said almost verbatim, she looked at me and then hugged me tight. Serena stepped to the side to allow us a private moment as mom wept silently against my chest.

I couldn't speak around the lump lodged in my throat. Carlton was just eleven and much too young to do any kind of drugs.

"But he'll be okay, right?" I asked when I could talk. I needed to hear her say it.

"Yes. They're going to keep him tonight and he'll be home tomorrow." She pushed back, wiped her face with the back of her hand. "No need for you to stay here all night, your dad is going to stay. I'm going home to get a few things and you can drop me back off." She looked up at me and then at Serena. "You asked to use the car tonight, and I said yes."

"We'll do it another time," I said before she could go any further. "I'll take you home to get what you need and then we'll come back here."

She wiped her eyes again and nodded.

Turning, I leaned forward and brushed a kiss against Serena's lips. "I'll call you later, let you know how things are going. Thanks for coming." I looked at Terri.

"No thanks needed," Terri said, wrapping her arm around Serena's shoulder.

The four of us walked out together. During the silent drive home I couldn't get the comment about Carlton eating my snacks or drinks out of my mind. Dad allowed us to pick out whatever we wanted from the store and then brought it home for us. I kept my stuff in my room, but so did Carlton.

"I'll only be a few minutes," Mom said, disappearing down the hall to their bedroom.

"Okay." I headed to my bedroom, closed the door, and checked my snacks. The only thing missing was a few bottles of water.

Chapter Twenty-One

The entire drive back to the hospital I wondered what happened to Carlton. He'd been acting strange a few days before today, and dad's reaction seemed over the top. Mom placed her hand on mine. I glanced at her, watched her try to smile. Her lips trembled before she could speak.

"He'll be okay, it's not your fault." She bit her lower lip and looked out the window.

"My fault? Because he went in my room?" Confused by her remark, I pressed the brake and pulled to the side. "Why would you say it's not my fault?"

She shook her head and continued staring out the window.

"Mom? What's going on?" I pressed.

She sniffed but didn't say anything.

"Carlton? He's really sick isn't he? I mean sicker than we thought?"

"Yes," she whispered.

"What's wrong with him? Did I do something?" The thought of doing anything, however small, against my brother cut deep like a knife.

Inhaling deeply, she turned to face me. Her familiar face wet with tears tugged on my heart. "The drug poisoned his system, they're working on him, but he's not responsive, not yet. By calling for help when you did... you saved his life, we wouldn't have made it in time." She squeezed my hand. "Thank you."

"He's my brother, why're you thanking me for taking care of him?" A sharp pain pierced my skull, the car darkened. I closed my eyes tight to block it.

"Reggie?"

I heard the fear and panic in her voice and fought the reddish-black fog in my mind to answer. "I'm okay, that happens every now and then." Leaning against the headrest, I took several deep breaths before opening my eyes.

"How long have you been having these headaches?" she snapped. Her weepy demeanor evaporated like the morning dew.

"A week."

She threw up her hands and stared at me. "Why won't my children talk to me?" She pointed at my chest. "Why didn't you say something? There's no reason for you to be in pain like this, either of you." She shook her head. "Start the car, I need to get these things to Bobby, he has to change from his work clothes." She crossed her arms and stared out the window.

"Sorry, just didn't want to bother you since it doesn't last long." That had to be the lamest excuse ever. A quick glance at her deep frown said she agreed with me. The drive to the hospital was done in silence. I didn't know what to say and wondered why she was so angry about the headaches. They weren't anything compared to what was happening with my brother.

We walked down several corridors together and then into a room where Carlton lay with his eyes closed on the bed. Dad sat in a chair on the other side holding his hand. When we entered, his eyes blazed when they landed on me and then he turned away.

"How's he doing?" I asked, moving to the opposite side of the bed, looking at Carlton's face. Lying there, he looked so much younger, peaceful in sleep.

"A little better, they've done all they can, now we wait," dad said, taking the bag from mom and heading to the bathroom.

I placed my hand on Carlton's forehead and then his cheek. "Listen up, Bro. Whatever's going on in your body, I want you to fight it. You can beat this. We're counting on you." I placed a kiss on Carlton's forehead. "Wake up, don't scare us like this." I couldn't keep the pleading from my voice, but not having Carlton in my life scared the crap out of me. The door closed, I didn't look away from the small figure on the bed. I covered his hand and squeezed lightly.

"Fight, Bro," I whispered, wishing I could give him my strength.

"Pull up a seat before you fall and hurt yourself," mom said, pointing to a chair.

I wiped the moisture from my face and dragged it close.

Dad came back out of the bathroom.

Mom placed her hand on Carlton's leg, while dad and I covered his hands. The silence stretched with no change. I prayed to every God I'd ever heard of and made up a few.

The nurse came in, checked his vitals, and then left. Her expression gave nothing away.

"This makes no sense," I blurted. "Why's he still out of it?"

"They gave him something to rest, to help heal," Dad said in a low voice. "It was close, we almost lost him."

"Did they tell you what he took? What kind of drug did this?" I demanded.

"They did, it's some long name," mom said.

"What is it? I'll look it up." My gaze flew from her to dad. Neither looked at me. "What did they say it was?" I pulled out my phone, prepared to type the name into the search engine.

"I don't remember," she said at length.

"Huh?" Confused, I turned in my chair to look at her. "What'd it start with?"

Eyes downcast, she shook her head. "I can't... remember."

I stared at her a few seconds longer and then shoved the phone in my pocket. "It's okay, no problem. Now isn't the time anyway. I'll check it out later." She looked up, her eyes clouded with concern, and then nodded.

Time dragged.

Hungry, I offered to go downstairs to grab us something to eat. Dad gave me a twenty. I left with their orders of burgers, fries and soft drinks.

"He took his brother's dose, poisoned his system." The whispered words caused me to stop and move closer to the corner.

"How did that happen?"

"Not sure, parents are torn up about it. Blame themselves. He might not make it; we'll know in the morning."

Chest heaving, I leaned flat against the wall until the footsteps faded. *"Brother's dose?"* What did that mean?

"Are you alright?" A security guard standing nearby watched me closely as he asked.

"No, my brother's sick and I don't know why or what happened to him. No one will tell me the truth."

"Where are your parents?" He took a step closer. Although his eyes held a mixture of empathy and compassion, I didn't trust him.

"Inside, I'm going for dinner." I moved to go around him.

His hand whipped out as if he'd stop me, but missed. "That's not a good idea right now, go back inside and talk to your parents," he ordered.

What the hell? I moved toward the staircase and jogged down to the first floor. Instead of going to the cafeteria I headed to the car, jumped inside, and peeled out the parking lot. That security guard spooked me.

"Brother's dose?" The words mocked me as I headed to the park. I needed to think. My cell vibrated. *Serena.* I picked up. "Hey, be outside in a few, I'll swing by to pick you up."

Veering sharply to the left, I changed directions and headed for her house. Dressed in jeans, a tee-shirt and sneakers, she walked around to the passenger side and slid in the front seat. I pulled out and headed into town. We drove in silence until we reached the hospital and I parked in the lot across from it.

Jumbled thoughts collided and I tried to make sense of them. Serena pulled her long hair into a ponytail without speaking. I watched her long, tapered fingers move quickly through her silky hair. Still she asked no questions.

"Carlton almost died." The words tasted bitter on my tongue. Unwilling to see her reaction to my pain, I stared straight ahead, locked in gray misery.

She gasped and touched my hand. I grabbed hers, allowed it to anchor me and the twisted thoughts crowding my mind.

Frowning, I faced her. "I overheard a nurse telling someone he took his brother's dose and it poisoned him."

Her eyes widened and the other hand flew to her mouth. "What? Dose of what?" Her eyes swept over me and then returned to my gaze.

I told her everything that happened since I left her at the hospital.

Confused, she shook her head. "You? He drank a few bottles of your water? There's drugs in your water?" The incredulity in her voice matched my tumbling thoughts perfectly.

"Mom forgot the name of the drug though. Crazy right?" I needed to hear the whole idea couldn't be true.

"Very. You look healthy and haven't been sick."

I nodded, fighting to slow down my heart. "Something happened to him." Opening the car door, I met Serena at the front of the car and took her hand. We walked in silence down the road. Reaching an empty, quiet spot between the park and hospital, we sat on a bench.

"What if..." I stopped and looked around. "What if that's got something to do with all this... the Rewind?"

She frowned and then winced.

"See, that's what I mean, it hurts to remember the name of the game, to remember anything. What if they've been giving us something to eat and drink that messed with our minds?" I said, rubbing her back.

"It hurts to remember. If I read my journals, the moment I try to remember those days, it hurts so bad I almost pass out from the pain," she admitted.

"Exactly, that started happening to me this week."

"I told mom about it and she said to stop trying." She paused. "So we've been drugged this whole time, something's messing with our minds or memories?" Serena asked.

"The more I think about it, the more sense it makes. Next question, who's paying for all of this? Is the drug legal?"

"Don't think so," she said slowly.

"Think they're testing the drug on us first, like guinea pigs?" Dread rolled down my back as I realized it was the only thing that made sense.

"Could be," she hesitated. "I don't feel sick as long as I don't try to remember. Mom, dad and I discussed high school next month, college, job opportunities for him, and what we'd like to do. Spent time hanging with Amazing and Kelly, shopping, getting our hair and nails done with no problems." With a tortured gaze, Serena stared at me. "Is that wrong? I can't remember the faces, names, or anything about anyone in my journals. How can I ever go back?"

I held her trembling body close wanting to ease her fears as mine spiked. People, places, and events before Rewind blurred and disappeared like ghosts. A vague memory of someone saying we'd forget during the 30 days but at the end still make a choice. For some reason that eased the tension rolling through me. This was what I'd signed up for, but not Serena.

"No, it's not wrong. What's wrong is taking away your choice. If you had both memories, past and present, you could make the choice based on your heart and knowledge. Let's hope they didn't steal that from you, me, and everyone else who played the game."

"Game? What game?" she asked.

I wrapped my arms around her shoulder and pulled her close. "Never mind, I've got this." I placed a kiss on her forehead and stared at the hospital in the distance.

Chapter Twenty-Two

Gasping, I sat up in bed holding my chest. I took short breaths and closed my eyes against the darkness in my bedroom. The clock in the corner glared the number thirty in bright neon, and then the words "*Shelly, Do you want to Rewind?*" scrolled across the screen. Seconds ticked by as I stared at the curve of the S and then the entire name, as if I'd learn something new or receive a shaft of inspiration on what I needed to do.

Moonbeams streamed through the mini-blinds and danced across my bed in the quiet early morning hours. *What happened?* Something scared me awake, my racing heart reminded me. Looking around my bedroom I tried to recall bits of my dream. Or had something happened before I'd gone to bed?

The adrenaline ebbed and my eyelids grew heavy. I pulled the comforter beneath my chin and rolled onto my side. A flash of light rolled across my vision. A woman who seemed familiar stood behind me coaxing me to ride a red tricycle.

"Come on Shelly, show mama what you can do."

Remaining ramrod still, I waited to see what happened next. A floodgate of information and memories opened, burying me with their intensity. Tears pooled in my eyes as I saw images of mama, Griffin, Roger, and Grandma Jan. Snapshots of me on my computer playing games, ghosts of the energy I'd received when I won or played with my clan swamped me.

"I play games? Is that what the martial arts is all about?" I whispered in awe as I watched me focused in front of a monitor, my hands in perpetual motion. Another snapshot of mama and I at the store, in the car, in the house. More images of me and two boys much younger. Mama didn't smile much, but neither did I.

Rashan! What happened to her? Had she returned home or was she in the game somewhere else? When her image crossed my mind I smiled, happy to see her. So many good memories when were younger, not as much the older we got.

Good times with Griffin, my stepdad, aunt, and clan. Eyes closed, I lay on my back watching, remembering and enjoying the warmth of family. We weren't perfect, but it was still good and the one thing I wanted above everything, family.

The images came slower now. Me with the boys, me playing games, me with mama and Grandma Jan. A hollowness filled my chest as I stared at the images of my face and wished I recalled what I'd been thinking at those times. Was I happy? Content? Why'd I play games all the time?

Last night Terri and Greg reminded me of a choice I'd need to make soon. "Last week you and dad said you've decided to remain in the program after your 30 days?" I'd asked mom.

Terri nodded. "This works better for us. I can't imagine my life differently."

Both said they wouldn't pressure me or interfere with my decision and I appreciated that. When I asked them what to expect, daddy had smiled, promised it wouldn't hurt. On Terri's thirtieth day he remembered her waking up and telling him she'd seen her past and never wanted to see it again. She gave her answer after that and lost her old memories immediately.

I remembered Daddy's 30th day because he'd made his decision later in the day, after dinner. We talked about some of the things he remembered, his mom, dad and brother. He'd been surprised his old memories didn't disappear until midnight.

Moving slowly, I groped around the nightstand and picked up my phone.

"Serena?" Reggie answered slowly.

"Sorry to wake you. But something strange happened." We'd been discussing the possibility of being test subjects for some drug company and had been searching the internet for information. So far we'd discovered hundreds of companies that ran all kinds of tests, but hadn't zeroed in on a particular one yet.

"No worries. What happened?"

I told him about the memory blast.

"Seriously? No pain? You remember everything?" His voice raised on the last word.

"Yes, and no pain. Must have something to do with the 30th day." I bit my lip, wondering what I'd do. And what would happen to us if I returned home? Holding the phone close to my ear, I rolled onto my back and stared up at the ceiling.

"So... did you leave a boyfriend behind? Someone waiting for you to come back to him?"

I snorted and then smiled. "Nope, no one." I refrained from mentioning I hadn't dated anyone or wore make-up in my old life. I wondered what mama would think if she could see this new version of me.

"Good. I'm glad the guys at your school and neighborhood are blind and dumb."

Laughing, I covered my eyes. He always knew the right thing to say. "Don't know about all that. Seems I stayed at home babysitting and playing video games. From what I saw, I didn't have much of a social life."

"Brothers? Sisters?"

"Two brothers, my mom, stepdad, uncle, aunts, cousins, grandma. Our family's not that large."

"Bigger than mine."

True, he'd lost his dad at an early age and even though he never said, I knew it was a sore spot. "Strange." I bit my lip and watched the moonbeams dance.

"What?"

"I miss them but I don't. Does that sound weird? Or make me a bad person?" I whispered, unsure how to put my feelings into words.

"Nope, don't sound bad and you're not a bad person, you're honest. Maybe that's what today's all about, know what I mean?

You have to make a choice, stay or go. It rocks you got your memories back so you can do that."

"I don't want to leave you, Terri, or Greg. It's crazy, but they... Right now, all of this is so different from my old life, if I hadn't lived it I wouldn't believe it could happen." I paused, thinking of the gaming. "Why would I play games all the time and not hang with friends like I do now?"

"Could you hang with friends back then?"

I thought about it for a moment. "Not really. I had joined a couple of clubs at school and had to quit to help out at home. Don't get me wrong, I love my brothers, but mama couldn't pay after-school care anymore and needed me to help."

"And you babysat every day?"

"Yeah. Grandma moved in last month, she's not doing well." My thoughts drifted to the extra care required for her. How had mama and the others coped with me gone? Grandma wasn't my responsibility, neither were the boys, but family helps each other, sticks together to make things better for everyone and not just one person, according to mama anyway.

"You watched her too?" His voice deepened and my cheeks warmed.

"Sometimes if Mama needed help." That had been my standard reply every time Rashan asked why I couldn't do things with her. She never bought into that creed, and went her own way.

"Who helped you?"

His question pulled me back into the here and now. "What?"

"Maybe that's why you spent so much time gaming. You needed friends, people to chill with, and they did that. Here, you're able to hang with me, Amazing, your friends, and you spend a lot of time with your parents, going to movies and stuff. You stay busy and don't have all the responsibilities that you had there." He paused. "You do realize you set things up that way, right?"

Tears pooled in my eyes as my throat tightened. I covered my face with my palm and tried to take a deep breath, but the words he'd spoken hammered into me. I wrote all those changes. I wanted a different life. I wanted friends, and parents who spent quality time with me. Guilt, dark, sticky and ugly, covered my soul, making it hard to see past my selfishness. Everything from the past thirty days had been about me, not anyone else. Torn, I tried to make peace with my mistake and envisioned life at home with mama and the boys again. My mind and heart screamed no. Maybe if I didn't remember the past thirty days with Reggie it'd be easier to settle.

"Serena?"

"Shelly."

"Huh?"

"That's my name, before Rewind."

"Okay. Did I upset you?"

A lone tear rolled down my cheek. "If anyone had told me I wasn't happy back then, I would've argued with them. Hell at 16, what did I know?"

"You know."

I sighed. Reggie wouldn't let me hide or get away with anything. "Okay, maybe I resented not being allowed to do things, but that's a part of growing up with family. Lots of teens help with the younger ones."

"Sometimes, not all the time. You didn't have time for yourself except online, right?"

"Yeah. Some Saturdays I had to watch the boys while mama went grocery shopping or something. If I pushed, I could've hung out on Saturday nights, but it wasn't worth the bother."

"Why?"

"Cause that might or might not happen. I got tired of canceling and just stopped," I snapped, surprising myself. "Sorry, just hadn't thought about that in a long time." It had been a sore spot, mama and I argued about her taking over my free time constantly until I stopped asking. She'd called me selfish. Maybe I was, but I didn't want to be stuck at home watching kids at 14. Two years later, nothing had changed.

"No problem, you have a lot on your mind to think about. Just... just don't disappear without saying bye."

Once again tears filled my eyes and my heart twisted. "I wouldn't do that," I whispered. "You're my... my..." I didn't know how to express what filled my heart when I thought of him. Did I love him? Possibly. But outside of family I had no experience with that emotion and wasn't sure I should say it. And if I did say it, would that mean I wouldn't leave? That I'd choose to stay because of him? Could I do that? I didn't think so.

Regardless of what I felt about babysitting and no free time, I didn't want to lose mama or my family, that much I knew. My heart clenched at the thought of not seeing Greg and Terri again. I loved them, they'd been great parents and had taken good care of me, but they weren't family.

"What is it you need most in the world?"

"Huh?"

"This helps, just answer," he said.

"I need a lot of things," I hedged.

"I know but narrow it down to that one thing you need most. It's there inside, what is it?"

The moment he said that I saw her. That little girl sitting in the red chair at the daycare. Left behind, forgotten and believing she hadn't been important enough or that something was wrong with her. Months, probably years after that scarring event, I'd been afraid of mama leaving me behind. There had been that nugget of uncertainty that she hadn't left me by mistake. That she'd regretted having me and I couldn't risk not being with her again.

"You there?" Reggie asked.

I cleared my throat and fought back more tears. "Yeah, just thinking about what you asked and you're right. I need my family."

My heart broke over the possibility of not seeing him later or tomorrow or the next day. Of not holding hands, walking down the street, or swimming in the pool, or watching a movie. Would I ever meet someone who accepted me completely? I doubted it.

"See, that makes it easier, doesn't it?"

"I guess. How's Carlton?"

"Good. I told you he came clean to the parents, said he'd been in my room, stole stuff. Dad put a lock on my door, but I don't use it much. It's easier to not keep nothing important here than to make a big deal out of it. He's just a kid."

I sensed he didn't want to travel that lane and changed directions. "Thanks for being you. I don't know how I would've made it this past month without you."

He didn't say anything for a long while. "I love you."

My heart clenched, goosebumps covered my skin. I wanted to sing and dance with the moonbeams, but first I needed to hear him say it again. "What?"

"Love you. Don't tell me you're surprised."

I was and I wasn't. I'd told myself it was possible, but I was scared to think about it. "How do you know?" I scooted up, leaned against the headboard, and pressed my hand against my mouth to keep from giggling or sighing or melting into a poodle of goo. No one outside of family ever loved me or showed it every day. I intended to bask in this moment.

"I just know." He paused. "I can't imagine being here or anywhere without you. Every day I wanna see you, talk to you, or just watch you walk." He snorted. "I sound like a chump, but it's real."

I extended my hand over the comforter and tried to catch the beams of moonlight. Exhaling, I closed my eyes and clenched my fist. "No, you don't. I love you too."

"How do you know?"

"I just do." Unlike Reggie, I really didn't know how to explain the way I felt when he looked at me or the gooey feeling inside when he kissed me. When I woke up or went to sleep I thought of him.

"Oh you do, huh?"

I smiled at the relief in his voice. "Yes, I do." I paused. "But I can't stay. What are we going to do?"

"Soon as the sun's up, I'll be over. We'll figure out how to be together after we both return home."

"But I won't remember anything."

"That's what I heard, but don't worry, we'll figure out something. I'm not about to lose you."

Warm tingly things filled my chest. Together we'd work this out and be together. "I don't want to lose you either."

"You won't. Get some rest, I'll see you around three or four after I clean out the garage and some other things for mom."

"Love you."

"Ah... love you too."

Chapter Twenty-Three

Terri and I stepped out the car, grabbed our bags and headed for the house. I glanced at my watch, it was after five in the evening. Reggie had been over earlier with plans to get together this afternoon to hammer out details of getting together after he left the game. He'd left to tackle a few errands for his mom, which seemed insensitive given this was my last day but I let it pass and spent a little time with Amazing and Kelly. They'd made the decision to remain with their new lives and didn't recall the game or anything from before.

The thought of never seeing or talking to mama again crippled me. I couldn't do it no matter how much I loved my new friends and life. Terri and Greg understood and said they wanted whatever I wanted.

Lunch had been fun and sweet. I had until midnight to type in my response regarding rewind, and planned to spend my last few hours with Reggie. He wrote his name on the sole of my foot along with his social so that I could look him up once he left the game. I gave him my social security number as well. It was the best we could think of and planned to expand on it later.

Before opening the front door, my cell rang. Frowning at the caller ID, I answered. "Hey Carlton." Things had gotten better between us since he'd been hospitalized and I'd convinced Reggie to spend more quality time with Carlton at home. Had he called to say good-bye?

"Hey, can I speak to Reggie?"

"Say please." I heard his mother say in the background.

"Can I please?"

"He's not here. He left two hours ago to help your mom with something." I turned and looked up and down the street, thinking he might be at the park or on his way here.

Carlton repeated what I said.

"Hi Serena, how are you?" Mrs. Thomas asked, taking Carlton's place.

"Good, thank you."

"I've been expecting that boy for over an hour, he hasn't made it home yet. What time did he leave your place?"

"Around three. He didn't go to lunch with us because he had something to do for you."

"He never made it here. Hold on."

There was some rattling and talking in the background. I heard Mr. Thomas' deep voice telling his wife not to worry. "Sorry about that, I get worried when I can't place my fingers on the boys. It's not like Reggie to disappear without letting you or me know where he's at. Hopefully he'll be home soon."

"If you hear from him, call me and I'll do the same for you," I said, trying to keep worry from my voice.

"Thanks, I appreciate it. He'll probably contact you first. Tell him to call home so I know he's alright."

"Will do." I disconnected and walked inside to tell Terri about the call.

Terri frowned. "That's not like Reggie, especially today. I thought he had special plans for the two of you tonight."

I sat in the high back chair at the kitchen island thinking over what Mrs. Thomas said. "We do have a couple things planned, that's the only reason I haven't answered the question yet." Reggie knew how important it was that I refuse Rewind before midnight. He claimed to understand, what if he was angry I wasn't staying with him? I crossed my arms and stood stiff. "If I don't hear from him in an hour or so, I'm going to log into the app and say no. I'm not going to wait for him." I stomped up the stairs to my room and showered.

"Of all the inconsiderate things. If you have a problem with my decision, tough. But don't lie and try to act as if everything's okay when it's not. Some kind of love, hmpf," I murmured while lotioning my arms and legs.

Staring at my naked image in the mirror, I pointed. "Why do guys say they love you just to try and control you?" I had no answer and looked at the clock on my dresser. It was after six pm. Six more hours to log in and cancel the Rewind. My shoulders slumped. I needed to say good-bye to Reggie first. I dressed in sweats and sneakers, pulled my hair up in a ponytail, and went downstairs where I left my phone.

No calls.

I called Amazing. "Can you check with Mark and ask if he's seen Reggie?"

"Hello to you too, Chica," she said, and then chuckled.

"Sorry, just... can you ask him?" I heard her talking to Mark in the background.

"No. Reggie said the two of you were hanging out all day," she said. "What's wrong?"

"His mom called here looking for him an hour ago, I don't know where he is." I refused to think anything bad had happened, but every horror movie I'd ever seen replayed in my mind.

"That's not like him. Anything we can do?" Amazing asked.

"Not yet. If he's shopping or planning something special, I'd hate to ruin it by sending out a posse. But if I don't hear from him in an hour, I may need you guys to help search for him," I said, hoping it didn't come to that.

"Whatever you need." Amazing said and disconnected.

I called Kelly, and Patricia, had them ask their boyfriends the same thing. No one had seen Reggie and everyone remarked it wasn't like him not to respond to my calls.

The next hour I couldn't focus. Greg had come home and offered to go looking. He and I drove around for an hour and stopped at Reggie's parents' house. Mrs. Thomas' voice reached us in the yard as she demanded her husband call the cops to search for her son.

A slight chill skittered down my back, my stomach quivered at her loud weeping coming from inside. Greg offered his hand and I took it. He squeezed my hand and we walked up the steps to the door.

Before we knocked, light flooded the porch and the door flung open. Mrs. Thomas stood wide-eyed in the doorway staring at us.

"Serena? Please... have you talked to him? Has Reggie called or sent a message?"

Swallowing around the lump lodged in my throat I tried to speak, but couldn't. I shook my head as my eyes filled in reaction to her distress.

"But, but where can he be?"

"He's not a child, stop worrying. He'll be home soon," Mr. Thomas said in a stern voice.

Mrs. Thomas stepped onto the porch and closed the door behind her. "I'm a mother, I know my children." She shook her head and took Shelly's hand. "This is not like Reginald. He always lets us know where he is, normally with you."

I nodded and licked my lips a few times. "That's true. I'm surprised he hasn't answered my calls, he always does."

Quick as a rabbit, she pounced on my statement. "So you agree something must be wrong? He could be out there hurt, needing us."

While I agreed it wasn't like Reggie to cancel a date without contacting me, I wasn't ready to say something was wrong. "I hope not."

"So do I, but I can't stop worrying." Mrs. Thomas looked over her shoulder toward the door and shook her head as laughter from the TV game show filled the air. "I hope my son is all right, otherwise there will be no peace in this house. We would not survive it."

"I'll call some friends and we'll start looking for him," I said to stop her from crying.

"Thank you, I'll go with you." She turned and walked inside.

"It's after eight, Princess," Greg said his hands on my shoulder. "I'll go with your friends and Mrs. Thomas while you go home. If we find anything, I'll call."

Before he finished, I was shaking my head. "I pray Reggie just forgot the time and is somewhere safe." I threw up my hands unsure what to think. "I'm scared," I whispered and leaned against Greg's chest. "This isn't like him, especially not today. Even if he didn't want to see me again, he wouldn't worry everyone deliberately."

"I know honey and we'll find him, don't worry. Why not write him a note, a letter, and when he comes home I'll give it to him."

That made so much sense, I hated to say no. But I couldn't leave yet, not without trying to help find Reggie, he wouldn't do it to me and I refused to do it to him. I sent everyone a text and asked them to meet at the park.

"I've got my phone. I can log on and cancel the Rewind from anywhere."

Greg hesitated, opened his mouth, closed it with a nod, and we left.

Chapter Twenty-Four

Nine cars crowded the small lot. Amazing and Mark stepped out of their car and headed toward us. Without saying a word, she wrapped her arms around me and held me close for a few minutes. Inhaling her signature strawberries and vanilla scent, I tried to tell myself Reggie was fine, but couldn't quite pull it off.

"It's okay, Chica. We'll find him." Amazing leaned back and searched my gaze. Whatever she saw must have concerned her. "Be strong for him."

I nodded and pulled the tattered strings of my heart together. Leaving Reggie and Amazing was harder than I thought. She'd stepped into the role of best friend without discussion and I couldn't imagine not talking to her again. My chest hurt as I stepped back and averted my gaze.

Clearing my throat, I wanted to say something hip like she always did, something that would let her know how much her friendship meant, but nothing other than sappy sayings came to mind, so I nodded.

"Come on, they're splitting up the town for the search, are you with your dad?" Amazing asked.

I glanced at Greg, who stood with the others to form the party. "Yeah, I think so."

"Good." She squeezed my shoulder as we walked toward the others.

A few minutes later, the town had been split into smaller sections and search areas assigned. I had no idea the town was over 200 miles long and 300 miles wide, and the fringes were wooded areas. Reggie could be anywhere.

Greg motioned for me to follow him to the car. "I need to stop by the house for flashlights and snacks."

I didn't want to go home to hear more reasons why I shouldn't be searching. "Okay, I'll ride with Amazing and meet you back home before midnight." I held up my phone. "I've got time to use this." I turned and jogged toward the other car before he could object. When Amazing saw me, she frowned but didn't say anything.

"Daddy had to go home first, I want to get started now," I said, sliding into the back seat. Uncertainty gripped me. Should I answer the question now and take a chance I wouldn't be taken immediately or wait until a quarter to midnight so I could help search for Reggie? I needed to see him, there were too many unfinished plans, unanswered questions for me to leave right now. One more touch, one more smile from him would quell the uncertainty plaguing me. I needed to know he would still be in my life. That urgency lodged in my chest and pushed me into the seat of the car. Love propelled me in the direction of the dark wooded area with my best friend to find Reggie.

"Oh, okay," she said, buckling her seatbelt. Mark pulled out and headed north. I glanced at my phone, almost ten pm. Time refused to slow down. I prayed for Reggie and hoped mama wouldn't be too mad when I showed up after being gone for a month. Memories of mama and Terri clashed, merged, and then split.

"What the hell?" I murmured, fighting to separate the past and present.

"Huh?" Amazing asked, turning slightly to face me.

"Nothing, just thinking." We needed to find Reggie fast. I fingered my cell phone and then pulled it out. The blue green Rewind app icon blazed bright. I pressed it. "Do you want to Rewind?" The question mocked me as I stared at it a few seconds longer.

"This is it," Mark said, bringing the car to a stop in front of the woods. "Take this." He handed Amazing a flashlight and then opened his door.

Amazing and I headed right, Mark went left.

"Reggie," I called out and then paused to listen for a response. Amazing called his name, and then Mark called as we spread out and looked behind trees, rocks, and boulders.

When we came to the fast running stream, tears rolled down my eyes. Something bad had happened and I'd never see Reggie again. The idea ripped into my chest, robbing me of breath. Bent over, I took in short gasps of air as dots flew in a weird pattern in front of me. A low, ragged sound filled the air. Arms wrapped around me as my legs lost strength.

"Chica, oh Chica, don't give up hope. There's still a lot of places we haven't looked," Amazing said in a low hoarse voice.

Sniffing back tears, I wiped my face with the back of my hand and walked with her toward the car. "No." I stopped and looked around. "We need to keep looking. He could be out here, hurt or something."

"Mark's looking."

"I need to look too." Pulling away, I took hold of her flashlight and walked deeper into the woods. "Reggie," I called. Behind me Amazing called his name.

Stopping, I tilted my head to the left and saw a light coming toward us. "Reggie?" I yelled.

"No." Cricket and Red strode through a thick patch of woods. "Heard about what happened and thought we'd help look too," Red said looking around. "How far did you go that way?" He pointed behind us.

"Quite a bit. Mark's searching that area," Amazing said, looking over her shoulder.

"We saw his car and started from the other end, figured we'd search from the road to the stream," Red said, holding his flashlight to the ground.

I edged around them and pointed my light toward more trees. "Thanks."

"Serena?" Cricket called as Amazing and I headed out.

Looking over my shoulder, I waited.

"Do you realize there's no signal out here?"

"What?" I had no idea what she was talking about.

She waved me close, we met halfway. "Today's the thirtieth day for both of us. I'm staying in, are you?"

"No, soon as I find Reggie I'm leaving." Hearing the words hurt.

"That's what I'm saying, there's no signal out here. It's after 11, you don't have much time."

"Shit," Mark yelled and then we heard a loud thud.

Amazing took off and I followed. The noise from the stream made his words sound garbled. Miscalculating the distance, Amazing slipped and fell in the mud. I reached for her hand and hit the ground hard. The breath left my lungs. Dots floated in front of my eyes as I tried to sit up. Slippery, my hands slid in the mud and I went down again.

"Damn it," I yelled, rolling in the opposite direction of the bank until I felt grass. "Come... come this way, Amazing." I huffed trying to catch my breath.

Red and Cricket crashed through the branches and stopped short of running into me. Amazing had a hard time rolling and clawed her way up the mound.

"Help Mark," she yelled to Red and Cricket as if they couldn't see the tall guy flapping and yelping in pain from the tangled branches a few feet away.

Red inched forward slowly. "Grab my hand," he told Mark as he leaned as far forward as possible without sliding in the mushy soil. They couldn't make the connection. Amazing inched closer and sank again in the soft mud.

"Get back," Mark yelled at her. His words lifted and were tossed with the wind.

Tears ran unchecked down Amazing's cheeks. "Chica, look there's blood on his forehead, he's hurt. I need to help him. I have to help him."

Muddied, I placed my arms around her and prayed for a miracle. Mark wasn't moving as much and Red couldn't get closer. I slid my phone out to call Greg or the cops or someone, but had no signal. "Please, please, not this," I prayed, watching Mark slide further into the water.

"Mark!" Amazing yelled, breaking free, falling and sliding forward. She grabbed his hand and yanked. Brushes cut into her skin but she held onto him.

"What if we make a human line and pull them up?" I suggested, needing to do something.

Cricket pulled a bungee cord from her pocket and handed it to Red. "Let's try this first. I have another one I can put in your belt loop Serena and I'll hold onto you while you reach Mark."

Red took the cord and inched forward. Mud squished and oozed beneath his foot but he didn't fall. A few minutes later, he leaned forward and dangled the end. Mark grabbed it with his other hand and dipped beneath the water.

Amazing screamed.

I gasped and moved toward her, unable to tear my gaze away from the spot.

Red yanked.

Amazing pulled but started to slide until she lodged her foot against a rock that was half in the stream.

Mark's arms and head re-emerged above the water. He sputtered and coughed.

"Help me pull him out," Red yelled.

I moved closer to Cricket, who'd put a hole in Red's pants with the sharp hook on the end of the cord and held it tight in her hand. "Hold onto his waist but don't slide into the mud."

Amazing strained and pulled on his arm.

Praying the cord wouldn't break, I wrapped my arm around Red as he pulled the cord. My heart beat so hard against my chest Cricket had to hear it. Mark tried to untangle himself as he was eased up. Amazing leaned back, her long black hair covered in mud. Strange I noticed that at a time like this. Her sudden pull jerked Mark forward onto the mud. We couldn't get to him without falling in. He half-covered Amazing, but she didn't seem to mind.

Mark rolled onto his side and pulled vines and branches from around his waist and leg. Lines of pain marred his forehead as he freed himself. He and Amazing looked at each other and then started laughing. He pointed at the mud on her face while she pointed at the mud in his hair. Personally I 'd laugh for joy to have made it out of the cold water alive. When Mark tried to scoot forward Red cautioned him to remain still and we dragged him through the mud onto solid ground.

I offered Amazing my hand.

"No, that's how we fell the first time. I've got this." She lifted herself and scooted back a few times, and finally reached more solid ground. She stood, ran to Mark and wrapped her arms around him tight.

"Sorry about that," Mark said, sounding embarrassed. "I didn't realize the ground was that soft or what those branches were. Won't make that kind of mistake again."

"I'm just glad you're safe," Amazing said, wiping mud off his face.

He placed a kiss on her lips. "You shouldn't have come down there, but thank you."

"I couldn't lose you like that."

Her simple statement tugged on my heart. I wanted to cry or scream that I didn't want to lose Reggie either, but remained quiet. Right now this was about Amazing and Mark's miracle. Things could've been very different. No need to be selfish.

"Thanks man," Mark said to Red. "I appreciate your help. You too, Cricket."

Amazing turned and looked up. "Thanks so much, I don't know what we would've done if you hadn't come along."

"No problem, we heard everyone was looking for Reggie and joined the search. Cricket thought of this area after we left Main Street," Red said, removing the bungee cord from his pants.

"Did you finish searching this area?" Cricket asked.

"No, we were over there when Mark fell." I pointed in the area we'd just come.

Mark stood slowly and brushed mud from his clothes, spreading it everywhere. A large hole and several tears ripped across his shirt and pants. "I need to shower and change, these pants are all torn up."

Amazing held his hand while watching him like a hawk. "Okay, give me the keys, I'll drive."

He nodded and handed her his ring of keys. She looked at me and I followed behind her. "Thanks so much Cricket, Red."

Cricket looked at her watch and then at me. "No worries, it's five minutes to midnight."

My brow rose. "Why do you keep mentioning the time? Do you know something about Reggie?"

Eyes narrowed, she pointed a finger at me. "This isn't about Reggie or your cousin or anyone else you might want to blame. This is serious and it's about you. Don't you get that? This isn't a game anymore, it's our lives. Good or bad, we choose. You choose. Time is running out and I'm trying to help you, but if you don't want it, fine." She spun around and headed toward the cars.

"Wait."

Cricket stopped and looked at me.

"I'm sorry. I don't want to play the game, but I couldn't leave Amazing and Mark, I miscalculated."

Amazing started the car and I turned to go meet them.

Cricket looked at me. "Why'd you wait so late? You should've done it this morning."

"I wanted this last day with Reggie, Greg and Terri." I moved through the bushes, scared of what might happen in a few minutes. I'd messed up again, should have answered the question earlier and took my chances of being pulled away immediately. I didn't and had no one to blame but myself.

"It's different with each person. Brenda left the game as soon as she said no. Others remained a couple hours before they were removed. This morning Red lost his memories right away, I still have mine, so I understand, but you cut it too close," Cricket said, huffing alongside me.

The car came into view. Waving goodbye, I hopped into the back seat and pulled out my cell phone. Amazing backed up and then headed to the main road. Three minutes to midnight and not one bar. I tapped the Rewind app.

Nothing happened.

Precious seconds ticked until the tires hit the asphalt road. Amazing pressed the gas and the car took off. I stared at the bars, hoping for a signal, and continued pressing the app icon. Less than a minute and I had no signal, no activity, nothing. Not again, damn it. Biting my lower lip, I cursed the mud, the situation, and Reggie. In another minute I'd be stuck in a past I created. Fuck Rewind, I needed my old life back.

Sweat rolled down my face. Stuck in this new life without Reggie? I couldn't imagine it, life would be worse than with mama and the boys. I had to go back. My finger pressed the icon and then tapped it several times.

"Come'on, come'on," I murmured, hitting the icon. It blinked and the game opened. "Do you want to Rewind?" I searched for the box to click no. It wasn't there. My cell rang.

Bright lights flashed across my vision, blinding me temporarily. My head spun, an acrid taste hit the back of my tongue. When I opened my eyes, I looked at the caller ID and answered. "Daddy?"

Chapter Twenty-Five

"Reggie? Where are you?" I heard my name and tried to focus on the voice but couldn't. Ice cold air blasted against my face and arms, wakening me. Opening one eye, I quickly shut it against the glare of the overhead light and rolled to the side. Large squares of coral colored tile covered the floor. Shadows danced in a corner behind a large chair and lengthened along the concrete wall. The barren room wasn't one I'd been in before, but I was familiar with the tile.

Stretching, I threw my legs to the floor and held my head in the palms of my hand to stop it from spinning. What had they shot me with? Fuzzballs lined my throat, it hurt to swallow. My stomach clenched and unclenched from either hunger or the aftereffects of something that had entered my system, probably the latter. At least I had on pants and at tee-shirt. A pair of sneakers lay near the chair.

Bleary-eyed, I looked around and saw a room just large enough for a regular-sized cot, small table, and chair. A large window took up one wall, a metal door on the other, and nothing on the other two. Thirsty, I searched for something to drink, and saw a can of club soda on the table. Before I stood, the door opened. Toro Moreno entered the room, pulled out the chair and sat, watching me.

I grabbed the can, popped it open and drank it down while preparing to hear his BS and hide the fact I planned to help Serena escape the game by answering the question before midnight. In retrospect, it was a dumb mistake that might have cost her life.

My stomach clenched at the idea of leaving Serena without saying good-bye. Neither Toro nor Karo would believe I cared for her, not after all the women I'd dealt with. Somehow Serena had wiggled into my heart, I cared for her.

"Toro." I nodded in greeting.

"Reginald," he said, tapping a tablet. "Good I see your memories have returned, are they in tact? Any pain or anything out of the ordinary?" He continued writing on his tablet.

Other than hating this whole fucked up situation? "No, I'm good."

"What did you think you were doing by agreeing with your target that she should return home?"

Busted. I sighed and returned to the cot. When Serena said she wanted to go home after I reminded her that she'd made her choices, I'd ventured off script and agreed with her. Even promised to find a way for us to meet after my thirty days. Somehow my programming slipped, or genuine emotions canceled my directives, but I'd have helped her leave the game permanently if I'd had the chance.

"I thought I could change her mind easier by going along with it, but was pulled out before I had a chance to work my magic." It wasn't the best idea to aggravate Toro, my immediate supervisor, but I had wanted to spend the rest of the day with Serena to make sure she got the happy ending she wanted.

"Hmm, I don't know about magic. Looking at your half-assed reports, there was nothing to insure she'd stay in the program."

"She would've stayed," I said stubbornly, not wanting to show my hand because it was empty. I had no good reason not to pressure Serena into remaining in the program.

"Because she fell in love with you? So have half a dozen other girls over the past three years, that's nothing new."

"None of them left the program," I said through gritted teeth.

"True, but those females made that clear on the thirtieth day. Shelly Bryson did not. Despite all your magic, she planned to return home. Even worse, you didn't report it immediately or try to stop her. As a minor I'm sure you understand why she will never be allowed to return to her family, not in the same way she'd left like the others for sure. Is that why you didn't report her decision, to save her life?"

From the moment Serena mentioned she was underage I knew she couldn't leave, her reappearance could set off a chain of events that would never be allowed to happen. Maybe that's why I listened to her dreams and co-signed her conspiracy theories.

"I was taken before I could seal the deal. We had a date planned and I intended to have her so busy at the stroke of midnight she'd miss the time."

Toro stared at me a few moments longer and then smiled. "I can see that. She really cares for you. But that's no excuse for these reports. Half of them don't mention the pain she experienced or her reservations with remaining in the program. Fix those immediately before I turn them into Karo's office. He's been interested in her case."

"Yeah?" That surprised me. Karo had been promoted to oversee all testing sites and we hadn't talked in a while. It would be good to see him, hear what he thought of all of this.

Toro nodded and continued tapping on the tablet. "Lucky for you she decided to stay in the program."

"What?" I didn't believe it. After setting things up to run out her time, she remained? How'd that happen?

"She never rescinded. Her father tried to get her to do it several times, but she didn't. It's all recorded. Karo will be happy."

"That's..." A sneaky suspicion crawled up my spine. "What happened?"

Toro didn't look at me. "What do you mean?"

"She wasn't going to stay. I hadn't gone back to seal the deal." I jumped up as what happened slammed into me. "Fuck. Fuck. Fuck." I turned and looked up at the ceiling with my hands clasped on top of my head. My heart raced as I saw her in my mind calling my name. "She's looking for me isn't she? That's why she didn't log out of the game, she was searching. Yes, she would do that. She would think something happened to me." I spun to face him, my face on fire as I gritted out the words. "You son-of-a-bitch, you planned this. You knew she wouldn't leave if I were missing."

Toro's face tightened as he returned my glare. "I hoped she cared enough to look for you so that we could complete our jobs. You aren't the only one who gives an account for each person recruited. My ass is on the line too. I wasn't about to lose it so you could take a chance on fucking her into submission. This way, she made a choice without interference."

"That's bullshit and you know it. No way would she have stayed if I wasn't missing. How's that not interfering?" My fist clenched as I took a step toward him. I'd broken more rules than one. After five years working for Karo, I'd fallen hard for one of my targets.

Toro pushed back and stood. We were similar in height, but I was larger, heavier, and a hell of a lot madder.

"You didn't make her stay or look for you. She wanted to do it. Just as she wanted a new past, now she has it. Once again you're not grateful I saved your ass. Be glad that was your last assignment. You'll be free of this job and have time to spend that bankroll you saved up." Toro walked out without seeing my face crumple at the idea of never seeing her again.

The cracking in my heart felt cold, like blocks of ice replacing flesh. Serena and I had connected on a visceral level, sharing parts of each other no one else knew. She shared her beautiful, clean soul. Somehow love for her took root in me when I wasn't looking, something no one else ever had. How will my days be without seeing her smile or hearing her voice? Dark? Lonely? I've always been alone, but this crippling sense of loss was new, and I didn't know how to navigate around it.

I dropped onto the cot, imagining what Serena had gone through when she discovered I was missing. Hell, Mrs. Thomas and the others probably took it hard as well. They would receive a special serum that would erase me from their memories and in time they'd forget having an older son.

But I wasn't as sure about Serena. She had my journal and photos. Had I wanted her to remember me even then? *Yes.* Sure, a lot of stuff in the journal was fabricated, but there were kernels of truth. Dad had died early. I'd lived with my uncle. But there were no happy memories there. The man had been a pedophile and tried to violate me the first night I lived under his roof. It hadn't taken long for me to get tangled into the system and fall through the cracks. I'd always been big for my age and signed up for Rewind five years ago while living in northern California at the age of thirteen.

At that time, Karo worked intake and saw through my lies. Instead of turning me into children's services or tossing me out, he investigated my situation and kept me with him. Initially, I traveled with him and his team, doing odds and ends in-between tutoring sessions. When I turned fifteen, I looked much older, and he allowed me to enter the communities as a watcher. I sent regular reports on any anomalies with the serum. Occasionally I was assigned to hook-up with a target who might give the company trouble later on. Serena had been my last assignment and I'd failed.

"Why didn't you leave while you could?" I whispered raggedly.

Chapter Twenty-Six

Karo strode into the conference room where I'd been waiting.
His dark hair gleamed beneath the lights. At some point he'd
discarded his suit jacket and wore a pressed shirt with an open
collar. Years ago, when I first met Karo I'd been scared shitless.
The man had a way of looking at you with those dark, pine green
colored eyes that made you think he saw your soul and found it
lacking.

At thirteen he'd been huge in my mind and his wiry frame
had looked a lot larger than it did now. Even though I was now
taller and bigger than my mentor, the man still scared me on
multiple levels with his unpredictability. A person never knew
what to expect with Karo, so much depended on what happened
before he entered a room. I knew Toro had passed on my reports
and that I could be in trouble.

"You little shit," Karo said, pulling out the chair and sitting in
front of me. "What happened on this assignment? We almost lost
the Bryson girl."

"Hello to you too," I said, realizing by his tone he wasn't
angry, just curious. "I was pulled before I could change her mind."

He stared at me a few moments and then leaned back in the
chair. "Tell me about her."

"Huh?" I hadn't expected that. My feelings for Serena/Shelly
were too new. I didn't want to share them with anyone.

"Tall, blonde, pretty blue eyes, nice body... the pictures show
her well. Tell me about the Bryson you dealt with, she has a strong
will it seems." He paused without taking his gaze from me. "Nice
girl?"

Hesitant, I mimicked his move and leaned back in my chair
while watching him. "She's a nice girl, smart."

"What makes her nice or smart?"

"Just the way she treated other people and how she processed information. Wasn't a whiner, but didn't back down either. Took up martial arts, has a mean drop kick. I'd hate to be on her bad side." I chuckled remembering watching her practice at the studio last week. She'd made some cute sounds as she executed her moves. "Nice."

"Martial arts? I thought it was drama and wondered how you handled a drama queen," Karo said with a straight face.

I laughed and sat up. Toro had been thorough in his reports. "Yeah she did that too, but hadn't gotten far. I suppose she'll do more." I had bought her a DVD with the play Annie after she told me it was one of her favorites. Lying on her bed watching it had been a fun time.

"Your reports are sketchy."

I shrugged and didn't bother defending myself. Karo knew me too well to lie and I didn't want to explain.

"That was your last job. Where are you going from here?"

The change in conversation surprised me and then I remembered who sat across the table. A master manipulator, Karo would get back to my feelings for Serena before he left this room. "Maybe go to the beach before heading to the University."

"Beach? Sounds like fun. Wish I'd known, might've been able to set something up."

Smiling, I leaned forward wishing we could hang out again. "I can change things around so we can make it happen. Been a while since we hunted honeys on the beach."

Karo laughed, showing even white teeth and breaking the somber canvas of his square face. "Indeed it has. Things have gotten busy, but if I can arrange it I'll let you know. You ready for college? Got everything you need?"

"Yeah, as far as I know, everything's ticked off the bucket list, why?"

"Bryson's not doing well." He slid a few pictures across the table.

Eager to know more about her, I spread out the pictures. My heart clutched as I stared at her face. One photo showed Serena doubled over crying with Cricket nearby. I wondered how that happened. The two weren't friends. Another showed Serena sitting on a park bench staring straight ahead, Amazing sat next to her holding her hand. The other photos were similar shots of Serena grieving. "Didn't she get the serum to forget me?" I asked, my voice low. The light in her eyes had gone out, she appeared listless, a shadow of her former self.

I'd done that to her.

"Yeah, Thomas, his wife and the kid are forgetting, but not her. She remembers and it's not good."

"Can I go back in? Give her closure?" I asked knowing the answer but hoping he'd do it this time.

"No. You've been gone a week and a half. Most have forgotten you, just like the others, she'll forget soon. Plus, there's no viable reason to have you watch targets after the thirty days, you know that."

I did, but that didn't stop me from wanting to see her again or missing the sound of her voice. "Why tell me she's not well if I can't help her? If I can't see her?"

Karo looked at me with a raised brow. "So it's true, this girl caught your heart? You have feelings for her?"

If it were anyone but Karo, I wouldn't answer. It wasn't anyone's business where my heart lies, but Karo had stepped in and was the only father figure I'd had in years. "She's special and I hurt her. I don't think I'll ever forgive myself for that."

The silence lengthened.

"Bryson has a cousin," Karo said, watching me.

I nodded, Serena mentioned looking for Rashan.

"She's staying in the program, refuses to go home. Her situation is becoming complicated."

Uncertain why Karo shared the information with me, I nodded slowly. "She's the same age as Serena, has one more year of high school and then college. Maybe you can get her in early."

"Thought about that, like I said complications." Karo tapped the desk while staring at the wall. "Serena and her family are moving from BellaVista. We set it up so Greg Hemper got a better job in Texas. He'll be housed in a community where we own a major share, it's not as restrictive as Bella, but far enough from prior locations to be safe. Even if someone walked up to one of them and swore they were related, Hemper or Bryson won't remember." He waved his hand. "Quite frankly Bryson's becoming too difficult to handle in BellaVista. Others are forgetting, but she isn't and is asking too many questions."

I frowned. "She remembers her birth parents?"

"No. That's over, she doesn't even have the headaches any more, at least nothing's been reported. Despite additional doses of the serum, she still remembers you. That's the problem."

"Because others are forgetting?"

Karo nodded. "We're monitoring her and her parents, but they need a change of venue. Hopefully it'll help her adjust."

My shoulders slumped at the announcement. I didn't know which state BellaVista was located in other than it could only be seen from above. Beneath the town were labs and offices monitoring and supplying test subjects with basic necessities. How long had the town had been there? I didn't know but I held out hope that I'd be able to return one day to apologize to Serena.

"I did that to her."

"This assignment was no different than a dozen others. Why do you feel bad?"

I glanced at Karo, read his sincerity and released a long stream of air. "I like her."

His lips quirked. "Like? All of this moping around for the past week and a half for someone you like?"

My gaze flicked over his face and then down. Instead of the mahogany table, I saw her smile reflected in the glossy top and swallowed hard. "She's different than the others. Have you ever met someone who didn't try to hide who they were? Who accepted their faults without making excuses or blaming other people? She didn't want or need to be fixed or tried to use me in any way." I shook my head trying to line up my thoughts. "When we were together... she saw me, understood that I wasn't perfect, probably knew I hid something but never pushed, never called me out."

"Did she know the real you? I mean, did you relax enough with her to share your truth?"

"Some. I told her about my uncle and leaving home. Told her about college and what I'd like to do later with my life." Heat rushed to my face and I turned aside. When we'd laid beneath the stars on the blanket in the park and made plans for the rest of our lives, I'd laid my heart bare. We'd talked for hours. I'd forgotten my assignment, the company, Karo, everything. At that moment in time, Serena had been the center of my world as our imaginations burst free and danced in the sky together. It had been exhilarating and liberating. We'd laughed and crafted a new world where our love sustained us.

I wanted that future with her.

"Everything except she was your target? That you'd been sent specifically to make contact with her to keep tabs on her progress? How would she feel knowing that?" Karo asked in an even voice.

"She'd be hurt, maybe devastated," I said after a few moments of self-loathing. "Probably hate me."

"But you were never supposed to fall in love with her," Karo said softly. "No employer can dictate matters of the heart. That was all you and Bryson."

Unable to speak around the lump in my throat, I nodded.

"You admit this? You are in love with this girl?" Karo pressed.

Sitting back in the chair, I pinched the bridge of my nose as I thought about the question. Love? I wasn't sure what that meant. Certainly my father had loved me while he lived. Did I have any experience with love since then? Not that I recalled. Sure I cared about a lot of people, many were targets and people like the Thomas's, whose lives I intruded for a brief moment. But in nineteen years of living, I've never experienced this gut tearing sensation of disappointment of letting someone down. My heart never ached with wanting to see a person's smile or hear their laughter. The idea of never touching or sharing a moment with Serena hurt like something heavy crushed my chest. Unbearable to imagine, so I didn't. In the back of my mind I harbored a hope that we'd beat the odds one day, that our love would act as magnets drawing us back together.

"Yeah, I believe I am."

"But you're young, your whole life is ahead of you. Think of all the girls you'll meet in college; in time you'll forget this one."

"Karo... Man, you never forget your first love. I'll never forget Serena. That doesn't mean I won't survive or date other females. Just that I'll never forget."

His eyes narrowed as he continued staring at me. "Ideally a person can be made to forget anything, that's what I do."

I didn't say anything.

"So you'll excuse me if I disagree." Staring at me, he tapped his upper lip with his finger for a few seconds. "Tell you what, I'll make a deal with you. Go on one last job for me, and in forty-five days I'll tell you where Serena's family moved. You can go and see her then. If she remembers you, you can stay, but if she's forgotten you, move on."

My heart leapt for joy and then stuttered. I knew Karo. "This last job, does it have anything to do with Serena's cousin?"

He looked at me and shook his head. "No, not at all."

"How long is this next assignment? Will it interfere with school in the fall?"

"No, it shouldn't. There are a lot of unknowns and not a lot of people I trust to handle something like this. You'd be doing me a personal favor."

That sealed it. I owed the man my life and hefty bank account. "Consider it done."

Without taking his gaze off me he nodded. "Would you like to Rewind?"

I chuckled. During my assignments I was given a different mixture of the serum that blurred memories, but never destroyed or replaced them 100%, that was why Carlton became ill. The two drugs didn't mix well, especially the dosage Carlton had taken.

"Not particularly. Do I need it for this last job?"

"No, you'll need your memories intact to make reports and take instructions."

When he didn't say anything else, I sat back in my chair and watched him. No telling what was going through that mind of his, or how it'd impact me.

Karo cleared his throat but didn't move otherwise. "In order to reinsert you in Serena's life, I'd need to wipe your memories. You'd no longer be employed by the company and you wouldn't be able to explain your disappearance to anyone."

Frowning, I placed my hands on my thighs and forced them to remain still. Something in his voice cautioned me to think through everything he said. "Like the people who refuse to remain in the game and are released?"

"Yes, something like that."

Surprised, I met his gaze. "But how will I remember Serena?"

Karo's steepled fingertips pressed against his chin. "You tell me."

Chapter Twenty-Seven

Rain splattered on the roof of the patrol car as it drove down the street toward my home. I'd told mom I was going to the library and would be home in time to go shopping for school clothes and supplies. I hadn't made it past the park. It called to me. Memories of Reggie and I sitting on the bench or grass floated through my mind.

Reggie.

My heart clenched at his name. When would the pain ease? Would I ever know what happened to him? Where'd he go? Daddy and the others searched everywhere for him and couldn't find a single clue. The cops didn't find anything either. After two weeks they stopped looking. Not me. I expected him to return any day. I imagined him sitting with me on the bench or on the sofa explaining what happened, and then us laughing about it. We'd promise to make sure it never happened again.

Every day I listened to each excuse why Reggie hadn't yet returned. My friends stopped mentioning him and my parents allowed me my fantasies. Today I'd sat in the rain with my arms wrapped around my waist shivering on that damn bench, waiting. Every day I waited to hear something, anything from him.

But there was nothing.

The car pulled into our driveway and stopped. "You can't keep doing this, Serena. He's gone, I wish he'd said goodbye or something so that you'd have closure, but he didn't. This is your last year of school; you have your whole life ahead of you. Don't let what happened with him ruin your life," the police officer said.

I'd heard some variation of the same words for the past three weeks. They were lumped with the others in a file called, "You don't understand." Rather than respond to his unsolicited advice, I nodded, and slid out the car. Mom opened the door, a worried look on her face as she stood holding a large blue towel. She waved to the patrolman before wrapping me in the warm terrycloth.

Without speaking she ushered me into the kitchen and placed a warm cup into my hand. Fragrant cinnamon and lemon teased my nose as I brought the cup to my lips. The sweet taste of honey rounded out the drink as it slid down my throat, melting the ice from the inside out. I toed off my sneakers while mom dried my hair.

I sneezed.

"Bless you," mom said.

I laughed.

Brow raised she looked at me as I continued to laugh.

"I sat in the rain thinking about a guy who didn't bother to tell me good-bye, Mama."

She didn't say anything but continued drying my hair.

"Hell, I might have the flu, get sick or something, and he'd never know." I paused and took her hand. Eyes filled with sorrow and compassion looked into mine.

"He's gone and he's not coming back," I whispered, hearing the admission from my lips for the first time. It stung, but not as badly as the first time I thought it.

She didn't say anything and I was happy. I needed to have this Sunday morning moment on my own. "I loved him. And it hurts that he didn't love me the same way. But he's gone and not coming back." I wiped the tears from my cheek as the words reverberated in my mind. I needed to hear them, to say them to make it real.

Mom cupped my cheeks and placed a kiss on my forehead. "Whatever you need to deal with this, let me and daddy know."

I nodded and swallowed hard.

Daddy walked in, wrapped his arm around mom and placed a kiss on my cheek. Mom kissed his cheek and we stood silently for a few seconds.

"I have a job offer in Houston," he said, watching me closely. "It's more money, a house, and a big step up in my career."

"That's great, honey," mom said.

Numb, I tried to feel something, anything, but couldn't. Leaving would make it harder for Reggie to find me, but he might never return. "I'm a senior."

He nodded. "I know and that's the only reason I hesitated to accept the job. But a change might do us good." He squeezed my shoulder and then hugged me close. "I miss your smile, the light in your eyes. Seeing you happy or content again is my sole mission in life. Think about it, I have a couple days to give them an answer." He placed another kiss on my forehead and walked toward the stairs.

"What do you think, Mama?"

"Like your dad said, a change might do us good." She walked to the other side of the island and placed a pan in the oven.

"What about my friends, Amazing, or Patricia or Kelly?" Even as I said their names it seemed one was missing, but I couldn't place a face or name.

"They'll always be your friends, Serena. Maybe you can plan a get together for Spring Break or something. I know you don't like to play online anymore, but you can video chat or exchange texts."

I nodded, sensing she really wanted to move. "What if... what if Reggie comes back and we're gone?"

"His parents or Amazing can tell him where you are, even give him your new phone number if you want. We're moving to Texas not another planet, he can contact you there just as easily as here," she said, smiling.

Nodding, I pulled the towel closer and stood. "When... when will this be over?"

She stared at me and then wrapped me in her arms. "I don't know, baby. The pain will dull over time, but there are so many unanswered questions, it makes things so much harder. Just take things slow, one day at a time."

Inhaling, I swallowed the pain and confusion. "I can't keep doing this, maybe getting away is the best thing. Everywhere I go here I see him and remember things we did together. That's not helping, it makes it harder. So... maybe a new place... well, that might not be a bad idea." It didn't hurt as much to say it as I thought it would. "I'm going to shower and change, be back in a bit to help." I moved up the stairs with determination to move forward. Did I still love Reggie? Oh God, yes. Probably always would. But the bastard had left me.

When I reached my room, I locked the door and stood in front of the mirror. Blond strings and clumps of wet hair lay limp on my face, head and neck. Red-rimmed eyes stared back at me. I'd lost weight, my face looked gaunt like one of those zombies on TV. I was in no condition to drop kick anyone, I'd really let things go.

Seconds passed as I stared. What the hell was I doing? I touched the dark circle beneath my eye with my fingertip gently and then my cracked lips. This wasn't me. I refused to allow this to be me.

"You said you loved me and I took you at your word. You said you couldn't imagine a day without me but you left, vanished without a good-bye. It would have been kinder to break up first, to take your love back." Anger, bitterness, and shame, a toxic cocktail, swirled just beneath the surface. "I don't want to ever go through this type of pain again. I swear I won't." I watched my lips, it sounded like me, but it wasn't. I transitioned like a butterfly into a person I never thought I'd be, bitterness over his betrayal had changed me.

"I loved you Reggie, and I hope you're not hurt or dead anywhere. But I can't keep living like this, waiting and hurting." I paused. So far the pain wasn't overwhelming, I could do this. "Now I'm moving away and leaving you and this town behind." I paused and straightened when it didn't hurt as bad. "If we ever meet again, I hope we can be friends, but I'll never love..." No, that wasn't what I wanted to say. "If we ever meet again and you have a damn good reason for treating me this way, maybe we can be friends."

The was nothing left to say, nothing left to feel, nothing left but the void surrounding my mind when I thought of him. Most importantly, I'd gotten through the break-up and went to shower. After washing and conditioning my hair, I blew it dry and took time with my appearance. Styled my hair in a simple flip with bangs, and applied light make up, I soon resembled my former self. Dressed in a pink jogging suit, I looked in the mirror again. This time my smile reached my eyes.

"Reggie, you blew your chance at my heart." I pointed to my image in the mirror with narrowed eyes. "Don't ever do that bullshit again. Never give your heart to the point you forget yourself. Got that?" I waited a beat as the words penetrated and dug deep. I'd given too much and received little in return. That wouldn't happen again.

"Got it."

Chapter Twenty-Eight

Karo continued staring at me across the table. I didn't know what to say. On the one hand I'd be free to be with Serena again, we could live the future we discussed. But I might not recognize her or have any memory of that future. Years of living and working with Karo saved me from wasting time arguing or complaining. At his core, Karo was a master manipulator. There was always a way to get what you wanted if you took the time to see things from his perspective.

"What if the serum isn't strong enough and I'm able to find her anyway? Will that impact your research?"

His brow rose and then he smiled. "I'm not in charge of research, but that's an interesting point. Initially I wanted to use the main serum on you, but there is another strain fresh from the lab that might work better. You'd still create your past for imprinting, but it locks it down within fifteen days instead of thirty. It's what we give employees when they give two weeks' notice."

"And you want to use me as a test dummy?" I curled my lip so he'd see my thoughts on his idea.

"Well... it's been tested numerous times, just not on anyone I've monitored. You can read the information and test results if you'd like."

"No thanks, I'll pass. Thirty days is fine. I've seen that work."

He smiled. "True, but the new formula allows you to change your mind between days sixteen and eighteen. You'll have more flexibility if things don't go well with your lady. Think about it before you say no."

Call me cautious but I wasn't interested in anything I hadn't seen work. "About re-creating my past, when do you need that?"

"Before you go on this last job."

My heart slammed against my chest as I looked at my fingernails. "Would it be okay if I keep you in it?" I hated sounding needy but Karo had become a staple in my life. Knowing we'd still have a connection steadied me.

For several seconds he didn't say anything and I was too nervous to look at him.

"Yes, that would be fine. You'd need to make up a new role for me. I'll help you with that."

"I was thinking you'd be my older brother, or uncle, something along those lines. Family I spend holidays and celebrated stuff with." There I'd said it. When I thought of family, Karo was front and center. He didn't deal with his biological family at all, at least he hadn't during the time I lived with him. We'd acted like two orphans and clicked.

"I see. Okay, we can make it work since we won't be in the same towns and visits would be scheduled."

Relief swamped me as I looked up at him. "Thank you. There are a lot of things in my past I want to forget, but not everything. You saved my life and I don't want to ever forget that."

Karo nodded slowly and lowered his gaze to the table before clearing his throat. "All right, we'll deal with your new past and your quest to find your lady love later. I hope she appreciates all you're giving up for her."

"Rewind?" Is that what he meant?

"Not just that, you'll move to a new state, go to a different college, be alone in a new area with only a vague memory of her. I'm only telling you the name of the town, not her address or anything else. You're on your own with love to guide you," he said with a hint of sarcasm.

Karo hadn't moved an inch during our negotiations, which sucked. For a few seconds I hesitated and almost changed my mind. Could I find Serena? So much depended on where she moved in Texas. In a large town it'd be difficult, almost impossible, especially if I used the old serum, which replaced memories daily. Wait, Karo agreed to be in my future even though you weren't supposed to take anything from your past. Maybe there was a gray area. If I wrote Serena into my past, I wouldn't forget her. That's it! I'd have Serena's picture next to me when I wrote my past so that when I stepped into my present she'd be fresh on my mind.

"What?" Karo asked, watching me.

"I plan to write Serena into my past as well," I said, waiting to see what he'd do.

For a few seconds he stared at me and then the corners of his mouth turned up. "You've learned how to manipulate the system."

If I had, it wasn't intentional, but that wasn't important. "So I can bring elements from my past into the new past?"

"Only in situations like this where I know what's going on and agree. Otherwise, no." He didn't raise his voice, but I sensed something disturbed him.

"Thanks," I said, re-energized and ready to get started before he changed his mind.

"Do you remember Josh and Pete?"

His casual question threw me for a loop and it took a moment to switch gears. "The couple in BellaVista? I played ball with Josh. Max was his mate. Who's Pete?" An image of a tall oriental guy with dark eyes and a quick smile rose in my mind.

"Max was Pete's new name."

I nodded.

Karo nodded. "Josh and Pete didn't work out. Pete left on day thirty but isn't responding to the shots to reverse his memories. His folks just entered him into a mental facility. He's being treated for schizophrenia."

"What? How'd that happen?"

"We're not sure, that's why you're going in as a physician's assistant. One of our people was hired as a doctor and you'll be assisting her. She'll send samples of his bloodwork so we can see what went wrong." He paused. "This is really important. I need you to focus on this while you're there. Stay to yourself, limit your involvement with staff so that when you leave it's not a big deal."

"Okay."

"To make matters worse, Pete told some online friends about Rewind, and his reappearance after the thirty-day mark caused them to contact his parents. It didn't gain any traction, but we're looking into it."

Serena mentioned she and Pete played games together, in fact she'd played games on several sites with a group of friends. Had they contacted her parents? Would that be an added complication for her? Karo never said, but that was a possibility. If the company thought anyone could expose them, that person disappeared, so I remained silent.

"No matter what, Pete will eventually be placed in one of our facilities where he can live his life peacefully. When the time comes, I want you to accompany him to the new location, make sure he's settled. Then you'll be done."

"Any idea how long all of this will take?" Sounded like a huge job where so many things could go wrong. It could take a long time.

"No more than six weeks."

The hope-filled bubble of seeing Serena soon, deflated. "Six weeks?" Doubt laced my words and I didn't bother hiding it. So many things could happen in an uncontrolled environment. Pete's family, governmental agencies, staffing, the list went on.

"That's the target, otherwise he's lost to us and will remain in a mental facility for the rest of his life. Now do you see why this is so important? We can help him regain some of his memories, enough to live a good life, but we need to move fast. We've already lost a week."

Nodding, I stood. "When do I leave?"

Karo stood and handed me a flash drive. "Your suitcase is on the chartered plane taking you to Georgia. Everything you need is on this drive."

I headed to the door and then turned. "After this, Serena and college, agreed?"

"Definitely. I'll get you registered at the University, secure your residence, and spin you around three times so you can begin your search." He laughed, walked over and slapped me on the shoulder. "Thanks for handling this for me, I appreciate it and will make sure your pay is deposited so you'll have a bigger nest egg for school." He paused and we stared at each other. "I'm proud of you."

For the second time in thirty minutes my throat tightened and I couldn't speak, so I nodded and walked out the door.

Karo looked at the closed door for a few seconds and then returned to his seat. Seconds passed and he didn't move, couldn't think past the idea that Reggie wanted him to remain in his life. He'd picked up on the hesitation in the kid's voice, knew he'd been prepared for rejection, and it had been on the tip of Karo's tongue to say no. But not because he didn't want the relationship, he already thought of Reggie as a kid brother, the only family he had.

Karo knew he lived on borrowed time. Sigman would order his demise as easily as he'd ordered countless others if he messed up or outlived his usefulness. No one was indispensable. In Sigman's and the Board's eyes, the only thing that mattered was the success of the program, which went beyond money. Power over the lives of so many was just as potent.

He closed his eyes and thought how he'd play this hand. In order for Reggie and Bryson to remain alive, he'd need to sell their usefulness in the program. Reggie was on his way to deal with Pete, who'd been undergoing Berkhorn's treatment for a week. The numbers were good, but they needed Pete isolated so they could track his progress. Reggie would handle that.

Next, he needed to sell Sigman and Berkhorn on the viability of continued treatment for Serena and Reggie on a long-term plan.

Ideas to accomplish his goal raced across his mind. He could do it, save them both, but the timing needed to be perfect.

A light tap on the door gained his attention. He waved Toro inside.

"We're all set?" Toro asked.

Karo glanced at the young man and nodded. "You have forty-five days. After that, he'll be in Texas, determined to find her."

Toro smiled with the confidence of a man who knew his way around women. "That's more than enough time. When is her family moving?"

"In a couple of weeks. Things are almost lined up. Just so you understand, her memories should only be of the past she created as well as her initial thirty days."

The young man nodded. "Bryson is a wild card, Sir. For some reason she's had spikes where her past merged with the present. That's why Dr. Berkhorn wants additional tests run with the new formula. I understand how important this test is."

Karo drummed his fingertips on the table without speaking. "The formula is en route?"

"Yes, Sir. Dr. Berkhorn says she must consume it once a day for two weeks, but change is noticeable within three days."

"Have a case of water sent to her now in BellaVista."

"Yes, Sir. But who will watch her?"

"Her parents, her friends. I'd rather she begins taking the new formula now in a controlled area where she can be taken to our clinic on property if there is a problem."

"And the added benefit that the incubation time for the drug would be over before travel." Toro paused. "Will I still need to watch Bryson?"

Karo looked up frowning. "Yes, of course. Not only watch but become her friend, we need to be sure this version of the drug does what it's supposed to and document it. If it completely patches holes, we'll be able to give it to targets with stronger will-power like Bryson in the future. If not, we continue tweaking until we do."

Toro nodded. "Yes, Sir. I'll send the cases to BellaVista for her and prepare for the Houston job."

"Good, keep me posted."

Chapter Twenty-Nine

I slept through the flight to Houston. Yesterday, Amazing, Pat and Kelly had taken me to lunch and threw a mani-pedi party at our favorite nail salon. We'd spent hours talking about school and boys. All in all, it had been the perfect send off and we planned to get together during spring break, and maybe attend the same college.

I hadn't been prepared for the humidity. It slammed into me the moment we left the airport with our luggage. My chest hurt from trying to breathe in that heat. We didn't waste any time picking up the lease car from Intercontinental Airport, and quickly headed to the freeway. It seems we drove for hours, but it wasn't that long before the GPS instructed us to turn off the highway and head north. By the time we reached the gated community, I was wide awake with expectation. Large, beautiful homes that could grace the cover of any magazine lined the road. We made several turns and finally pulled into the driveway of a large two-story house with a wide porch, fenced back yard, and dark shutters which contrasted nicely against the white walls.

"This is home for a while," daddy said, opening his door. I cringed as the outside heat attacked the cool air inside the car. How would we survive in this weather? So far I wasn't impressed with this slice of Texas. Mom handed me a cold bottle of water, which I gulped down before sliding out of the car and moving quickly to the shaded porch.

Daddy keyed in the code on the door, and we went inside, appreciating the cooler air. "It's furnished," I said, looking at the large living, dining, kitchen space done in light shades of blue and cream. "You told them what you liked." I sat on the sofa smiling at mom.

"Yes, I picked out most of the furniture, our personal things will be here in a few days. Soon this place will feel like home." She sat next to me and held my hand while daddy walked through all the rooms.

"It's hot." I looked at her.

"I know, no one mentioned that," she said in a low voice and winked.

"There's a pool back here," Daddy said.

I jumped up and ran toward his voice.

Mom laughed and followed.

"It's big," I said, looking at the screen-enclosed pool and Jacuzzi. A large grill, refrigerator, and storage cabinets sat on one side. An outdoor dining table and six chairs were arranged near that area. Loungers surrounded the pool. Outside, the fence and a few tall trees ensured a modicum of privacy. Kneeling on the paved patio, I placed my hand in the water. Cold.

"Now this is what I'm talking about, this is epic," I said. Mom hugged dad and they kissed.

"Let's see the rest of the house," mom suggested.

"In a minute." I removed my sandals and placed my feet in the water. Leaning back, I closed my eyes, the cold water below and the humid heat above clashed. It felt wonderful. The hair rose on my arm and I opened my eyes to look around. I couldn't shake the feeling someone watched me. Moving slowly, I backed up, entered the house, and caught up with my parents. My heart beat so hard I thought I'd pass out.

"You okay?" daddy asked, staring at my face.

Uncertain what just happened and aware of everything I'd put them through over Reggie, I cleared my throat and tried to smile. "Yeah, what's back here?" I walked inside and saw what was obviously the master bedroom. "Now this is definitely you, mom." I ran forward and fell on the massive bed. The cream, gold and peach combination and dark furniture had her stamp all over it.

"It does look good, doesn't it?" She said, her tone smug.

"Yes." I jumped up and finished looking at all the rooms while thinking about what had just happened at the pool. By the time I convinced myself I'd been imagining things, my clothes were unpacked, and my bed made.

Mom and I headed to the nearby grocery store because the cupboards were empty. An hour and a half later, we returned home. As we unloaded the car, two teenage boys walked by the opened garage. At least I thought they were teenagers, they may have been older. One looked Hispanic like Amazing, the other reminded me of Red, Cricket's boyfriend, with his strawberry blond hair and tall lanky build.

"Hey, what's up?" The blond stopped and looked at me. Daddy came outside and took most of the remaining bags inside. I moved in their direction with my hands stuffed in my back pocket.

"Nothing much."

"Just moved in?"

"Yeah."

"I'm Wayland, this is Toro." He pointed to his silent friend.

"Serena."

"Cool. Are you in high school or what?" Wayland asked.

"Yeah, Senior." I glanced at Toro. His dark gaze never wavered reminding me of the incident on the patio.

"Any idea where you're going to school?" Wayland asked.

"I can't remember the name of it, but I start next week." I'd been given a choice of a nearby private or public school, and couldn't decide. They both had good stats. In the end my parents chose.

"If you want, we can introduce you to others in the neighborhood, there aren't a lot, but enough so you'll know somebody on your first day," Wayland offered.

"So both of you are in high school?" My gaze flicked from Wayland, who could pass for high school, to Toro, who looked older.

"No, just me. He graduated last year," Wayland said.

I glanced over my shoulder, ready to escape the heat. "It was nice meeting you guys, hope to see you around." I took a couple steps backward, watching them watch me, and then turned to walk into the garage.

"Who was that?" daddy asked when I made it to the kitchen to help put away groceries.

"Toro and Wayland, who's still in high school. He asked where I'd be going next week."

"You told him about the private school?"

"None of his business. Plus, I couldn't remember the name." I sat on the stool and wondered if I should mention the feeling I had before, or how creepy it was Toro didn't say a word the whole time.

"We need to go car shopping tomorrow," daddy said, tapping me on the nose.

I perked up at his reminder. I'd gotten my driver's license before we moved. During the week, mom and I would share a car since she'd started a graphics design business and worked from home. "You know what I want."

He laughed and walked into the family room.

I went upstairs to my room to shower and change. I heard noise on the patio downstairs and looked out my window. That eerie feeling of being watched returned and I looked everywhere, but couldn't see much because of the tree blocking the view. I closed the blinds and pulled the curtains tight before heading into my bathroom. The jittery feeling in my belly persisted when I finished and dressed. I stared at the window, wondering if I could be seen and then shrugged it off. My cell rang. I looked at the caller ID and smiled.

"You're Amazing," I said with the right amount of practiced flare.

"Yes, I am," she said with good humor. "How's everything going? Tell me you hate it and plan on running back here."

Dropping onto the bed, I laughed and gave a recount of my day. For a few moments it seemed like she was around the corner and we could meet for burgers and fries.

"Someone was watching you?"

"I'm not sure, but it felt weird and no, it wasn't the heat."

"Okay, tell me more of the hunky guys walking around in shorts and flip flops."

"Thanks for your concern, Bestie."

"No, I know if you were really worried you'd have told the parents. Now give the deets, Chica. Are they hot and spicy?"

I thought of Wayland and Toro and snorted. "Not that I've seen." Of course, I measured each guy against Reggie and they came up lacking. Amazing knew that and didn't call me out on it.

"No. Hmmm, maybe I'll wait to visit until you meet some hotties, keep a lookout for me."

I chuckled, pleased she didn't press the issue for me to start dating again. That wasn't happening anytime soon. "Will do." We continued talking and laughing about stuff that didn't matter to anyone but us. The conversation lightened my mood, and when I went downstairs I'd forgotten about the feeling of being watched.

Chapter Thirty

I pulled into the driveway, grabbed my books, and headed inside. The heat seemed bent on melting me and I refused to give into more complaining. Instead, I hefted my book bag on my shoulder and went to grab the mail. A late model BMW slowed and stopped. I refused to look at the car as I removed the contents from the metal box.

"Hi Serena," Toro said, getting out of his car and heading toward me.

My muscles tensed with each step he took in my direction. When would he stop? I wasn't interested and had been very clear on that front. Tight-lipped, I nodded. "Toro."

"Did we get off on the wrong foot? I get the feeling you don't like me for some reason? Did I do something to offend you?" His voice softened and he managed to sound as if I'd hurt his feelings.

"The first time we met you acted weird, staring and not saying anything." I looked at a postcard from a martial arts studio I'd visited last week. Mom thought it might be a good idea to get back into it since I'd enjoyed it so much before. I wasn't sure. But I'd signed up for drama club. So far I liked the group and volunteered to work the soundboard, with two other guys, for an upcoming play.

He blinked and straightened as if he hadn't expected that answer. "Wayland was talking."

He asked, I answered. I shrugged and turned to go inside without feeling guilty or anything.

"So because I didn't talk that first time you're offended? Or just don't like me?" His tone said 'how childish' or 'that's ridiculous.' Since I didn't like either interpretation, I shrugged again.

"May I ask where are you from?" he said to my back as I reached the step leading to the porch.

"Why? I haven't asked you any personal questions," I said over my shoulder and continued up the steps.

"Wow. Have you always been this rude? Unfriendly? Did somebody hurt you or something?"

I stopped and looked at him for few seconds. Tall, dark hair and eyes, nice body, killer smile, Toro wasn't unattractive, not by a long shot. But I just didn't like him. Something about the way he carried himself didn't jive with me. "I've been told I've always been like this." I saluted him and headed inside the house. When I didn't hear his car leave immediately, I watched him write something on a piece of paper and then place it on my windshield before returning to his car. He looked at the house again and then drove off.

For several seconds I stared at the paper on the windshield. Curiosity pulsed in my chest. What was his angle? I'd been in Houston for three weeks, had made a few friends at school and a couple in the neighborhood, but nothing like in BellaVista. Amazing and I still talked every night. I smiled thinking of what she'd say about Toro's note.

Mom's footsteps came close. "Why are you staring out the window?" She moved to the side and looked out as well.

"Toro left a note on the car."

Her brow rose. "Did he? While you watched?"

I shrugged.

She opened the door, walked outside, and picked up the note. Smiling, I wondered if Toro were someplace watching and what he'd think now. She handed me the folded paper and we moved into the kitchen.

"Whoever made you so cold, I'm not him." I read the note a few more times and laughed.

"What?"

"Reverse psychology." I read the note to her.

"Hmm, I see what you mean. Why don't you like him?"

"I can't explain it. He's oily, slick. His smile doesn't feel right, there's something off about him, something not right," I said, struggling to find the words to express my gut.

"Okay. That's good enough for me."

I grabbed a bottle of water and some chips. "Thanks, I don't know why he keeps trying."

"It's the thrill of the chase. You said no, and I'm sure you've been blunt." She eyed me with her patented I-know-you look.

I laughed. "Very, but he keeps trying. That makes no sense. Vanessa, a girl who lives around the corner, has this huge crush on him and won't speak to me over what she thinks is going on. As far as I'm concerned, those two would make a great match." Vanessa was pretty with dark hair, a heart-shaped face, and blue eyes. She had an exotic look and large breasts, which she played to her advantage. I still wore an A cup.

"For some men, it's all about the hunt or chase or whatever word they call it. The more you say no, the more their egos tell them to make you change your mind. Makes little sense to us, but that's the way of it." Mom placed a large casserole dish into the oven and faced me. "Follow your instincts and don't give him the time of day. In the end you'll be glad you did."

Jumping off the stool, I grabbed an apple from the bowl and headed to my room to get homework done. When I closed the door, I pulled out the paper and read it again.

"*Whoever made you so cold...*" Images of Reggie flashed across my mind. Had he done that? Made me cold? I didn't think so. Besides, not wanting Toro had nothing to do with Reggie and everything to do with Toro. *What about the others?* I exhaled and dug out my laptop.

Since starting school I'd been asked on several dates, which I declined. I hadn't given my phone number to any guys. None of them interested me. There was no spark. Nothing, and that was okay because I knew I wasn't broken, just disinterested. In time that'd change when I met someone... interesting.

Chapter Thirty-One

The moment I entered Greg Hemper's office I was grabbed and slammed against the wall. Unrelenting pain stabbed the back of my head and ran down my back. "Give me one reason why I shouldn't beat the shit out of you and toss you down the garbage disposal," Greg gritted with ice cold blue eyes. A better reaction than I anticipated since no bullets were fired. After the last assignment of getting Pete settled, I didn't have the patience to wait until Serena's father was in a better mood.

I arched my back to relieve the pressure, but he held tight. Although we were similar in height, he outweighed me by several pounds and none of those were fat. Besides, I needed his help.

"Can I talk to you for a few minutes?"

"Hell no, Reggie. Whatever you have to say, sell it to the movies. Just stay away from my daughter," he snapped and released me.

"Please, I don't have a lot of answers, but I would like to explain what I do know." I straightened my short-sleeve polo and stepped away from the wall.

He prodded my chest with a pointed finger. "I trusted you. Opened my house and my heart to you, allowed you to date my princess and you broke her heart. There's nothing you can say that'll change that, so leave and don't come back."

Two days ago I'd arrived in Houston. I'd missed school this semester and would start in January. The apartment rented on my behalf was midway between the campus and downtown. As soon as I slept for twelve hours, I'd searched for Greg Hemper in every bank in Houston until I found his office. I'd driven across town to ask for his help with Serena.

"You've forgotten a lot of things, Greg."

He stared at me for a few seconds. "Why are you here? How'd you find me?"

"I just finished a job that I barely remember." I met his gaze. "I don't remember much except Serena. Her smile, her laugh, her scent. The past 60 days thinking of her kept me sane, and alive with hope."

He frowned. "What are you saying? You were someplace you don't remember?" He didn't offer me a seat, but he hadn't thrown me out either.

"It's all in patches, as if certain parts have been cut out, leaving the rest, which makes no sense." My stomach tightened, as I crossed my arms over my chest and unclenched my jaw. "Georgia. Somehow I left BellaVista and wound up there. I think I worked in a clinic, which makes no sense because I wouldn't do that." Frowning, I looked at him as if he had answers.

"Sounds like a sorry excuse to me," he snapped, taking a few steps in my direction.

I straightened and met his gaze. "Look, I'm not going to let you knock me around, no matter how much you think I deserve it. Serena wouldn't appreciate it and regardless of what you think, I'll find her. She'll at least listen to what I have to say before judging me."

He clenched and unclenched his fists a couple times without speaking. "What are you doing here?"

I'd cut my hair low, and now I ran my palm across my head. He knew there was only one reason I'd risk a showdown with him. I guess he just wanted to hear me say it. "I'm looking for Serena. The way it ended before... it was wrong. I need to make this right."

"We searched everywhere for you, where'd you go?" He continued staring at me, an unfamiliar twist to his mouth as if he smelled something bad.

"I don't know. I woke up in a different place and couldn't return." Struggling to remember, I walked in a tight circle and then held onto my head. "God it hurts when I try too hard, like a knife in my mind."

"Serena experienced that," Gregg said softly, his eyes changed from chips of ice to sky blue. "I remember Terri telling me about it, but it passed. And you've been someplace else all this time?"

I didn't blame him for the disbelief in his voice, but I couldn't explain where I'd been or why I recalled some things and not others. "Yeah. As soon as I could I boarded a plane and flew here."

"What made you choose Houston?"

"Good question, I don't know why. That morning I woke up on a plane, the flight attendant gave me a large manila envelope with the address of my apartment, keys to my car, information on school, and bank accounts."

"Bank accounts?" He walked to his desk. "What banks? Do you have that information?"

"Yeah. I need to stop there later today." I pulled out the paper from the folder, looked at the bank information, and then wrote it down on a piece of paper before handing it to him.

Greg read the information and his brow rose. "That's a prominent bank. Give me a moment to see what I can find out." He waved to the chair in front of his desk. Grateful to have help, I took the seat and pulled out the picture of Serena I'd kept. This photo had been taken at the park on our first date. My finger traced her lips curled in a smile. Bright blue eyes laughed into the camera on my phone. She looked happy.

"Reggie?"

I looked up and met Greg's stern gaze.

"This account has one lump deposit a week ago. Did you open it?"

"No. I can't remember the name of my bank, but this one's new, I think."

"You had another account with them, but it was closed two months ago, after you disappeared." He stroked his chin while looking at the monitor. "Someone closed it for you but it doesn't say who." He glanced at me. "You're 18, right?"

I nodded. "Nineteen, almost twenty."

"This is odd, I can't get more information, it's blocked."

If he couldn't get answers I knew I couldn't. "How's Serena?" I'd held off as long as I could.

"Good, in school, dating." He continued tapping keys and didn't look at me.

"Health-wise?"

That stopped him. His brow rose as he met my gaze. "Never better." After a few seconds of charged silence in which I thought he dared me to disagree, he returned to the monitor. I hadn't thought of fixing things with Greg, my goals centered on Serena. Boy, I'd been wrong. Greg acted as her gatekeeper, Terri would be worse I supposed. Before I could reconnect with the girl who occupied my dreams, I'd need to prove worthy by her parents.

Straightening in my seat I returned everything, including Serena's picture, to the envelope. "I'm sorry for disappearing, for causing you and your family pain or worry. I'd never have left Serena on my own. Never would've betrayed your trust or hurt your wife. Please accept my apology."

When the first words left my mouth, Greg turned and watched me with a narrowed gaze. Nostrils flaring, he allowed me to finish, and now sat watching, weighing my words.

"If what you say is true, and it's hard to believe it is, then you may have had no choice in the matter." He pointed to the monitor. "Someone's been playing with this account. I plan to check a few more things before accepting your apology." Our gazes clashed as he leaned forward with his hands clasped on his desk. "If you're sincere, if you've lost your memory, then do this. Wait a few days before seeking Serena. Tonight I'll talk to my wife, she may want to see you first, hear your story, see if you're on the up and up. I don't know. What I do know is we never want to lose our daughter again the way we lost her when you disappeared."

"I didn't mean --"

"What you meant to do or not doesn't change what happened or the fall-out afterward. For weeks she cried herself to sleep, wondering if you were dead or alive. There was no closure. If I could've found you, I would've shot you between the eyes."

"Mr. Hemper, if you would've found me then I'd have been happy. I hate not knowing. Not feeling complete, as if chunks of my life are gone." I snapped my fingers and then closed my eyes briefly, not wanting him to think I was some young punk. "I disappeared, that's true. But against my will, you can take that to the bank."

"Will you give us some time to think of the best way to handle your re-introduction into my daughter's life?"

Everything inside twisted and rebelled at the idea. I clenched my fist but didn't look at him. "How much time?"

"A week."

My head snapped up. "No." The man was on drugs. It'd been over 60 days already and Serena had no idea what happened.

His eyes chilled. "Five days."

"No," I gritted out. "Two days."

"Not including today."

A sinking feeling hit my stomach. Had I just made a deal with the damn devil? "Will you tell me where she is?"

He shook his head. "You've got two days to find out everything you can, I won't help you."

What did I expect? That he'd welcome me with wide arms? Be the same Greg who laughed at my jokes or talked sports? In some region of my mind I'd expected that Greg to return. I'd always like him and had been sure he'd help after I explained. Pride in shreds, I wrapped my tattered dignity around my shoulders as I stood and headed toward the door. Alone in a new place left me cold. Love. Friendship. Where were those things now? At some point I'd made a wrong turn and love left me vulnerable. Had I made the wrong decision to come here?

"Deal?" Greg said as my hand touched the doorknob.

Tight-chested, I cleared my throat and thought of the return drive, the empty apartment and lack of anything to do. Two days until I know if it'd been worth it. "Deal," I said and walked out.

Chapter Thirty-Two

The parking lot of the mall wasn't too crowded at this time of day. I pulled into a spot near the store where mom bought her favorite bath scents and perfumes. The lady made them specifically for her, and had called to tell me the basket I ordered as a late birthday gift was ready. I glanced at my watch and groaned. I didn't have much time. The past few days mom had been acting weird whenever I was late from school or wanted to go anywhere. Today I'd left school a few minutes early so I could pick up this gift, but I still needed to make it home on time.

Running from the parking lot to the doorway I pushed my sunglasses up my nose and entered the large glass door. Cool air brushed against my skin, energizing and propelling me around the corner to the small scent shop.

"Hi," I said to the unfamiliar clerk while searching for Magda the owner. "I'm Serena Hemper. I'm here to pick up my special order.

Smiling, she nodded and walked toward a hall. "Yes, one second."

Opening my wallet, I pulled out a credit card and silently thanked God for daddy. The clerk came right back with my order. The large basket filled with creams, lotions, and oils looked festive and perfect, even though it was late.

"You like?" She turned it so I could see everything.

"Yes. It's great. Do you have the gift bag?" I looked around for the bag Magda had showed me when I placed the order.

"Yes." She placed the basket in the bag with tissue paper, and handed me the card.

I wrote a short apology for being late and placed it in the bag. Pleased with my gift, I handed her the credit card along with my ID.

Errand completed, I headed back to the car thinking of mom's expression when I gave her the bag. Smiling, I pressed the button and unlocked the car.

"Serena?"

Good lord, not Toro again. Without looking or responding, I walked faster.

"Wow, so it's like that? You won't give me a chance to explain either? I came all this way and you won't even hear my side of the story?"

Everything inside me froze. The voice, the words... it couldn't be. Slowly, as if moving too fast would break the illusion, I turned and looked across the parking lot. My hand flew to my mouth as I stared at Reggie standing in front of a black BMW. Blinking fast, I took another breath. He hadn't moved. Instead he stood stiff, acting as if something kept him in place.

"Reggie?" I whispered, scared to say his name. Scared to be wrong again. Scared he'd disappear. Instead he walked toward me and I met him half way. Tentatively, I touched his face and shook my head. "You're here? How? What?" Thoughts tumbled over each other, I had so many questions. My emotions crashed and rolled in a huge ball of confusion. No question I was happy to see him alive, but then anger over his leaving the way he did slammed into me. Shame over how I'd handled his disappearance washed over me, and then fear that he'd toss aside my questions and leave without explaining gripped my chest.

"Yes, I've been looking for you."

I looked at the mall and then back at him. No one knew I'd be here today. "At the mall?"

He shook his head and held out a small black bag. "I'm returning a watch I bought the other day. Had no idea you'd be here. But I'm glad to see you. Is there any way we can talk? I'd like to explain what happened." He paused, and I wished I could snatch off his sunglasses and see his eyes. "At least I'll tell you what I remember."

"Sure, let me call mom and tell her I'm going to be late." Skin tingling in anticipation of hearing what he had to say, I stole another glance at him from the corner of my eyes. He still looked good, and I wasn't sure how I felt about that after everything I went through.

"Mom, I'm at the mall and will be home a little later." I frowned as she questioned me as if I was lying. "I can take a picture of the mall and send it to you."

She didn't say anything for a few seconds. "That's okay. When you get home we need to talk about something."

I glanced at Reggie wondering if I'd be telling them about seeing him today. "Okay, see you in a bit."

Holding the gift bag high, I looked at him. "I've got about an hour, hour and a half tops. That's more than enough time for you to tell me what happened." Silently I congratulated myself for not sounding weak or falling apart or touching him despite how badly I wanted to.

"Anything you give me is fine. Talk here or someplace else?" He surprised me with the softly spoken question.

The Reggie I remembered would've taken my hand and walked me to his car. "Here's fine. We can sit in the car." I headed for the driver's side while he slid into the passenger's seat. It felt weird looking at him from this angle, but I didn't say anything.

"First, I want to apologize for everything. I don't know what happened. One minute I left your house headed home, the next thing I remember I'm in Georgia somewhere working. I can't remember anything from that point until I woke on a plane heading to Houston five days ago." He spent the next ten minutes telling me what he did remember and then stopped. "It's wild and I don't know what else to do or say other than I'm sorry my life's all jacked up."

"You expect me to believe you came here for me and you've been here five days." I pointed to the bag on his lap. "You've been here long enough to go shopping, get a place, and buy a car... riiiight. I'm on your mind alright."

He opened his mouth and then closed it. "I love you Serena, always have. Like I said, thinking of you is what kept me going. Hearing you make light of what I went through to see you, to be with you... hurts like a motherfucker, but that's on me. I wanted this, a chance." He shrugged and turned away.

My stomach dropped at his response. Throat tight, I tried to apologize but couldn't. The things he said didn't make sense, no one forgot that much. "So you have amnesia? Is that what you're saying?"

"Not according to the doctor." He looked at me with a wry smile. "No lie. I never would've left you without saying goodbye. I don't know what happened or why or even where I've been for the past months, but I never forgot you. Not one day did I forget your smile or hear your laugh." His fingertip touched my chin briefly.

My breath caught as tingles shot through me.

A thousand questions raced through my mind, but I couldn't ask one. Twin fairies stood on my shoulder, one said I should forgive and reminded me of my love for him. The other screamed for me to run in the opposite direction and never speak to him again as it reminded me of the pain I'd endured when he disappeared.

Self-preservation is a tricky thing. Reggie may have forgotten a lot of things in the past two months, but I remembered everything clearly and refused to open myself up again.

I sighed, drawing his attention. "This... this is a lot to take in," I said, watching him closely. "It's hard to believe."

He nodded and then held a flash drive high. "This is all I have left. I'd hid it with a few things and it was still there." He raised his sunglasses to rest on his head and met my gaze. "Watch it, and then tell me what you think. If you don't want to talk to me again... I'll leave you alone." His voice broke and then strengthened at the end of that sentence. "But this may help you understand." He placed it in my outstretched hand.

"Understand what happened to you?"

In a typical Reggie move, he shrugged and opened the door. My heart swelled at seeing remnants of the guy I'd fallen for. This serious side of Reggie confused me. I didn't know where he was coming from. Uncertain I was ready for him to leave, I got out of the car and stood in the door. "So I don't get your phone number?" Internally I cringed at the question I hadn't meant to ask. *Please, please don't make fun of me.*

"Sure, give me your phone."

We stared at each other a few seconds before I reached into my purse and then handed my phone to him. He tapped the screen and then his phone rang. "There, you have it. Feel free to use it any time."

He turned and headed to the mall.

"Reggie?" I called out when I saw he wasn't going to look back.

He stopped and looked at me.

"Thanks... for explaining," I said, heat filling my cheeks. God, could I be more pathetic? I didn't want him to go, I wanted to take him home and have things the way they used to be. But that wasn't possible. I'm smart enough to know that, but I couldn't just walk way. Instead I waited until he entered the mall, and then sat in the car for a few seconds looking at the flash drive.

Mom called and I started the car without answering. Boy were they going to be surprised.

Chapter Thirty-Three

I pulled into the driveway, grabbed mom's gift, and headed inside. Mom met me at the door with a worried gaze.

"Are you okay?" I asked, holding the gift bag behind my back.

She sighed. "Yes, there's something I need to tell you, to talk to you about and... well, I don't want you to get upset."

The way she watched me put me on defense. "You've been acting weird lately, is that what you want to talk about?" I moved sideways, not ready to give her gift, not when she stood holding her hands tight in front of her. Whatever bothered her must be deep.

"In a way, let's go sit down." She turned and headed to the family room without noticing or commenting on the bag in my hand.

I placed it on the floor next to the sofa and waited.

"The other day daddy... well, I'm not sure how to say this, but it seems Reggie's tracked you down."

"What?"

Her gaze met mine and she looked as if she'd cry. I wanted to tell her it wasn't that serious, but hearing Reggie and dad's name in the same sentence stopped me.

"He went to Greg's office a few days ago to apologize, explain, and ask to see you. Daddy checked a part of his story and says it true, but the rest of it, not knowing where he's been... we aren't sure about that. He agreed to wait a couple days before seeking you out. Greg's been driving around town before coming home at night in case Reggie tried to follow him."

"What?" I shook my head trying to grasp everything she'd said. *Daddy trying to ditch a tail?* Reggie went to see daddy first? I wasn't sure how I felt about any of this.

Mom patted my hand and made a soothing sound, totally misunderstanding my reaction. "I've been worried how you'd react to his showing up here, but you don't have to see him if you don't want to. Greg made that clear and Reggie agreed."

My heart dropped and for a few seconds I couldn't think. "He agreed not to see me?"

"If you don't want to see or talk to him, he promised not to make trouble or push his way into your life again. Daddy made it clear we didn't appreciate what happened before. I think he grabbed Reggie or something."

"What?" My eyes widened as I turned to her. Reggie didn't start or run from fights, I couldn't imagine him and daddy punching each other.

Mom nodded. "For how he treated you."

"But..." I held up my hand and released a breath. "Let me get this straight. Reggie's in Houston, he went to daddy's office?"

"Yes, our last name isn't real common, and Reggie is smart."

I hid a smile at her defense of my ex and continued. "He agreed to what? Wait a couple days before looking for me? Why?"

Mom's gaze slid toward the floor before returning to me. "Daddy asked him to give us time to prepare you, to see how you felt and what you wanted to do." She leaned forward and took my hands. "I know it's a shock after all this time, but I think you should at least listen to what he has to say. If for no other reason than closure and to ask all the questions you need."

Should I mention Reggie at the mall? He looked good, but sounded different. Sad almost.

He hadn't been looking for me, it had been what? Luck? Coincidence? That was such a leap with all the shopping malls and places in Houston.

"Serena? You don't have to --"

"Just thinking, that's all. This is a lot to take in. Reggie... I want to know what happened." I met her concerned glance and picked up the bag from the floor. "This is why I went to the mall to get your birthday gift. It's late, but I wanted to get that lotion you like and had to wait until she could make another batch."

Seeing her eyes widen and glisten in surprise made my day. With slow moves she opened the bag and took out the contents, commenting on each one. When she finished, she pulled me close and kissed my cheek.

"Thank you, I can't believe I didn't see that bag when you walked in."

"Your mind was on other things," I said. "Plus, I ran into Reggie at the mall."

The smile on her face froze and then morphed into a confused expression. "Reggie? At the mall? Today? Just now? You saw him? Talked to him?"

I nodded and waited.

She put the bottle of lotion on the table while watching me. "He told you what happened?"

"Yeah, you're right, it's hard to believe." I started to tell her about the flash drive but didn't. Maybe after I looked at it, I'd mention it later.

Her shoulders dropped but she didn't release my gaze. "He sounds determined, sincere."

I nodded and stood, not ready to discuss all my mixed up feelings right now. "Yeah, but so does Toro."

Mom frowned. "That boy's a nuisance, I'm glad you didn't go out with him."

"I haven't gone out with anybody."

She nodded slowly. "That's true."

Quiet, I headed to my bedroom and placed my book bag in the corner. I turned on my laptop, dug the flash drive from my pocket, and inserted the disk. A half bottle of water sat on the desk and I finished it off while waiting. My cell beeped, Amazing. I didn't want to talk to anyone right now and let the call go to voice mail.

There were two files on the flash drive. One said Shelly, the other said Reggie. For some reason I clicked Shelly first. Several files labeled journal and a video appeared. I pressed the video and sat back in surprise as Reggie and I appeared, seated next to each other in the park back home. Apparently, I was Shelly. For several minutes we talked about the possibility of a drug that altered our memories and how so many things didn't add up. Although we didn't find proof, we made the video in case we lost each other. He gave me his memories and I gave him mine.

Hands trembling, I replayed the video three more times hoping for a flicker of memory, but there was none. The fourth time I watched the video, I muted the sound because I couldn't believe we were serious, and simply watched the way we looked at and touched each other. The look in his eyes as he stared at me tugged at my heart, he *had* loved me. Probably still did. The way I leaned against his chest as he spoke took me back to a place where he'd become the center of my world. Those had been good times.

Frowning, I stared at the video. Why'd we make this? Or say those things? Were we preparing for today? To be separated? I clicked on his name, the file opened and the same video was beneath a few journal entries. I opened the first one and didn't stop until I read all four. There wasn't much I didn't know. What about the other?

Butterflies filled my belly as I returned to Shelly's file and opened the first journal. Each page told a story of a girl I had no idea about. It was interesting to read, but I couldn't relate to her dilemma. She played a game and lost her memories? That was crazy. By the time I got to the last journal, she'd met Reggie and was falling in love.

Seeing Amazing's name stopped me cold. I knew all of Amazing's friends and there had been no one in BellaVista named Shelly. I re-read that page several times trying to remember and couldn't. Closing my eyes, I leaned against the headboard and tried to think. A game that recreated memories... I couldn't buy that. But something had happened. Uneasy, I pulled out my cell and called Reggie.

He answered on the second ring. "Hey."

"This video... I'm having a hard time believing the conspiracy theory," I said.

"Me too, but that's me and you in the park."

"Have you read the journals?"

"Several times. Something about mine don't ring true, but it is what it is. I can't see you complaining over playing a game either."

My cheeks warmed at the first journal entry when she'd sounded like a wimp. "Yeah, that threw me too. So what do you think this means?"

"Fuck if I know. I stored it in the lining of a jacket and had it with me when I arrived. When I realized it was there, I cut it out and watched it. In a way it answered a lot of questions, but I'm still in the dark. I just don't remember and may never get my memories back."

"That sucks."

"Tell me about it. Some days I walk for hours trying to remember and come home exhausted so I can sleep. Other days I don't bother getting up. There's this dark hole and it's fucked up."

"Yeah, what are you going to do?" I still wasn't sure what to believe, but somehow we were in this together.

"Live one day at a time. Karma's a bitch, I must've done something, somewhere, sometime, that's kicking my ass right now. I missed this semester, so I might take a trip or two, try to get my head straight before next term. Why the hell you moved to a place so damn hot?"

I laughed at the re-emergence of the Reggie I knew. "Daddy's job, plus I needed to get away. It was too hard staying there." My voice sobered.

"Babe, if I could re-write history, change what happened, hell, I'd like a chance to kick the son-of-a-bitch's ass who took me, I'd do all of that." He paused. "I never stopped loving you."

My heart clenched and I closed my eyes to shut out the world that said I'd be crazy to believe him or the wild story of him losing his memory. The words dug deep, unlocking the door to my heart. Tears filled my eyes, but I refused to allow them to fall. Never again. "I thought something bad happened to you. I couldn't eat or sleep." I scrubbed the tears from my cheek and inhaled.

"Serena, I'm so sorry. I knew you'd be worried and tried to get back to you to let you know what happened. But for some reason I couldn't."

"Couldn't or wouldn't?" I snapped as the pain from that time flowed through me. Who knew unlocking my heart would release everything?

"Couldn't for sure," he snapped. "I'd never treated you like that before, what makes you think I'd do it then?"

I had no answer and remained silent.

"Damn it," he growled. "I can't remember and when I press too hard my head hurts really bad. Your dad said it happened to you once."

Vaguely I remembered telling mom about my headaches. Biting my lip, I took a leap. "What if someone tampered with your memories?"

"Or yours."

I rolled my eyes at his stubbornness. "What can or will you do about it?"

For a few seconds he didn't speak. "Not much I can do. Guess it'll be like those people abducted by aliens who knows something happened but can't prove it."

"And when they try to prove it everybody thinks they're crazy," I added, understanding his dilemma.

"True. I have an older half-brother, Remi Karo. Wonder why he's not in those journals. Growing up I looked up to him, smart, good looking, great dude. I might visit him while waiting for school to start."

"Have you talked to him?" I asked to cover my surprise that he wasn't all alone as I'd thought.

"Several times. He wants me to move to Florida, go to school there, says I can stay with him."

"Oh. So you're leaving again? Why bother contacting me? You didn't have to do that."

"Yeah I did. I had to apologize and explain, that's what you do when you hurt someone you love," he said in a soft voice.

"Love? Love's got you leaving again?"

"Give me a reason to stay."

My chest tightened, fear had me on lock down. "What about school? You moved here to go to school."

"No, I moved here to find you. To be with you. If you've met someone else and don't want me, I'll leave."

Same Reggie, he wouldn't let me hide, demanded I be honest. "There's no one else," I whispered.

"Thank you, God," he yelled.

I chuckled. "You nut."

"Scared shitless that you'd moved on. Your dad said you were dating."

Smiling wider at daddy's interference, I pushed several strands behind my ear. "There's a couple guys sniffing around."

"Sniffing is cool as long as you aren't interested in them and they don't push boundaries," he said.

Warm from his affection, I closed my eyes and allowed the good memories from before to flow over me.

"What happened? You went all quiet," he said.

"Just thinking, have you contacted Carlton or your mom?"

"Who?"

"Carlton, your brother," I said, more alert.

"I don't... I don't have a brother named Carlton. My mother died when I was two, my dad when I was ten. I didn't know Remi until I was 12."

"Short, dark tan complexion, curly hair, light brown eyes, he followed you everywhere and broke into your room." I gasped as that memory spiked. "Carlton told Cricket about your past."

"He did? Why?"

"I don't know. I can call and ask her. Do you remember Mrs. Thomas?"

"No."

What the hell was going on? How could he forget his mama? I couldn't imagine daddy or mom not being in my life. "You lived in BellaVista, that's where we met."

"Where's that?"

"It's..." I frowned. "It's in... I don't know. Let me ask daddy."

"Okay, let me know. Maybe I'll go back there to fill in the blanks. Thanks, that helps a lot."

Hope stirred in my chest. "You remember?"

"No, but you do, so it must be true. It's more than I hoped for, knowing I have a small brother. I've always wanted more family."

"Do you remember anything about BellaVista? Mark? Amazing? Kelly? Russ? Josh?"

"That last name sounds familiar but not the others."

I frowned. "You and Josh weren't that close, only played ball together. You hung with Mark and Russ all the time."

"Did I? You have pictures of them?"

Scrolling through my phone I sighed. "No, this is a new phone and I didn't save the pictures. Amazing probably has some, I'll ask her when we talk later tonight. She and Mark plan to get married after they graduate in the spring. I'm the maid of honor."

"Cool, maybe I'll remember them after I see a few pictures."

"Strange you don't remember anything from there."

"I remembered you and your parents."

A knock sounded on the door. "Dinner's ready," Mom said.

I looked at the clock. "We've been talking for over two hours, time for dinner." Unsure where we'd go from this point I waited to see what he'd say.

"Okay, can I call you later around ten?"

Relief removed the tension that had held me tight. "Yes. I'll ask daddy where BellaVista is and let you know."

"Are you going to show them the drive?"

I thought about it for a few seconds. Mom and I were really close but I wasn't a hundred percent sure I wanted her to read ramblings of me calling another woman mama. "Not yet, let's see if we can figure a few things out first."

"Okay, I didn't mention it to him the other day. He tried to kill me when I walked in his office. Your old man got skills, it would've been tough knocking him on his ass. Got a lot of respect for him handling things that way. A man ought to look out for his kids."

Not sure what to say, I logged out, placed the flash drive in my pocket and stood with a lot more questions than when I sat down. "I'm going to eat."

"I'll call you later and thanks for talking to me without calling me crazy. I've called myself that a lot of times recently."

"You're a lot of things but not a liar or cray cray."

He laughed and clicked off.

I squared my shoulders, looked into the mirror for a few moments. "He came back for me and I still love him."

Chapter Thirty-Four

Blistering sun rays beat down around the patio outside my apartment which faced the community pool. A few college students and a lot of professionals who lived in this complex lay on chaise loungers or on the edge of the pool with their feet in the water as if the heat was of little consequence. Perhaps one day I'd become immune to the heat, but since I hadn't reached that point I remained beneath the shaded area of the patio with a standing fan on high.

Two women walked by my unit and waved.

"Hello ladies," I responded with a respectful nod and zero interest in my voice. That's been the way it's been since I arrived and I think word's gotten around that I'm not looking. There hadn't been anymore knocks on my door or females stopping at my patio to talk.

They smiled and continued toward the pool. My gaze dropped to the sway of their bikini-covered bottoms. Earlier I'd played with the idea of going to the pool and decided against it. Serena and I had agreed to give our relationship this last chance. Going to the pool without her would send the wrong message and could undermine all the progress we'd made so far.

Almost 20, I wasn't ready to get married, but I didn't want to play around and lose Serena either. There's something about her that calms the anger inside and makes me feel stronger, but not in an arrogant way. There's this look she gives me, not quite a smile, her lips curve at the corner and her steady gaze sparkles, conveying her trust and solid belief that I'll do the right thing. That look feeds me, makes me strive to be better, to earn another look. I search for it in every conversation or decision we make.

For years I dealt with females so I wouldn't be alone. Living on the run was hard, but I'd been big for my age and always attracted older women who taught me how to make and keep a woman happy. It'd been a game I mastered without emotions.

When I met Serena, she had this innocence about her. Learning she was a virgin shocked me. Thirty minutes into our first conversation I realized this sexy, smart, kind, beautiful female, had little experience with guys like me. Since I'd never dealt with anyone younger either, we were both on unfamiliar turf, but we connected. I'd taken a chance and shared my life both the ugliness and the decent parts, something I'd never done before.

As my best friend and woman, she accepted and understood me. We clicked without the sex. I snorted and took another drink. If that wasn't love, shoot me, because I didn't normally go down like that. But I let her set the pace and it worked. When we came together it'd be right, special. But damn it was hard waiting.

Been almost a week since I saw her at the mall, and even though we saw each other every day and talked every night since then, she hadn't been to my place so we could be alone.

Today I planned to change that. Had my A-game ready to bring her here, grab some Chinese, and watch a movie I'd bought. I smiled thinking it'd be nice having her to myself. I took another long pull of water and decided to get a beer when I went back inside.

I heard a noise, looked over my shoulder and waited to see if it came again. For what I paid to live in this place the security better be top notch. Since I didn't hear anything, I continued watching the ladies sunbathe at the pool while wishing my lady was here with me. Standing, I tossed the empty bottle into the trash and went inside to get a beer. The moment my feet touched the ceramic tile floor, someone rammed into me, knocking the small table near the door to the floor in a loud crash. Fire spread through my side as I doubled over trying to see. I caught a glimpse of dark pants and dove for his legs. *Son-of-a-bitch come in my house and attack me?* I'd kill the bitch.

My fist connected with his thigh.

He countered with two punches to the top of my head. I released one leg but held onto the other as he tried to kick me away. Reaching out, I grabbed something hard that'd fell from the table and hit his thigh as hard as I could. He groaned but didn't yell. I hit him again and he kicked me in the head.

Dazed, my grip loosened enough for him to break free. He limped toward the front. Still holding the heavy object, I stood slowly and went after him. Dressed in all black, even his head and hands were covered. The only thing I saw was his dark gaze and some pink flesh around his eyes. How the hell he walked in this neighborhood dressed like that? Someone had to see him.

"Motherfucker, you walked in the wrong door," I yelled as he tried to open the front door, but it required a key and I never left the key on the door.

Chest heaving, he pulled something from his pocket and faced me. "Your choice, either let me leave or I drop you here and leave the way I came."

Spikes of pain radiated from my skull, I thought I'd be sick as I tried to make sense of what he was saying. "Are you asking me to let you get away after you broke into my crib? Are you serious?" My grip tightened on the metal book end as I prepared to throw it.

"No. I'm telling you I'm leaving. I'm not supposed to hurt you but I will if that's the only way for me to leave." He inched toward the window behind him.

"Wait, hold up. What do you mean you're not--?"

"Just consider this your lucky day, you get to see sunrise tomorrow. Now do I shoot you or will you be smart and not try to stop me?" He waved the gun, I saw it clearly.

"Get the fuck out of here," I said, holding my head as he climbed out the window and disappeared. I went to the window and looked out and around but didn't see any sign of the dude. I closed and locked it. Was I bleeding? I looked at my hand. No.

Should I call the cops or security? What did he mean by not hurting me? In the end I decided spending more time at the shooting range would be my best bet.

I took the keys from my pocket, opened the door and walked outside to look around. Cars were parked in the lot, but there was no one walking around that I could question. Dude had simply disappeared.

Son of a bitch my head hurt. Moving slowly back inside, I grabbed a bottle of water, two Ibuprofen, and sat on the sofa. As the adrenaline ebbed I stared at the water. "What the fuck just happened? I'll be damned, got punk'd in my own place." Rubbing my head again, I picked up the table and straightened everything.

Had I been robbed? I went to my bedroom, looked around, nothing seemed out of place. Checked the bathroom, walk in closet, and the spare bedroom without noticing anything out of place.

Pissed someone violated my privacy, I searched online for security companies and made an appointment for someone to come Monday morning. As soon as I hung up, my brother Karo called.

"What's up, Bro? You ready to plan that trip?" The last time we talked we'd agreed to plan something before I started school in January.

"Not yet, I've got a lay-over in Houston today, got any free time to hang out?"

I punched the air and whooped forgetting about the pain in my head or the break in. I didn't spend much time with my brother and wanted to see him. "Any time. Let me know, I'd like you to meet Serena."

"Your first love?" he said dryly and then laughed. It had been a running joke between us. Karo didn't believe in love.

"Yeah, Man. Serena." I didn't laugh because it wasn't funny; he knew I was serious about her.

"Ease up, no disrespect intended. I'd love to meet the lady that slayed your ass."

Happy to see him, I looked for my keys. They were still in the door from when I went outside. "For real, want me to pick you up?"

"No, I got a car. See you in a bit, it'll be nice to catch up. Everything good?"

I told him about the dude who broke in. After assuring him several times I was alright and nothing was taken, he clicked off.

Smiling, I checked my stash of beer and snacks. There was enough to start, if I needed more I'd run out and get some. I started to call and share my surprise with Serena and then decided to wait until I saw her later. With another glance at the window the guy left through, I went to shower. Karo would know ways to keep burglars out, I'd make sure to ask.

Chapter Thirty-Five

Saturday mornings, daddy went to play golf. Today he promised to return in time to take mom to some event in town she'd been raving about. Reggie planned to come over around three and we'd have a few hours alone, the first time since he'd returned.

Lying across my bed with my laptop and Shelly's journal on the monitor, I decided to check into her story. Maybe she was missing, or her parents searched for her? Daddy hadn't remembered where BellaVista was located and he searched for it. Plus, Mrs. Thomas denied having an older son, and didn't remember Reggie. That had been such a surprise for mom and dad they now believed something had happened to Reggie's memories and Mrs. Thomas' too.

I wanted to be sure my memories hadn't been screwed with. The idea that daddy or mama weren't my real parents sent a chill down my spine. What if I was one of those missing teenagers whose parents never found them? I wanted to know, but then what? What would I do if the journals were true and my name had been Shelly?

Heart in throat I stared at the flash-drive and was tempted to toss it in the trash. I didn't want to change my life but I needed to know the truth. Placing the drive in my pocket, I headed downstairs to grab a snack. Daddy walked in with a case of water and placed a few in the refrigerator. Mom walked into the kitchen and he whistled.

"Give me a few minutes to get cleaned up." He swatted her on the ass, grabbed a bottle of water, and left us in the family room.

Mom and I grabbed bottles and sat on the stools. "Reggie's coming over?" she asked.

I nodded but didn't meet her gaze. I planned to go to the library to dig into things.

"We haven't talked about sex yet, but do you need protection?"

I coughed, sputtered, and spewed some water.

She handed me a paper towel. "Here."

Wiping water from my face, arms and clothes, I didn't look at her. Reggie and I talked about it and decided to just let things flow. I believe he planned to take me to his apartment later, it'd be the first time I visited. I was excited and ready to be intimate with him. So many nights when he'd been gone I'd wished we'd had sex or made love as Amazing said. Now that he was back in my life I wanted to do everything with him. From the moment I met Reggie, I claimed him as mine, he was it for me and there was no reason to wait. But I couldn't talk to mom about it, not yet.

"It's important you have protection," Mom said.

Since my face was on fire I knew it was red, she had to know I couldn't talk about this. "Mom, please, don't."

"What? I can make an appointment with the doctor, you can get a prescription."

Amazing and I had gone to the clinic in BellaVista, I just never took the pills. They were in my drawer. "I'm okay, thanks."

Our gazes met and then she smiled. "Just be careful, and prepared."

Did Reggie say something to her or something? I wanted to crawl under a rock, instead I tried to smile, and act as if I had it all together. "Can we not talk about that? Please?"

She patted my hand. "Of course. Remember you can talk to me about anything." Standing, she walked out into the hall and disappeared.

Guilt sucker punched me over her last comment. I didn't want her to know I doubted my parentage. She'd be crushed. Still thirsty after the first bottle, I grabbed another while pretending to watch

TV instead of waiting for them to leave so I could do some online searches without interference.

A few minutes later, they walked into the family room smiling. Handsome in his light yellow polo and dress slacks, daddy strolled through first. Mom's fitted white dress showed off her slim figure and nice tan.

"Be back later, have fun and don't stay out too late," Daddy said.

We'd never talked curfew since moving here so I assumed it'd be the same as before and waved them off. When the car left the driveway I clicked off the TV and fetched my laptop from my bedroom, intent on using the family room so I could see Reggie when he arrived.

I typed Shelly Byron into the search engine. My finger hovered over the enter key. So much could change with this. Did I really need to know? How would I look at mom and dad? There was so much riding on this. My heart cracked and I lowered my hand, the next second I pressed the key.

Several news articles appeared. Mouth dry I clicked on an article from a Kentucky TV station and watched the video. A woman, Linda Chesney, the screen had her name, asked for information to find her daughter Shelly and niece Rashan. Two pictures flashed on the screen and I gasped. With a few tweaks the blond could be my twin, but I didn't recognize the dark-haired girl. A man, the dark-haired girl's father asked for prayers for the girls and mentioned a reward. I stared at the picture of Shelly Bryson for a few seconds, waiting for an aha moment or a flash of recognition.

Nothing.

Sure we looked alike, but without the journals I wouldn't believe for one moment we could be the same. Even if we were, I mean, *are* the same, I have no idea who she is. Stumped, I read three more articles on the missing Shelly and then searched a couple missing person's databases.

One online photo gave a good, clear shot of her face. Blue eyes, like mine, seemed sad, distant, like she didn't laugh or have fun. Her long, blond hair appeared dull and was pulled from her forehead with a white headband, highlighting pimples on her forehead.

Without thought, my hand flew to *my* face searching for signs of acne. Mom had placed me on a skin and hair care regimen in middle school. I'd never had acne and certainly never pulled my hair back like that. Still, we could be twins. Wouldn't that be funny if her mom had two girls separated at birth?

Linda Chesney. I ran a search on Shelly's mom. There wasn't a whole lot more other than her Facebook and Linked-in pages. The social pages had a lot more information. Pictures of Linda, two small boys, her husband, and a couple with Shelly. I frowned over the lack of family photos on her page and then searched for Shelly's social media pages.

Instead of a real life picture, an avatar of a blond Zena with a whip of truth strapped on the side of her hip and cross blades strapped to her back filled the slot. The banner was a fight scene from some game.

"Seriously? Games? No drama or martial arts?" I scrolled down her page amazed by all the game references. "Is this all you did? Play games?" I looked at the pages she liked and clicked on some of her friends. All were gamers.

"Well, this proves we can't be the same person. I'd never spend all my time playing games." After clicking a few more of her friends, I returned to her page wishing I could see her last entry instead of all the public gaming stuff. Send her a friend request? I chuckled and searched some of the others like Rashan, her father, and then Reggie. Why wasn't I surprised Reggie didn't have a Facebook page or any social media pages? What would he think of all of this?

My brain was full of static from information overload, lots of thoughts zipping around but nothing concrete to help come to some sort of decision. A weight pressed against my chest as I stared at the pictures. The people in the journal were real. My fingertips pressed against my lips to keep them still, to keep the sound of denial from pressing forward, to silence the questions I'd need to ask if this was true.

Should I contact Linda? And say what? "I could be your kid, but I don't remember you or anything about you?" That sucked.

Reggie's car pulled into the driveway. Shutting down the laptop, I played with the idea of having a twin sister somewhere in the world. It'd be epic, but who'd be our mom? Terri or Linda? After returning from my room I grabbed another bottle of water and looked outside to see why Reggie hadn't come inside yet and groaned.

Toro had parked his car behind Reggie's and was getting out. I grabbed my purse, hurried down the steps to meet Reggie and send Toro away, hopefully for good.

"Hey," I said to Reggie, who'd just stepped out the car wearing fitted jeans, a rust colored polo, and looked at Toro.

"Hey Babe, who's this?" He nodded at Toro, who leaned against his fender, blocking us in.

"Toro, name's Toro. Does that mean anything to you?" Toro asked, watching Reggie.

I stepped forward, ready to ask Toro what was his problem.

"No, should it?" Reggie said, his head cocked to the side. He pushed his sunglasses up his nose and leaned to the side.

Toro shrugged.

"Move your car please, we're heading out," I said, hoping to diffuse the tension in the air.

"I didn't know you had a guy in your life. Wish you'd told me."

Even though Toro spoke to me, I had a feeling the comment was directed to Reggie and that wasn't good.

"Now you know," Reggie said in a hard voice. "Is there another reason you're still here?" He moved to stand in front of me, his legs apart and arms loose on his side.

Toro looked at me and then at Reggie. "You made your choice?"

I stared at him as if he were high on drugs, never had I given him any indication I was interested in him. Rather than respond to his question, I turned, opened Reggie's car door and slid into the passenger's seat. *Arrogant asshole.*

A few seconds later Toro left.

Reggie returned to the car and pulled me into his arms for a hot kiss. "That was sexy as hell, a very classy way to answer a question."

Pleased by his response, I waited until he started the car. "Before we go, I need to lock the house. I found some serious stuff." I held up the flash drive.

"Lock up, my brother stopped through town on his way to San Diego. He's only going to be here a few hours. I really want you to meet him."

I looked at my sky blue cotton pants, blue and white striped short sleeved blouse, and then at him. "Should I change?"

Reggie laughed, a nice robust sound that always made me smile. "No, if you change for anybody it should be me."

"Good answer," I said, rubbing the short goatee on his chin, gaining a smile from him. For some reason he thought the extra facial hair looked good and I agreed. I armed the alarm, locked the front door, and made it back to the car in a less than a minute.

We drove across town and entered another gated community. "There are townhomes, condos and apartments in this development. My place is back here." We pulled into a numbered parking space. Inside I was surprised at how big the place was and how nicely it had been decorated.

"Who picked out the furniture?" I asked, touching a red and cream glass vase.

"Don't know," Reggie said, wrapping his arm around me. "It was like this when I moved in."

"Oh...you rented it furnished?"

He nodded, took my hand and walked toward the back. On the patio a man sat talking on the phone, and then stood as we approached.

"I expect you to take care of that within the hour," he said, smiling at me before looking at Reggie.

What had I expected of Reggie's brother? It was obvious they didn't have the same parentage. Reggie's parents had been black. Remi had dark eyes, and his thick wavy hair was smooth like daddy's, but his dusky complexion, several shades lighter than Reggie, tagged him as mixed. Indian, European? I had no idea.

"Serena, my brother Remi Karo. Karo, my lady, Serena."

Smile still in place, Remi stuffed his phone into his pocket, reached out and hugged me. "Karo to family and friends," he said. "She is much too pretty for you, Bro." He placed a kiss on my cheek and released me. "But I'm glad to see you're happy."

He and Reggie bumped fists and we headed inside. "I have time for a meal, shall we order in or go out?" His gaze flitted from Reggie to me.

"I'm good with anything," I said, even though I had eaten at home and wasn't really hungry.

"There's a restaurant nearby that I always visit when I'm in town," Karo said. "I'll introduce you to the owner, make sure they take care of you whenever you need a good meal."

Reggie smiled and we headed to the door. "I wish you could stay longer. I was telling you about the problem I'm having remembering things--"

"Wait until after the meal to talk of that," Karo cut him off. "I'm hungry and want to eat first. When we come back we'll discuss it, okay?"

"Solid," Reggie agreed.

Chapter Thirty-Six

The restaurant was in an industrial part of town, a good twenty minutes from the apartment, but it was good seeing Karo, I'd missed him. The food had been okay. A little bland, and the soup had a funny aftertaste. Serena picked over her food without eating much and I didn't blame her. All in all, I doubt I'd be returning there any time soon no matter how much my brother raved about it. I glanced in the rear view mirror at Karo's car following us back to my place. During the drive Serena talked non-stop about the restaurant, the area it was located, and the people who'd watched our table. Sounded as if she'd switched things up a bit.

"What'd you say?" I asked. She'd been talking about searching online for the people in her journal, something I hadn't thought to do.

"What do you think I should do? Contact Linda, Shelly's mom?"

"Why would you do that?" Had I missed something?

"If me and Shelly are the same person, shouldn't I tell her I'm okay so she won't be worried?" She paused and shook her head. "That makes no sense. If I'm Shelly and she's my mom, who's Terri and Greg? Besides I don't know Linda or any of the people on her Facebook page." She turned in her seat facing me. "There were only two, no, three pictures of Shelly on her mom's page, what do you think of that?"

"Huh? Not everyone's into that stuff."

I felt the sting of her gaze and once again wondered what I'd missed.

"It just seemed as though she could've had more pictures of her missing child, that's all."

Uh oh. "Didn't you say you couldn't see Shelly's private stuff? Maybe her mom's other stuff is private too."

"Good point, I didn't think of that."

I grunted and turned onto my street. "What time you gotta be home?"

"Regular curfew. Hey, I don't mean to be funny or anything, but you and Karo don't look anything alike. Is he Indian or Scottish? What's his nationality?"

She always tried to be politically correct and I didn't care about that stuff. "His mom's white, I don't know much more than that."

"Oh. Why didn't you stay with him instead of your uncle when your dad died?"

I snorted. "Guess his mom wasn't having it. He's just ten years older than me."

"He looks older."

I stopped to tell security my brother was behind me and we drove through.

Serena yawned and I looked at her. "Tired?" I tried to keep the disappointment from my voice since I had plans for us that required her alert participation.

"No. I don't think so anyway."

"Good, this is your first time at my place. I have something special planned for later."

"So you don't think I should do anything? About Shelly and her family? I should just leave it alone? Stay with Terri and Greg while these other people wonder what happened to their kid?" We spoke at the same time and then looked at each other.

I pulled into the garage without answering. Those were loaded questions and I knew better than to tell her to forget everything and be happy with me even if that's how I felt. Hell, my past had holes large enough for a tank to drive through, but I focused on my future. However, if I wanted to share the present with Serena, I needed to step correct and give her questions serious thought.

"First, let me say you should do what's in your heart. Think everything through, there are a lot of pieces to this puzzle, including both sets of parents and families. I cannot explain the journals, the missing girl who looks like you, and the fact you have no idea who those people are. It's a huge mystery. No matter what you decide I've got your back. If you want to fly to Kentucky one weekend, I'll get us tickets so we can look these people up and talk to them. If something foul went down, Terri and Greg could get in trouble." I scratched my head. None of it made sense. Greg was no criminal; he wouldn't take someone else's kid.

She covered her mouth and stared at me. "I don't want them to get in trouble."

"What do you want?" I placed my hand on the door handle and met her worried gaze.

"The truth. Don't you want to know the truth too?"

I shrugged and opened the door. "You read my journal, that's my truth. No surprises or secrets."

She slid out and met me at the entrance into the kitchen. "Seems I should know the truth."

I pulled her to the side and leaned against her. Gently I spoke into her ear. "Tomorrow I'll ask if you can go with me to a rave in Vegas. It's a three-day event. If your parents say yes, we'll fly to Kentucky so you can find the truth. Deal?"

Nodding, she wrapped her arms around my neck. "Deal, but think of something better than the rave, they'll never go for that."

"Family reunion? My mama's side?" I asked, teasing.

"That might work," she said, her brow furrowed.

Karo was waiting inside, otherwise I would've explained I'd been kidding. Family reunion? Me? Never happen. She kissed me before I could move. It wasn't often she acted first, but I always liked when she did.

We broke for air and touched foreheads. She had to feel how much I wanted her, but that would wait until Karo left. "Let's go inside, we'll take care of this later." I took her hand and placed it on my crotch.

Her cheeks reddened but she didn't remove her hand until we walked inside.

Karo's gaze swept over both of us and he pointed to a bottle of champagne on the counter. Impressed, I lifted it, read the label, and sat it back down. "That was good food." Karo glanced at his watch, sighed noisily and popped open the bottle. Foam spilled out onto the floor. He poured three glasses and pointed to them.

"A toast." He picked up a glass.

I handed Serena her glass and raised mine.

"When you said no one forgets their first love, and that you'd find Serena because you loved her, I didn't believe you. There's been some bumps and a few problems along the way, but I'm happy to say you were right and I was wrong." He lifted his glass. "Here's to making great memories with your lady."

"Now that's something I can drink to." I tossed back the champagne, it tickled going down.

Serena smiled wide and took a sip. She started coughing and laughing. "It tickled." She touched her nose and I wrapped an arm around her waist, pulling her close.

Karo chuckled. "You two... there are a few things I need to correct before I leave. Reggie, you mentioned a flash drive, where is it?"

I pointed to my den. "Laptop, why? Ready to talk about it?"

He nodded and his head continued bobbing.

"Serena, where's yours?" he asked.

"In my pocket." She pulled it out and we both stared at it in the palm of her hand.

Karo took it. "Stay right there." He turned and walked down the hall.

"Where else would we go?" Serena asked, frowning, and then laughed. Her teeth looked whiter than normal and I tried to touch one. "Stop that." She pushed my hand away.

"Why you always pushing me away?" I leaned down until my forehead touched hers.

"I don't push you away. I want to be with you all the time, don't you know that?" Her voice softened and sounded like flower petals.

Flower petals? Where'd that come from?

"Okay you two, let's get you comfortable." Karo got behind us and pushed me. "Go to your room, take off your shoes and lay down, we'll talk in there."

"Where?" Serena asked, frowning.

"Reggie's bedroom, you'll just get there sooner rather than later," Karo murmured.

"Word," I said, pleased I'd finally be alone with her in bed. Wait, did he say we'd talk? Now? In the bedroom?

Two of us couldn't comfortably walk down the hall side by side, but I didn't want to let Serena go, so it slowed things a bit. Karo kept mumbling but didn't leave as I thought he would. When we entered my bedroom I opened both arms and smiled down at Serena.

"Ta da... what do you think?" I watched as she looked at the bed and then back at me with a sly grin.

"It's big."

"Yes it is," I said and winked.

"Kids, can we get this over with," Karo said, stepping from behind me. His movements wavered a bit and then straightened.

"Whoa," Serena said as she reached for the footboard and steadied herself. "I'm dizzy." Concerned, I headed toward her but Karo grabbed my arm and pushed me toward the side.

"Hey," I objected, but he pushed me again.

"Get into bed both of you," Karo said with a touch of impatience in his voice.

"Not with you in here." Serena crossed her arms and stared at him.

"That's not cool with you in here, Man," I said, sitting on the side of the bed trying to hold my head up. My eyelids drooped and I didn't fight when he lifted my legs and placed them on the bed.

"This is what I get for becoming involved, attached," Karo mumbled. "Leave your clothes on Serena, at least until after I'm gone, then you guys can do what you want."

"I wasn't taking them off anyway." She sat onto the bed and looked at me.

I moved her soft hair from her face and stoked her cheek. "This isn't how I planned the day, Babe."

"Can the two of you listen to me for a few minutes? I really do have a plane to catch and this has to be corrected before I leave."

"There's buzzing somewhere," I said, trying to locate the source of the sound between my ears. A thousand pins raced up and down my arm. My eyelids drooped before I could tell Karo what I felt.

"What's the matter, Reggie?" Serena asked.

"Listen, don't move. If you stay in bed for a few hours everything will be fine," Karo instructed.

"What are you talking about? What happened?" I whispered, forcing out the words.

"The medication's taking effect." Karo's palm rested on my chest. "It's okay, Bro. Rest a while, it'll pass, I promise. You have my word everything will be perfect for you and your lady. You won the bet, I won't renege."

"What medicine?" Serena asked.

"Not now, let me get Reggie settled first," Karo said.

The bed dipped. Serena's warmth left, leaving me cold as the darkness pulled me under.

"What did you do to him?" Serena's question was the last thing I heard and one I'd love to know the answer to.

Chapter Thirty-Seven

Standing on the other side of the bed I watched Karo stand over Reggie, watching him sleep. Nervous about how Reggie fell asleep so fast and Karo giving him medicine, it took everything to remain still and wait. Who was Karo? Reggie hadn't mention him before, not that he told me everything, but a brother? He would've mentioned him, or had he and I forgot. Not that it mattered, Reggie claimed Karo and that settled the matter.

"You are a complication," Karo said without looking at me.

When I realized he was talking to me, I frowned. "Complication?" That didn't make sense.

He glanced at me, the joking, happy-go-lucky guy from the restaurant was gone. Cold dark eyes swept across me, leaving goosebumps behind. "You didn't eat or drink much at the restaurant."

"I'd eaten at home before Reggie picked me up, I wasn't hungry. Sorry that complicates things for you." Had I offended him? Why did it matter if I ate or not?

He stuffed his hands in his pocket, turned and faced me. "Did Reggie tell you he had a visitor today?"

"Huh?"

"Someone broke into this place, he didn't mention it?"

Brows furrowed, I shook my head. "They didn't hurt him." It was more of a statement than question. I'd noticed the bump on his forehead when he picked me up, but had gotten sidetracked with everything about Toro and Shelly.

"No, but they were here to take him out." He paused and watched me closely. "Do you understand?"

"Take him out?" My voice cracked as I thought of what those three words meant. I swallowed hard and looked at Reggie. "Why?"

"So you do understand, good, that will make this easier. As to why, it has to do with his memory loss, contacting people, that type thing."

"But... that doesn't make sense. None of this makes sense." Dread rolled down my back, tightening my chest. I looked at Reggie again. "What did you do to him?"

"Gave him medicine."

"Will it hurt him?"

"Of course not, he's my brother and will always be protected."

My eyes widened as the silenced lengthened. "What's going on?"

He glanced at Reggie and then shrugged. "This isn't unusual, sometimes minor patchwork is required to help cement fractured memory loss. When he wakes everything will be fine."

Relief flowed over me and stopped when I met Karo's steady gaze.

"As I said you are a complication. But you're also a gambler at heart so I'll put all the cards on the table and allow you a choice."

"Choice?" That should sound good but it didn't.

He nodded and took a step closer. "Listen carefully, I'm only going to make this offer one time. You'll never be able to say you didn't choose, because you will make a choice today on how you live the rest of your life."

Tension rolled off my shoulders knowing I'd have a life to live. "Thank you."

"Save your thanks until you hear your choices. You can return to Kentucky, to the life of Shelly Bryson with Linda and Griffin Chesney as your parents. Or you can remain here with Reggie, Terri and Greg. Choose."

"Is Linda my biological mother?"

He didn't say anything.

"I don't know Linda and Griffin. What would happen if I showed up at their house?"

"What do you think would happen?"

Hell, I didn't know. "They'd ask questions I couldn't answer, probably take me to the doctor or something. Will I ever remember them?" I searched his gaze.

He looked at his watch without answering.

"How can I make a choice without knowing if I'm related to Linda?"

"It's your journal, your notes. You know who she is, now it's time to choose. Go back to Kentucky and forget the past few months, or remain here and forget Kentucky, you will *not* have them both."

Butterflies filled my stomach as my head buzzed with possibilities. I let out a shaky breath. Everything hinged on what I choose, and once done it could never be undone. My pulse pounded in my temples. I can't think straight.

I spun around and looked at Reggie lying across the bed with his eyes closed. Terri and Greg, the only parents I knew flashed across my mind. Amazing, Kelly, my new friends at school. How could I possibly leave them?

"Will she ever find out what happened to her daughter?" I asked to ease my conscience.

"No. But she's doing okay. Time to choose, this offer won't last much longer. If I leave here without an answer, you won't be here when Reggie wakes. Now choose." A muscle twitched at the corner of his right eye, his mouth formed a straight line. His arms hung loosely to the side but I was certain that could change in an instant.

"Give me a second to think, this is a big decision. It's not fair."

He snorted. "You have parents who love you, what's not fair about that?"

"Parents who didn't give birth to me, what happened? Did they steal me from Linda and Griffin?"

"No, not even close. They're the parents you chose."

That made no sense. "What --"

"Enough," he said, his hand in front of him. "Think about what you really, truly want. It's there. You already know and I'm not holding your hand or allowing Reggie to save the day for you. No. This day you chose and live with that choice for the rest of your life."

I clenched my fists tightly, barely noticing the pain of my nails digging into the palms of my hands. Through a swirl of intimidating fears comes my mother's voice, casual and light. *"God gives us one life on this earth, make it the best you can. Whenever you have a chance at happiness, go for it. Pain has its own calling card and sometimes there's not a lot we can do about it. Choices today affect tomorrow, so be happy. Love, live and laugh."*

I closed my eyes as her words surrounded and comforted me. I don't know what happened with Linda Chesney, and may never know. But I'm happy with my life right now, with Reggie, mom and dad. I have a sister in Amazing and was on track for college in the fall. It might sound selfish to not want to return to a life with strangers, even if we were related, but I couldn't see giving up my future to live in the past.

"Serena or Shelly?"

My eyes flew open. He'd moved closer, less than an arm's length away. I wanted to look away but his gaze pinned me to the spot, demanding an answer.

From the floor of my heart, light as the wings of a butterfly, my answer came out on a whisper. "Serena."

His gaze flickered. He grabbed my hand and I felt a sting in my arm.

"Ow." I jerked back and looked down trying to see what had happened. Warmth radiated up my arm and spread across my chest. "What'd you do?"

"Saved your lives, well actually, you did that." His voice softened a bit at the end.

"What?"

"You made the right choice. Now the people sent to clean up this mess will leave the two of you alone." He paused. "Thank you for saving his life."

"Welcome?" I wasn't sure if I should thank him for scaring me the way he had, but he appeared genuinely grateful. "My parents?"

"All taken care of. No worries. Just so you know, you haven't been Shelly Bryson for the past seven months." He waved at the outfit I wore, pointed to my hoop earrings, and hair. "You're Serena Hemper, a sassy young lady with a bright future."

Should I be flattered? He did threaten me in a roundabout way, so I didn't say anything. Instead, I watched Reggie.

Karo clapped his hands drawing my attention. "Now, there'll be no trips to Kentucky or contacting Shelly's family, or the Thomas's again, consider that chapter closed. If I'd known about the flash drives... we'll make sure this doesn't happen in the future."

"What about the flash drives?" My fingertips and toes tingled as I rocked to the side and grabbed.

He waved his hand. "Not important.

"How did you know we were going to Kentucky?"

"I just know. Your laptops, computers, phones, everything is being wiped. No more holes, no more Kentucky, no more Shelly, no more talks of taking you out." He stared at me a few seconds. "Repeat after me. I am Serena Hemper, not Shelly Bryson."

I repeated it.

"I have never heard of Shelly Bryson or Linda Chesney or any of their family." I repeated the words.

"I have never been to Kentucky." After repeating that sentence my throat tickled and I grabbed a bottle of water. When I finished, Karo smiled. "One more thing, say Karo was never here. I have never met Reggie's brother."

I repeated those words and blinked a few times.

"Whoa." I reached for the footboard to steady myself. "Dizzy." My head grew too heavy to hold up. "You gave me a drug?"

He took my arm and led me to the bed. Grateful to be off my feet, I sat and then stretched out next to Reggie, searching for his warmth. Footsteps clicked on the floor and stopped.

"Nope, just did a little patchwork."

Chapter Thirty-Eight

Reggie and I walked along the crowded sidewalk of the Las Vegas strip. This morning at 11 am, Amazing and Mark were married. I stood as her maid of honor. It had been a beautiful wedding and small reception. The couple planned to relocate outside Toronto, Canada after their honeymoon. Mark had been accepted into some type of training program and Amazing would start college in the fall. It'd been great being with her again, but it hurt knowing we wouldn't see each other often.

Along the strip we watched a pirate fight, listened to Gondoliers sing as they paddled passengers along a hotel canal, and stared in amazement at the huge roller-coasters zipping in and out of a tall hotel.

"I didn't think there was a place in the states hotter than Houston," Reggie said in between licks of his fast melting ice cream cone.

"No kidding, it was too hot to sit by the pool today," I said, avoiding a small kid running from her mom.

He grabbed my hand and we headed up the walk to our five-star hotel, a surprise gift from Reggie. Last week I'd graduated from high school and Reggie finished his first semester. He planned to attend summer school to catch up. Since I'd be attending that same school in the fall, I'd enrolled in summer school as well. My parents weren't too happy, but we'd all go on a ten-day cruise soon, which helped.

"Excuse me," a lady said, stopping us in the casino lobby.

Glad to be out of the heat, I smiled at her. "Yes?"

"It's just..." She pointed and then shook her head while looking me over from head to toe. "You look like my niece." She chuckled. "I guess we all look like someone, but the two of you could almost be twins, except she didn't wear dresses or style her hair or do much besides play games."

My brow rose and I glanced at Reggie. He shrugged.

"Don't get me wrong, she's a lovely girl, lots of potential, but not a natural beauty like you." Her cheeks reddened. "Sorry, I'm babbling. It's just seeing you is such a shock. Lost two nieces at the same time. We know why Rashan left, her mama was crazy. My brother finally got the balls to do something about that. But Shelly, she was more grounded. Came as a surprise when she took off too. No question Rashan talked her into it, that girl was always trouble." Her gaze swept over me again and I felt a little uncomfortable with the intensity.

She shook her head as if in the midst of an internal debate and won. "Good thing Linda and Griffin didn't come. No, seeing you would've been too hard, might've had a relapse." She nodded as if she'd just made some type of decision. "Linda, my sister, Shelly's mom, finally quit working herself into the grave, stayed home with the boys and our mama for a while. Saved her marriage, that's for sure. Now she works from home doing consulting and things are much better." Her gaze widened. "They still miss Shelly, that won't change, just other things changed, know what I mean?"

Reggie squeezed my hand as I nodded and wondered how to leave gracefully.

"Mama's in a home now. It's better for her, she needs a nurse now, you see."

No, and I didn't want to be rude, but this whole conversation was odd. "We have to go to dinner but it was nice meeting you," I said, stepping to the side before she gave me more of her family history.

"Gail Penny, just got married last month, this is a late honeymoon for us." She smiled brightly, her hazel eyes bright.

"Congratulations, Gail." I took another step backward.

"That your fella?" She pointed to Reggie.

"Yes, he is." We hadn't done introductions and I didn't plan to. "Well, it was nice meeting you." I walked off feeling her eyes on my back.

"That was creepy," I said beneath my breath.

"Awww, I thought it was cute how she told all her family business to a stranger," Reggie said.

I pushed him and he grabbed me around the waist, pulling me closer. "You're always pushing me away," he whispered as the door to the elevator closed. I turned into his arm and leaned against his chest.

"I'm going to miss mom and dad when they move in September."

He stroked my hair and placed a kiss on top. "Yeah, but it's a good job. Plus, he made me promise we'd visit for the holidays even though I don't like snow."

I snorted thinking of Philadelphia and the general manager's position daddy had accepted. "It snows a lot there; maybe we could learn to ski."

"Whatever you want is fine with me. I'll let Karo know what's up so he could meet us."

I smiled and looked at him as the doors opened. "Finally I'll get to meet him. I called to thank him for my graduation gift."

"You talked to him?"

"No. I left a message." Reggie's brother had sent a gift card for my graduation and I planned to spend it before going home.

"He's been busy with work, but I got him to agree to spend Christmas with us, so we'll see him then."

"Epic," I said as we walked into our room and closed the door.

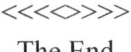

The End

The following is a preview of Rashan's story, Book II in the Siggost Chronicles.

Tonio picked me up from the library parking lot in his silver pick up. It was his pride and joy. The one thing he loved above all else and his first line of defense why he couldn't afford a kid. Eager to be one step closer to my new life, I slid in the front seat and leaned forward for a kiss. I received a quick peck on the lips. Big difference from the first time we got together. His tongue had been so far down my throat I had gagged.

"You okay?" he asked as he pulled onto the main road.

"Yeah, why?"

"Just surprised me when you called yesterday wanting to spend the night, that's all."

The light turned red and he looked at me. My heart dropped. The first time I saw him he reminded me of that actor in the Vampire Diaries, Ian Smolder. Sexy and handsome with a don't give damn attitude. I should've run the other way when he asked me out. I didn't. So here we were.

"I haven't changed my mind about having a kid," he said rather bluntly.

In the back of my mind I needed to believe the father of my child was a decent guy. That I hadn't made a complete fool of myself by choosing to give myself to him. Pity I couldn't stop hoping for vindication.

"It was a false alarm. I'm not pregnant." The lie tasted the way rancid meat smelled.

His lips curled into a boyish smile, making him appear much younger than his 20 years. "Why didn't you call and tell me before now? I've been worried. Couldn't sleep." His much larger, calloused hand grabbed mine and kissed the back of it. "You're on protection?"

Maybe I shouldn't be repulsed by his excitement, after all I didn't want to have a kid either. But seeing him all sweet and sexy now, when he'd been cool before, turned my stomach. He didn't look nearly as handsome anymore. "Yes, I'm well protected." No way to get pregnant while I'm pregnant. "But I still want you to sleeve up." Just because pregnancy was off the table, STD's weren't. Shame coated my throat and I looked away. Despite him not wanting me, more specifically our child, I planned to sleep with him rather than return home tonight.

"Whore. Slut. Fool." Mama's strident voice rang in my ear. Goosebumps flew across my arms as her venomous snarl flashed across my mind. Over and over, every vile name she had called girls who engaged in sex before marriage buffeted me. Tonio squeezed my hand, pulling me from beneath the onslaught of memories I hoped to erase.

"Yeah. Yeah, good idea." He winked, reminding me why I'd been attracted to him the first time I took my car to the repair shop where he worked. It was that boyish charm that reeled me in, and had me dropping my panties before common sense hijacked my thoughts.

"Hungry? Want drive-thru?" With the lie that I wasn't pregnant, his entire demeanor changed. He smiled, kissed the back of my hand again and kept his hand on my thigh. All the things a lover would do. His thick hair brushed against his shoulder. He faced the road, his side profile highlighted his firm chin and high cheekbones. Once I'd asked him about his heritage. He claimed to be a mutt, Spanish, English, Irish, Indian and African American all mixed together.

"Yeah. Sounds good." I looked out the window as we left the town where I'd grown up to a neighboring area in another county. I was officially on Tonio's turf. He seemed more relaxed as we drove down a main road and stopped at the light. He pulled out his phone and placed a call.

"Mable, this Tonio. Can you fix two chicken specials?" He looked at me.

I nodded that was fine. Truthfully I wasn't sure I'd be able to eat anything. Butterflies filled my stomach. By now, Mama would notice I was late coming home. Would she call Aunt Linda, Shelly's mom? I doubted it. Those two didn't like each other. If she was well into her bottle she might not notice I wasn't home. I just wanted this day to be over and tomorrow to start.

"I'll be there in less than ten minutes." He disconnected and tossed the phone into the small compartment in the middle console.

"You look pretty. Then again you always do," he said taking my hand again.

"Thanks." Heat rose to my cheeks. Butterflies took flight in my belly. My repulsion for him was slowly disappearing.

"You sure you can spend the night? I don't mind taking you home if you want," he offered.

"No, it's fine. I've worked everything out. My parents aren't expecting me until tomorrow. School's almost over, lots of sleepovers and stuff." Lies rolled off my tongue, surprising me how good I'd become. How would I ever attend another confessional?

"Good, I can't wait to have you all to myself all night." His smile turned into a sexy, leer, another thing I found attractive.

Since Tonio and I wasn't exclusive, something else I learned when I mentioned the possibility of being pregnant, I wondered how many women he'd said those words too. Not that it mattered... too much. This was our last night together. Even if Rewind was a bust, I would be leaving town.

Rather than speak my skepticism, I smiled, did a little gushing and then looked out the window. The sun had set. I was in another county an hour and a half from home. I took a moment and let that settle as he pulled into the parking lot of a small beige colored cafe.

"Be right back," he said, sliding out the car.

I nodded and pulled out my phone. Maybe I should call Shelly and warn her that I'd left. Even though we agreed to wait until I made a decision, she might tell Aunt Linda, who'd call daddy and they'd stop me before I reached Rewind's office. I pushed the phone back into my bag and took a deep breath. Indecision rode me hard. A part of me wanted the safety of the familiar, which meant staying behind and dealing with mama. Another part wanted a new, better start.

Tonio returned to the truck holding two large bags. I took them from him and sat them on my lap on top of my backpack. "Smells good," I said peeking into a bag, breathing the heavenly aromas.

"This place may not look like much, but they can cook," he said, as they pulled out the parking lot and headed toward his home in silence. Tonio rented one side of a duplex near the outskirts of town. It wasn't a bad place, the neighborhood appeared safe, quiet. Both times I'd been here before, people seemed to mind their own business.

He pulled up in front of his unit and looked at her. "Eat first?" His brow rose as he quirked his lips.

"Yeah, sounds good." My stomach had calmed, and the idea of eating held a lot more appeal. He took the bags of food and slid from beneath the wheel. I grabbed my backpack and slid out the other side. By the time I reached the front door, he was inside turning on lights and heading toward the kitchen. I locked the door behind me and took my backpack to the bedroom.

"You want ice with your sweet tea?" he yelled.

"Yes, thanks. I'm in the bathroom." I washed my hands and pulled off a layer of clothes. I didn't want to wear the jeggings right now and exchanged them for the jeans. Mama's mark had disappeared as I suspected. Once again, I turned from side to side to be sure there was no baby bump and was relieved my stomach was still flat. I packed my jeggings and shirt into my backpack, took off my sneakers, and after one last glance headed to the kitchen.

Tonio had placed the Styrofoam containers with our meals on the table. He produced real forks and glasses for our drinks.

"Thanks," I said taking a seat while he poured more tea into his glass.

"Welcome." He sat and tore into his food as if it would run away if he didn't shovel every morsel into his mouth right now. The first time I watched him eat I'd been amazed. He made a joke about starving third well countries, but I knew he felt self-conscious and tried not to stare.

My appetite came in waves or spurts. The food was good, but I knew I wouldn't eat it all. When I finished, I pushed the container away.

"That was so good," I said patting my stomach. "Thanks, I'm stuffed."

"Stuffed?" He looked into my container and then at me. "You haven't eaten that much. Want me to put it in the microwave for later?"

"Not really. I ate something at the library, probably why I'm not that hungry now." And another lie rolled off my tongue. Maybe if I stopped talking, the lies would stop.

"Oh." His gaze lingered on me before he pulled the food toward him. "I'll finish it."

I pushed back from the table, taking my glass and fork to the sink and washed them. Tonio came up behind me, placed his hand on my hip and squeezed. "I missed you," he said.

I wanted to believe him, so I did. "Really? I missed you too." I turned and wrapped my arms around his neck.

"Yeah?" He smiled while staring at me. "How much?"

"Lots," I said as he pulled me closer. Our faces were inches apart. My heart raced with excitement as he leaned forward and brushed his lips against mine. He really could be nice when he wanted.

"Mmm, you're so sweet." His tongue brushed across the seam of my lips tasting of lemony tea. I melted against him. Tonio wasn't a body builder by any means but he was strong, and it felt good being held in his arms.

We broke apart breathing hard. His dick pressed into my stomach as he moved back and forth, watching me. "Let's go to bed."

I nodded and tried to back away. He grabbed my hand, pulled me close for a quick kiss and without releasing my waist turned off the lights, checked the doors and headed to his room. I jumped on the bed face down, rolled over and looked at him standing in the door. Knowing he loved this kind of play, I took my time pulling the band from my hair, allowing it to spill down my back and cover my breasts.

"You've gotten bigger." He pointed to my chest.

"Really?" I played dumb. "This is the same bra size I always wear."

He stared at my nipples and then at my face. "You're beautiful. Can't believe you're here."

I smiled. His words soothed my battered pride and made me feel better about spending my last night with him.

"I wanted to be here… with you." At that moment I meant it. There was nothing or nowhere I wanted to be more than right here with him. Blood surged through me at his heated stare. I placed my hands beneath my breasts and pushed them together.

He licked his lips and took a step closer to the bed. "Damn girl," he said in a husky voice. "You got me shaking and shit." He held out his hands. They were shaking. Knowing I did that to him went straight to my head. It was a high no one had ever told me about. Women slaying men. I stretched my legs and slowly peeled off my clothes. It took a little longer because of the zipper but Tonio didn't mind. He remained in the same spot all but drooling as I showed more and more skin.

I was on fire. Hot with desire, feeling powerful and in control.

"Take off your clothes," I told him.

He blinked and then tore off his pants and shirt. After hopping around on one foot while taking off his socks, he finally stood in front of me, naked. The last time we were together he liked when I told him what to do. Did he want that again?

I laid back on the bed and opened my legs wide. He started to come forward.

"Don't move until I tell you too," I said in a sharp voice.

He froze, met my gaze and nodded. His cock jumped as he watched my hand travel down my stomach to the top of my hairy mound. "You want this?" I asked

"Fuck yeah," he said in a low voice that sent a thrill through me.

I placed my feet next to my hips, knees pointed to the ceiling. Tonio's gaze never left from between my legs.

"Taste me," I said. A video I'd seen a couple weeks ago showed a woman demanding her lover kneel and lick her. The man acted eager and excited like Tonio behaved now.

In a long fluid move he lay stomach down on the bed, his face between my legs. This was one thing Tonio excelled in. If there was a degree for eating pussy, and I think there should be, he'd be the instructor. He never rushed and never stopped until I got off.

First, he licked me everywhere down there. His mouth was warm, lips were soft and his tongue magical. One of his fingers entered slid inside.

"So fucking tight," he said. I felt the word vibrate through me and rolled my hips against his face.

"Do that again."

This time I grabbed his hair and pressed against his face. It completely sent me over the moon when he shuddered beneath my hand. I humped against his mouth as sweet tingles moved through me. I wanted more. His fingers pumped in and out of my vee-jay, making slurpy noises as he suckled and then grazed my clit with his teeth.

I screamed. The combination of pain and pleasure blew my mind. "Again," I grunted. He complied. I writhed like a snake against his face until he found the right spot and zeroed in. He latched down, flicked his tongue hard and fast, taking me on the ride of a lifetime.

My entire body erupted. I shook so hard from the top of my head to the tip of my toes. I couldn't speak as my vee-jay pulsed like a heartbeat gone wild. What a ride!

Tonio held on for a little while and then released me to ride the crest of pleasure. He blew against my lips and placed soft kisses between my legs.

"So good. So damn sexy," he murmured. "I'm going to clean you up and take care of you."

Too tired to speak, I nodded and lay on my back with my legs wide open. Tonio's idea of cleaning me up was to lap juices from my skin. With each lick, I regained energy. By the time he finished I was hot and ready to go. Would he allow me to tell him what to do again? Did he enjoy it as much as I did?

He looked up. Smoky dark eyes met mine. His intent was clear. He wanted me bad. In the space of that moment, every care, problem and concern disappeared. "Are you done?" I demanded, testing the waters.

"Yes."

My eyebrow rose. "Yes, what?"

He stared at me for several seconds before speaking. "Yes, Ma'am."

My heartbeat raced at the need in his gaze. I can't explain the pride and excitement that flowed through me from his words. "Come here," I whispered needing to touch him. He crawled and resting on his palms looked down at me. "Where are the condoms?" I asked.

The fire in his eyes dimmed a bit but he didn't move. "In the top drawer."

I reached over, opened the drawer and pulled out the box. "Hmm, ribbed. Sounds interesting."

He smiled.

I picked up a packet, opened it and took his cock in my hand. He jerked and closed his eyes as I rolled it onto him. With my hand holding his cock, I pulled him down and placed the tip where his mouth had just been.

Jaw clenched tight he stared at me, waiting for permission, something he'd done the last time we were together. I wondered how long he could hold out. His arms trembled beneath the strain of holding his weight.

"Please," he whispered after a few minutes and I nodded. "Now."

Tonio surged forward. I gasped at the full feeling as I did both times before.

"You okay?" he asked, his face near my head against the pillow.

"Give me a minute. It's tight."

"So fucking tight and good. You're killing me. Can't get you out of my mind."

His words were like spigots releasing moisture and easing the pain. "Now."

"Thank you." The words sounded as if they were dragged from his inner most self. His hips rose, pulling his dick halfway out and then thrust forward. I liked the closeness of sex this way, we were one in the sense his body was inside mine, but it was hard for me to cum like this. Tonio normally came after a few thrusts, especially if he was worked up like now.

Just as a warm curl of lust hit my belly, he yelled. It was over. We both were satisfied. The other times when we finished I showered and left him asleep. Tonight I would be staying.

"Damn, Rashan you're awesome. A natural Domme. I like that sometimes." He pulled me close and snuggled against my neck. His warmth chased away the chill in the room for a while. Today had been long emotionally and physically. I was drained. Tomorrow, was a new day and life.

"Next time, you wanna be the submissive?" he asked in a sleepy voice.

The idea of doing what he told me to do held zero appeal. I couldn't imagine it no matter how hard I tried. "I'll think about it." I scooted closer and soon was asleep.

Hello,

Thank you for taking the time to read the first book in my new series, Siggost Chronicles. The idea of a shadow group operating in the US isn't new. While researching MK Ultra, I wondered what it would be like if the research had a positive impact on unlikely test subjects. Using social media as a recruiting tool isn't new either. But when I put those elements together, I came up with these fascinating stories.

Are you disappointed Shelly didn't return home? That she found love and happiness while her parents suffered her disappearance? I struggled with that one. But this is book one of the series and if two teenagers were able to outwit an organization with billions of dollars at it's disposal, along with military backing, the stories wouldn't ring true. Sometimes bad things happen to good people is a matter of perspective. It's my hope that these provocative tales will provide the entertainment we all enjoy along with making us think beyond the box.

Shelly loves video games and plays a high-stake game that changes her life. In this game she shares her deepest fantasies and is surprised when they become a reality. An alternate reality that she appreciates and feels guilty about at the same time.

You're invited to journey with me through this new series. If you like fast paced action, suspense and great love connections like me, you won't be disappointed. Feel free to drop me a line,

SydneyAddae@msn.com. I will have a separate newsletter for Siggost Chronicles, if you'd like to join, https://goo.gl/rxVxDm.

I also write paranormal wolf shifter romances. Check out my list of books below. The first book in the series, BirthRight is a free read in all ecommerce stores. If you're a Kindle Unlimited fan, the next five books in the La Patron Series is in Kindle Unlimited for a limited time.

If you're interested, feel free to join my Facebook group, La Patron's Den, where discussions regarding Silas and the Wolf nation abound. Also, you can find me at my website, SydneyAddae.com.

Rewind is the first book in my new Siggost Chronicles Series and I'd like to ask a favor. When you finish reading, **please leave a review**, whatever your opinion, I assure you I appreciate it.

Thanks again
Sydney

Siggost Chronicles
Rewind

La Patron Series
BirthRight
BirthControl
BirthMark
BirthStone

BirthDate

BirthSign

Sword of Inquest

Sword of Mercy

Sword of Justice

La Patron's Christmas

La Patron's Christmas 2

La Patron's New Year – w/Catherine Marsh, & Leigh West

KnightForce 1

KnightForce Deuces

KnightForce Tres'

KnightForce Damian

KnightForce Ethan

Angus

La Patron's Den – Jackie's Journey

La Patron's Den – Alpha Awakening – Adam

La Patron's Den – Renee's Renegade

Knight Rescue

Booksets

La Patron Series Books 1-6

La Patron Series Books 4-6

The Sword Series – Books 1-3

Vampires:

Last in Line

Bear:

Bear with Me

Jewel's Bear

www.ingramcontent.com/pod-product-compliance
Lightning Source LLC
Chambersburg PA
CBHW070837280626

47161CB00015B/1028